IN THE

CARDS

A Kaybrum Chronicle

IN THE

CARDS

A Kaybrum Chronicle

EMILY K. BRAY

 Torchflame Books

Published 2023, by Torchflame Books

Paperback ISBN: 978-1-61153-574-7
E-book ISBN: 978-1-61153-575-4
Library of Congress Control Number: 2023914372

To the first audience,
and the next one.

CHAPTER 1

KORVO:

KORVO LAID THE CARDS ONE BY ONE onto the ragged metal edge that made up the roof of the Refuge. Even though the darkness felt like the sun was never going to return, Kor knew what was on the cards without seeing them. He could feel their stories rush up through his fingers and paint a tapestry across the night sky. Destinies that etched themselves one shuffle at a time.

Destinies that all looked the same. He sighed, gathering the cards into a pile with one hand. Kor scratched at his neck before putting the cards back into the leather pouch on his hip. The cards had been showing him a vague darkness that was coming, but the details were always too fuzzy.

Kor looked down at his right hand and stretched his fingers. Ever since he had left his home in Hadran he had a harder time understanding the messages the cards were giving. It was like things were getting lost in translation, like wool was coating the mouth of the fates, leaving their hints and headlines muffled. He massaged the bumps disfiguring his right hand. Acid could do that to a person. Acid could fray the connections. It left a permanent scar inside and out.

"Sitting up here all by yourself?" Aer pulled herself up the last rung of the rusted metal ladder that brought her to the edge of the roof.

"Is anyone besides you going to be stupid enough to come up here with me?" Kor took in the nightly dazzlement of color forced on her by the nightclub she sang for down the road. Bright red lips and painted cheeks masked her harsh features from the random passer-by, but Korvo knew her beyond the makeup. She was beautiful in the way that a sword is beautiful. She had purpose and severity. The club tried to hold her back with feathers and beads, but she was a spring ready for action. She was also his oldest friend. And sometimes, more.

"For a guy who always complains of the cold, you could find somewhere a little more protected from the elements," she said.

Kor just smiled and tapped his olive knuckles against the metal pipes around him. The smoke from the furnace below wafted in ripples to his touch.

"Plenty warm," he said; then he sighed, looking down at the papers Aer had brought him. He shifted through them without letting his eyes read anything of importance. The stacks of papers, the information from his sources, were only getting smaller every day. And just like the cards, he knew what they said without looking.

Nothing good.

"I think even if you were the richest person in all of Kaybrum, you would still sit up here." Aer drew her long, slim legs close to her body.

"But, at least, I'd own the building." The weight of what the building held forced its way into the ease of their conversation. Below them lay the prison where they 're-educated' young people with magic. Kept them from being nuisances to the public. Helped them find the 'right way.'

A chill ripped through Kor. He shifted so his back was directly against the smokestack. It wasn't hot enough to burn, but the heat did its best to penetrate deep into his bones. He still shivered.

"Admit you're cold," Aer said, placing a hand on his shoulder. Her warmth melted into him in a way that the smokestack's could not.

"It's only because you bring all your silly winds with you," Kor said, settling the papers in front of him with a rock so they wouldn't blow away. The winds were as much a part of Aer as his cards were to him. He could not separate her from them if he tried.

"You know I can't help that."

Magic trickled through them, connecting them to the elements of the universe. Every Magic's connection was unique, but it was part of them, just as much as breathing.

"Besides, I don't hear you complaining about the winds when they bring you information." Aer wiped the back of her hand across her lips, streaking lipstick across her face. The gray air made her face look haunted.

"Did they?" Kor asked, looking away from her.

"Perhaps." She plucked a feather from her hair and let it drop off the side of the building. Kor watched it float until it had been lost in the darkness of the morning.

"Bryce and Merin are already dealing with it," Aer said, picking another small feather apart.

"You sent Bryce and Merin without asking me?"

"Do I need to ask your permission?" Her tone was playful, but her eyes missed the sense of humor. Aer was always on edge. He knew better than to remind her that he was the leader of their rebellion. It would only end badly for him.

"Do you think they can handle it?" Kor asked finally. "Alone, I mean."

"They're not little kids anymore, Kor. You were doing much more dangerous things when you were their age." Aer finally let the skeleton of the feather drop. Kor didn't bother to watch that one. He rubbed his hand instead, pulling it into his lap.

"I just want—" he started. His eyes caught the crack of sunshine barely beginning to crest the walls of the city.

"To protect them. I know." Aer laid her long, thin fingers on Kor's shoulder again. He reached up and brushed them with his fingertips. Even the feeling of her skin felt muffled. He wondered for a minute what it would be like to hold her with both his hands at full capacity.

"Bryce has had too many close encounters with the Watchers lately. If he gets in another fight, he's going to get thrown into the Refuge again," Kor said heavily.

"Risks have to be taken in order for us to gain any sort of ground in this fight. You know that more than any of us."

Kor looked up at the sky to ignore the clear stare Aer had given his hand.

It had been five years, but he still wasn't used to it. Still wasn't used to the stares. Still wasn't used to the mumbled reading of the cards. Still wasn't used to not being able to clearly make out the Raven: the mark that all Magics were forced to wear. It was as if something that was so much a part of his existence had been wiped out. Like he would never be whole.

Magic wasn't illegal in the Northern Territory like it was in his homeland, Hadran, but it still wasn't accepted, especially in Kaybrum, the capital city. And they all, as soon as their powers manifested, were branded. The Raven brand, and any bogus reason, was enough for the Watchers to pull any child with magic from the street and throw them into the Refuge. Korvo, at seventeen, had a running count of how many days were left until he could never be placed in that putrid place. Labor camps, exile, those were more pleasant options.

"Will you do a reading for me?" Aer asked, holding his cards in her hand. He had been too lost in thought to notice her grab them.

Kor grasped for them, but she pulled them away letting the cards slide into her palm. She shuffled them slowly, and Kor sat back and watched the mix of the cards creating and dismantling destinies in front of him.

"Just a short one," he said, finally taking the cards. He tapped the base of his hand on the deck and split it one final time, stacking the two pieces together in reverse order. Aer nodded and sat back.

"Past," he said, drawing a single card from the top of the deck. The pictures began to form inside his mind as soon as he touched the card. Aer's past was as dark as ever. He caught snippets of things he knew: the nightclub where she worked, the Refuge, a dark alleyway, the feeling of blood slowing to a sludge from anger. What it would look like without his mangled right hand, he couldn't know. The hand had been that way since before he came to Kaybrum and met Aer.

Aer didn't ask him to elaborate on the past. For them, it was often easier to leave things unsaid. Nothing good came from reliving it.

"Present," he said before reaching for the next card. Aer crossed her arms in front of her like she was waiting for something. Kor hesitated. She gestured for him to get to it already. He touched the card. Immediately, a jolt of energy buzzed up through his arm and bounced in lightning streaks through his mind.

He flipped the card over and stared intently at the image before him. Three long swords were plunged into the breast of a bird, its wings outstretched, its head turned away as if looking at the storm raging in the background. The three of swords: upheaval.

"You feel them, right?" Aer smirked, leaning her back against the smokestack.

"And you sent Bryce to deal with this?" Kor said. His jaw hung for a moment, having a hard time connecting with the rest of his mouth.

"And Merin," she said. She looked at her reflection in the shiniest pipe near them and rubbed at the make-up on her face.

"The wind told you about whoever this is, right? Not one of our informants? We're the only ones who know about it?" Kor glanced up and down the streets of Kaybrum. With the intensity of the cards, he couldn't trust this to just anyone.

"The wind loves to find me all kinds of lost things. Even if they don't know they're lost."

"I'm not sure I even know what they've found, yet. And it's better we figure it out before someone else gets to them."

"Keeping secrets from people? That doesn't sound like you. Unless you saw something in the cards," Aer trailed off.

"It's not a secret," Kor said. He looked down at the card again. "Just a precaution."

Aer nodded.

Kor pulled his knees to his chest, a move he only would have done alone or with Aer. But he needed to pull everything in and think. The cards had felt alive again. They had the same electric tang they'd had before his readings became fuzzy. There was no doubt that whatever they were looking for reminded him of Hadran: beautiful, and hiding a deadly secret.

"But whoever they are, they're powerful. And right now, we need something to tip the cards in our favor," Aer said flicking the fluttering pages of the documents she had brought him. Kor nodded without really hearing her. He was still lost in his thoughts.

They sat in silence a moment before he realized he wasn't finished. He'd forgotten to pull the last card. The future had always been hard to interpret even before acid had mangled the flesh on his hand. He flipped the card over immediately to let the image help him figure out the snippets and impressions of time that came with them. Kor paused and looked at the card in front of him. He let his fingers walk over the black eyes of the raven scratched deeply into the card.

"What do you see?" Aer asked.

Kor stared down at the raven, trying to figure out a way to explain the impending doom the cards had been hinting at all night. Aer began singing a song under her breath. It filled Kor with the feeling of warm water and boats coming in from the harbor even though they were a hundred miles from the coast. It made him break eye contact with the paper raven and bring his focus back onto the wispy blonde near him.

"Bad news?" she asked in between verses of the song. The words of the melody were lost to Kor, who couldn't understand the language of the winds.

"Everything has been turning up the same," Kor shook his head and threw the cards back into their pouch without saying anything more. The sun now shone over the city walls and the stirrings of the street below them were beginning. The two sat in silence for a minute, watching the city of Kaybrum wake up to another day of living in the shadow of the Refuge.

AER:

Aer took a deep breath and began to sing softly again. She shuffled the papers she had brought in time to the melody. Kor raised his eyebrow, but he didn't move yet. She could wait him out. She watched as he thought. He was formulating plans, odds, and strategies. She let him. His yellow-green eyes were looking through the world to the future, a place she could only see with his help. The cards had been bothering him, but she knew better than to pry. They had long learned to let each other's demons go.

"You know," she said when his face relaxed and she could tell he had finished thinking, "I don't need the cards to know that things are changing."

"The winds are telling you the future now?" Kor reached up to smooth a piece of hair out of her face. She pushed him away. He let his head thump against the metal pipe and closed his eyes. Aer took the opportunity to look at him in the early sunlight. His forehead was creased and furrowed. Unease settled on his olive skin like a dark shadow. It made him look older when he led meetings. But up here, with only her, the deep-set frown just made him look worried. In front of the people, he was charismatic, sure, undaunted. But here, she could see the last few months had taken their toll.

"No. I'm actually reading the information Bethlem has gotten us." She thrust the papers in front of him again. Kor's brow furrowed deeper as he slowly read through the information. She knew it wasn't much. Mostly an increase in arrests for Magics.

"This many?" Korvo sighed rubbing at his temples.

"If you can believe the reports," she said.

"The horrible thing is, I do believe them, and I'm not even surprised," Kor said.

"Aren't you talking to the Council today, anyway?" Aer tried to get Kor back to sounding like his normal optimistic self.

"To try to get the school approved. But at this rate there won't be anyone left to teach."

Kor took a deep breath. And then another. He stood. His back straightened, his yellow-green eyes focused, and all the weight of the world carried by his seventeen years settled on his shoulders.

Something needed to change. Quickly.

When the wind had come and whispered to her just as the sun was dipping behind the wall that surrounded the city, telling her that something big and new and powerful had come, she hoped it would be the change they needed to finally make a difference for Magics. They needed something.

The wind whispered about it in excited, overlapping voices in her ears, and it felt like hope.

But she couldn't just bring him news from the winds. Kor didn't always trust it. Like a new puppy tripping over its legs and entranced by the smallest thing, the wind could get distracted. This news may be days, weeks, years old. But if she could explain the words of the wind to Kor, he might not give her that slight look of hesitation every time it brought her the news of the world. He would feel their urgency this time. He would know something was about to change.

KORVO:

"Think Bryce and Merin will be okay?" Kor asked more to himself than Aer.

"Best to wait for Bryce somewhere that's a little closer to the ground if you want to find out." Aer rose slightly and straightened the long, tan skirt and the collar of her jacket, revealing a slim strip of pale skin at the base of her neck.

There was a jagged black mark there, the same one found amid all of the acid burns on his right hand. The Raven's head that marked them for what they were. Magic. Hated and hunted. Kor fought the need to reach out and touch it.

The climb down from the top of the Refuge was always treacherous. Harsh winters and the public's blind eye had not been kind to the metal sides of the building. They were streaked with rust and ragged in places, but Kor had been coming here long enough to know all the little places where his clothes or skin might catch on an edge. This was his thinking place; the place where he could see the rest of the city, where the plight of his people could not be any worse. It was where he came and practiced his pleas to the City Council, where he ran risk calculations he did not think would go well, and where he had met Aer.

"Someday they are going to just put you in the Refuge out of spite for being on their roof," a familiar voice called from the other side of the street.

Kor smiled at Bryce.

"Good thing I'll know about that someday before they do," Kor said. He crossed the street and clasped hands with the younger boy.

"I thought you and Merin were supposed to be out looking," Aer said, moving across the street to join them. Leave it to Aer to scold them.

"We are. Well, we were, but we hit a little snag." Bryce leaned against the wall.

"Snag?" Kor asked.

"You guys always give us a sense of who you're looking for. The wind talks to Aer, the cards talk to you, but my plants don't pay any attention to the random passerby in the middle of the garden. And it turns out 'interesting and warm' doesn't really get us that far."

"I told you what the wind told me," Aer huffed.

"But couldn't they for once give us something concrete like hair color, body mass, birthmarks?" Bryce asked.

"I think you know the answer to that," Aer teased.

Bryce stuck out his tongue. He traced his finger over the moss growing from the crack along the side of the building. A small smile crept over his face as Merin appeared with her hands full of warm pastries.

"We searched the Wall District," Merin said. She handed out the food to the group. Kor took a bite and the flaky crust sat on his upper lip.

"We were about to go to the gardens," Bryce explained, "but we got a little hungry and wanted to stop and see if the cards had anything else to say. Maybe something that's at least a little useful." His grey eyes accused Aer of being ridiculous. Aer turned away with a huff.

"This is someone totally new. Not someone from the city," Kor said scratching the back of his head. That much had been clear, but the rest was like lightning. Quick to come to him, but just as quick to disappear.

"In a city of a half million people, that's really going to cut it down," Bryce said. He finished the last bite of his pastry and licked his fingertips.

"Can one of you come with us?" Merin handed another pastry to Bryce, who gobbled it up in three bites.

"Aer needs sleep," Kor said, "and I need to go to the Council." He paused, there was no need to worry them. "You'll be fine." He put his hand on Merin's shoulder, and the girl sighed.

"Where do you want to meet?" Bryce asked.

"Bethlem's at the usual time," Kor said.

Bryce nodded, and he and Merin went down one side of the street. It would have been easier for them to meet back here, but he couldn't convince Bryce to make it up the ladder. Aer thought he didn't like being disconnected from the earth. Bryce's powers, after all, came from nature and the top of the Refuge was the furthest from nature one could get. The tall roof might have allowed for quiet reflection, but it didn't comfort the way nature did.

Still, Kor knew better. Bryce was afraid of the Refuge. He used his typical bravado to keep it at bay: bragging about his time, meeting in its shadow, ignoring the slight shudder in his voice when it suddenly came up in conversation. But Kor recognized the extra flick in his eyes when it was mentioned after dark. He had done a reading for Bryce more than once and felt the depth of the darkness and the haunt of the stale air recycled through a thousand breaths heavy with fear. It was through Bryce that Kor knew the Refuge, and it was through Bryce that Kor vowed he would end this treatment of kids like them.

With Bryce and Merin back to searching, Aer put a final, hesitant hand on Kor's shoulder. It wasn't much, but with Aer, any semblance of touch was enough to give him strength. He turned and headed to his meeting with the Council. It wasn't the first meeting. It wouldn't be the last. But he had to keep trying.

BRYCE:

The ground clung to Bryce's feet as he walked, causing him to have a lurching sort of swagger. It looked cool and confident, but it was merely a charade, a pure coincidence that the Earth just connected with him in the same way that plants obeyed what he wanted them to do. Merin happily sashayed beside him, keeping time with his slow and steady gait.

Bryce let his eyes sweep around them, his head on a swivel. He was looking for Watchers as much as he was for the person Aer had sent them to contact. Merin looked forward down the path.

"Merin," he stepped up close to her and whispered in her ear, "we have company." For a second, he considered scaling the tree to his left and getting out of the way. He was not known for keeping his cool with any of the Watchers in the city, and while he wasn't afraid of a fight, he didn't want Merin to see him get tossed in the Refuge. Merin winked. Bryce's heart settled, but his fist didn't unclench.

"Miss, is this Magic bothering you?" the Watcher asked. He straightened his dark blue uniform and let his hand linger on the baton at his waist.

"Bothering? He was helping me identify the foliage," Merin said in a singsong voice Bryce knew was part of an act.

"Foliage?" the man asked. He walked in front of them, so he was staring directly at Bryce. "I thought it might be you, Segal."

Bryce spat. He hated his last name. It just reminded him of the family that had abandoned him.

"Who else knows the difference between the different trees in this garden?" Bryce leaned against the trunk of the closest tree, grinning.

"Miss, I'd be careful with riffraff like this." The officer pointedly ignored Bryce.

"But he seems so knowledgeable," she cooed. The man inched closer.

Bryce felt his adrenaline spiking. He rolled his fingers in and out of a fist.

"He's also very knowledgeable about the inside of the Refuge. Probably been up all night frequenting the Wall District doing who knows what," the Watcher scoffed. Bryce could barely hear what the Watcher said with the blood pumping so loudly in his ears, but if he laid a hand on Merin there was no way Bryce could stand for it.

The Watcher brushed his hand across Merin's cheek. Bryce moved toward the Watcher, his fist coming up, but Merin shot him a glance to stay still. The look in her blue eyes crushed any resistance he may have had. Bryce crossed his arms and leaned back against the tree, but he could still feel his blood rushing. The bark hardened beneath his back.

"Why don't you let me escort you to..."

"I'll be fine on my own, thank you," Merin cut him off.

"But, Miss, I don't think you realize the danger of hanging out with these Magics."

"Yeah," Bryce said. He refused to look at the officer. It would only make his blood boil more. "We're all hardened criminals. You can tell just by looking at us."

The Watcher glared and went back to Merin, leaning in close.

"The last two nights I've arrested at least five of these abominations. You wouldn't believe how dirty one of them was. Worse than this riffraff," he said, pointing at Bryce. "Looked like he'd slept in the streets his whole life. Looked a little like your friend Korvo, Segal."

"Well, then I bet you're tired and need to go home and sleep," Merin said. Her tone turned a little too harsh. The officer straightened, and one of his hands returned to his club. Bryce bristled, putting a foot against the tree trunk, ready to push off and stop anything that might happen next. Better him than Merin.

Merin placed her hand on the Watcher, and Bryce saw the man's eyes droop. There was no question Merin used the slightest trickle of her power to soothe him. The Watcher's hand relaxed, and the man turned without saying anything and ambled away from them.

Bryce smiled. "That was new. You can make 'em sleepy now?" Bryce asked, watching the dark uniform walk away from them without another thought.

"Something I've been working on. It's for getting a patient to rest."

Bryce laughed. Merin was always working on new ways to channel her powers. Hell, she had enough practice fixing him up after his fights.

"We're just lucky that you don't have the mark," Bryce said. He reached down to fix the cuffs on his pant leg. There was no point in hiding what he was. Rolled up, his tattoo was completely visible. He wore his Raven's head with a tinge of pride. Kor had taught him that.

Merin ignored his comment, pulling her sleeves all the way down to cover the bottom of her palms. Bryce didn't know what to say to her. He never seemed to know what to say to her.

They walked through the gardens at a leisurely pace. Bryce tended to the plants and the trees as they went, picking off dead blooms and giving a little green energy to places where the wind had torn through tree branches. More than once he and Aer had argued about the wind.

"Do you think he's really arrested that many people?" Merin asked, leaning down to smell some of the only flowers still in bloom during the winter months.

"Probably mostly just talk, but if the arrests really are picking up at this speed, Kor's going to need to know."

He picked at the edge of his thumbnail.

"Bryce..."

"Kor will keep us safe. He's going to make a difference for all of us and he's going to shut down the Refuge for good."

Bryce recited his mantra and took a deep breath. Merin didn't say anything, just reached over and grabbed his hand for a second. He could feel the positive energy flooding into his veins. He hadn't even realized he was that tense until the knots in his back began to relax.

"Do you really think whoever this is will be much harder to get on board than anyone else we've talked to?" Merin asked, twisting her curly chestnut hair back into the semblance of a loose braid on her shoulder.

"I think the powers that be," Bryce raised his eyebrows and lifted his chin back toward the tower of the Refuge where Kor always stayed, "think this one is important."

"Did Kor see anything else in the cards?" Merin let the tip of her braid tickle the underside of her chin. Bryce frowned.

"He hasn't been seeing anything good lately."

"That's because he keeps having to look at your face all the time," Merin teased. Bryce stuck his tongue out and slowly his lips turned back into an easy grin.

"Well, we can't all be perfect like you." He knew Merin would chase him for that comment. Merin didn't have the mark of the Raven. Her parents had used their money and their connections to keep her safe. A lot of Magics didn't like her for it. Not many Magics had parents around. If they were born to a non-magic family like Bryce had been, their families tended to rid themselves of the 'problem' as soon as they could. Bryce kept quiet as much as possible about her home life, just like he would keep any secret for Aer or Kor.

Especially Kor.

Since the day they met, Bryce would have followed Kor into a fire. Into hell. Into the Refuge.

Bryce had been thirteen when he made it to the city. He'd come from a small farming village a few hours away. After he was branded at ten, once his family could no longer deny what he was, his parents greeted him with side glances and whispered conversations. He endured three years of their silence. They didn't kick him out; after all, his powers were useful on the farm, but they hardly talked to him at all. Bryce left in the middle of the night for the capital, where he could be lost in a sea of people. It was better for his parents to have a missing son than one to gossip about and use.

Kor had taught him how to not be afraid. Not to hide. To be someone.

And Kor was going to make it okay for Magics to be safe.

"Do you think," Merin said, catching up to Bryce, "that maybe that creepy watcher arrested the person we're looking for?"

"I guess it's possible. We haven't heard anything that would point us in the direction of a new Magic in town. Even in the Wall District they hadn't heard anything, and Bethlem knows everyone."

"Exactly, what if they got picked up last night before they found their way to someone who would help them? That jerk said one of them reminded him of Korvo. So maybe someone foreign."

"They're probably still being held at the field office. It takes a while to process the first time." He remembered waiting in the cold, empty cell, waiting for what felt like hours without anyone explaining anything. He knew he was going to be put in the Refuge, but the anticipation worked on his nerves. Sometimes he still woke in a sweat dreaming about that first time.

"I guess we know where we're going." Merin turned on her heel and headed out of the garden. Bryce walked slowly behind her. The dirt stuck to his heels more than usual, making his legs feel about as heavy as his mind.

"How are we going to get in?" Merin asked.

"I figured I'd let you do all the talking." Bryce tried to put some levity into his voice, but it just wasn't there.

"I could say I'm there to see to his ailments. I'm sure he didn't come away from a run-in with Watchers unscathed."

"But then you'd reveal your powers," Bryce said, snapping his head up and stopping her with his hand. "You'd be hated like the rest of us. Until the Refuge is destroyed, you need to keep a low profile." His voice cracked a little. Merin pushed his hand off her shoulder gently.

"There are regular healers. I know how to dab a wound with a warm cloth just like anyone else in this city."

"So how will you explain me?" he asked. "I am not letting you go in by yourself. We're not even sure this person is the one Kor sent us to go get. And I am never leaving you alone with any creepy Watcher slime."

"You can act as my hired bodyguard. You can't trust all these random Magics, don't you know. Best to hire protection." She winked.

"I could even wrap his hands in vines to show we're on the Watchers side," Bryce said.

"They might recognize you."

She was right. He had been known for his vines getting him into—and out of—trouble. But when she wasn't looking, Bryce whispered a short mantra to the ivy growing up the pale grey brick that lined this portion of the garden and snapped a small piece off to put in his pocket. Just in case. You could never trust a room full of Watchers.

A plan in place, they walked to the station.

"This had better be him," Bryce muttered to himself when the building was within eyesight. It was made with shiny, silver-coated glass that reflected back the uneasy smile on Bryce's face. With a glance, he shifted to look at Merin's easy posture, her straight-edged shoulders, her fluidity. Her upbringing would get them through the door. He would just have to play the part and hope for the best. The vine in his pocket twitched uneasily.

He gave a sigh and crossed his arms across his chest to appear more like a bodyguard, but it also gave him the sense of relief of having something in between him and that reflection staring back at him.

CHAPTER 2

KORVO:

KOR KNOCKED SOFTLY ON AER'S DOOR. The sound echoed, a subtle apology for waking her hours before he normally would, but the Council had barely listened to his plan. He just wanted to build a school for Magics. Somewhere to keep them off the streets and allow them to learn the things they needed to make it in the world. A real place for education, not the sham of a re-education center like the Refuge.

The wind burst through the crack at the bottom of the door and the handle toggled in his hand, letting the door creak open, but Aer was nowhere to be found. The winds did things like this for her, and as Kor stepped into the small bottom-floor apartment, he immediately felt the bustle of the wind continue circulating. He was always amazed that the wind would stay confined to this small amount of space. That Aer could confine *herself* to this amount of space. But Magics got paid very little, and she refused any help to get a bigger apartment. He wished she would agree to live with him. But she was independent, and he had to respect that.

"What is it, Kor?" Aer called from behind the curtain Bryce had helped her nail to the wall for some privacy between rooms.

Kor didn't speak for a second, collecting his thoughts.

"Did they say no?" She put her hand out and pointed at a shirt that was thrown over the back of one of the kitchen chairs.

"No," he said, putting the light linen shirt in her outstretched hand. He turned to give her more privacy than the flimsy curtain provided. He was already invading her space; he needn't impose himself anymore. "Not exactly."

"So what did they say, *exactly?*" Aer stuck her head out from behind the curtain and looked at him. Her brows furrowed. He raised his hands.

"They wouldn't listen about the long-term impacts of educating all members of society. They said they wouldn't give government funds."

"So, we're dead in the water." She pounded her fist into the wall.

"Not quite. They allowed me to get permits to use the old maintenance building near the Wall District."

"Without any sort of funding, how are we going to run it?"

"We'll have to figure that out."

"We?" Aer huffed.

"Of course we," Korvo said, sitting down. "We ran the numbers. You know that getting people educated is our best chance. When people know how to, they can rise up. And if we run a school, the Refuge loses its most pleasant-sounding aspect of 'educating' young Magics."

"But what if people still don't care? They don't care now. What if we teach kids how to read, and they still see us as less? They have to listen to us for any of that to matter. Otherwise, we're just making nice while they still hate us."

"Where is this coming from?" Kor asked, but he felt it. It was the safest way, but he couldn't help feeling the ping of guilt for choosing this course. All the same, he had made his bed, and he would lie in it if it meant Bryce never faced the refuge again.

"The arrests keep growing. The Wall District is getting poorer and poorer. You heard from Merin that they plan on raising taxes again, and you know who that hits the most. Where are you going to get the money for the school?"

"That's why we need to do this, even if it's just me every day teaching children everything I know. We'll get the supplies. We always do."

Aer nodded, but her eyes were lost somewhere in the corner of the room.

"Did something happen?" Kor asked.

"It's just ... We might finally be able to fight back." Aer rubbed at the jagged Raven's head on her neck. "You felt the energy with this new person. Besides, what do we know? You and I can read because Bethlem taught us. We have street smarts, and that's what is going to give us the edge."

"Edge in what? I thought we agreed."

"I did. I do." She paused and sank into herself. "The world just seems too big. Too heavy to keep carrying on like this. It's going to kill you, Kor. You can't keep going on being perfect all the time. There has to be another way."

"That's why we hold up the world together."

"But your plans, they're long term. Can people hold on that long? Can people try to hold up this mess of a world for that long?"

"If they can't, they can hold on to hope. It's so light it floats on your wind," he said.

Aer smiled. The winds whistled around Korvo.

"And if you think you can't hold on, then ... you can hold on to me." Kor moved closer.

Aer's smile faded slightly. He had pushed her too far. He knew it. He turned to stare at the table. Aer didn't move.

"For a little longer," Aer said and sat in the chair opposite him. Kor didn't take his eyes off the grain in the wooden table. The silence dragged on.

"Do you think Merin and Bryce have found who they're looking for?" he asked finally.

"Still worried?" She leaned her head on her arm, stifling a yawn, and Kor felt worse for waking her up.

"They're just kids."

"Two years, Kor. They're two years younger than us."

"And two years can be a lifetime," Kor said. "More than a lifetime," he mumbled under his breath. Aer pulled her hair back into a bun at the top of her head, revealing the mark etched into her skin. "Much more," he whispered quietly enough that only the wind floating by Aer would notice.

"They'll be fine. Just like we were." She stood and grabbed her jacket.

"You're right." Kor followed her. She was. They'd be fine. But no one else needed to end up hardened like they were. He and Aer were the only ones who needed to juggle love, hatred, and the past. He and Aer were the only ones who needed to put their necks on the line for the coming revolution. He just wanted Bryce and Merin to live their lives.

Kor followed her out of the house. They walked without speaking for seven city blocks.

"Who do you think this new person is?" Aer asked when they entered the Garden District.

"Powerful. As long as I read the cards right," Kor said tapping the leather pouch tied next to his hip.

"You always read the cards right," she scoffed.

Uneasily, Kor ran his fingers over his bumpy, blotchy skin. "Sometimes things aren't as clear."

Aer nodded. Silence overtook them again. Kor could feel the breeze around him grow. He took a step to his left and let Aer have her room. The winds always flocked to her when she was deep in thought.

As they walked, Kor tried to remember the names of the plants Bryce had taught him. They were all different from Hadran. These lost their leaves in the winter and felt like paper to his fingers. Not the waxy lushness of the flora he was used to back home. He shoved his hand under the leather strap to touch the cards in their pouch. He let his thumb rub over their dusty edges, soft from wear and tear. Home. Why had the cards shown him home?

Hadran was somewhere he could never return. Magic was outlawed there. And while Kor had to admit being labeled, taxed, and ignored wasn't ideal, it was better than what happened in Hadran. That's what had sent him North. The promise of something better. Somewhere he could lead the fight for Magics. Somewhere the battle hadn't already been lost in politics that were ingrained in stone.

BRYCE:

The guard stopped Bryce after they let Merin go by. Bryce wanted to blame everything on the mark attached permanently to his ankle, but his clothes were also torn and patched, and Merin's were not. He knew that she smelled like summer rain and fresh linens, and he smelled like the musty dirt in the garden. He knew that spots of dirt were mixed equally with the freckles that covered his face.

"What is your business here?" The Watcher asked him.

"You're not going to ask her?" He pretended to be shocked.

"She's not a Magic. Nothing good comes from a Magic coming to a Watcher." The Watcher's hand went to his baton.

"He's my bodyguard," Merin said in her commanding voice, a tone that had only taken seven years of school and thousands of her parents' dollars to create.

"You sure you want a Magic to be your bodyguard? Isn't that who you're trying to protect against?"

"Are you going to bring your bare fists to a knife fight?" Bryce said leaning in over Merin's shoulder to be face to face with the guard.

"I heard there was a Magic brought in this morning that caused a little bit of a stir?" She was reaching. They had no idea if anyone had been brought in. It was a hunch, and it could backfire at any moment.

"Just a little one. But how is that any of your business, Miss?"

"I was called as a healer," she said without any hesitation. Bryce smiled. She might have had the commanding voice from her parents' money, but she had the lying on her feet from him. She had come a long way in the year they had known each other.

"Well, alright. I still don't think you should be so free with the Magics, Miss—"

"My business is my own." She turned, letting the edge of her braid come defiantly close to the guard's face without touching him. Bryce followed silently behind.

Once their eyes adjusted to the dark interior of the room, a woman at a desk waved them over. "Please sign in," she said. Merin signed fake names for them both. Bryce stood a good two feet away, making sure to keep far enough to stop anyone from recognizing him immediately. It would not be ideal if he ended up in a cell next to the Magic they had come to fetch.

"The room you are looking for is third on the left." The woman gave Merin a pleasant smile. She ignored Bryce completely.

Merin thanked her and headed down the hallway.

Two Watchers in special uniforms lined with gold trim stood outside the door.

"I'm here as a healer. This is my bodyguard," Merin said. They undid the bolt for her and ushered them inside.

"Are there always special guards for the cells?" Merin whispered.

"Those aren't special. Those are parade uniforms. Some bigwig must be coming by today. The quicker we get in and out the better it will be for everyone," Bryce whispered back.

"Agreed."

The room was cold and bare. There was no one in there except one guard and a small shadow of a shape at the corner of the room.

"Excuse me," the guard said. This one was in regular uniform. Apparently, they didn't expect the important people to deal with the prisoners directly. Bryce scoffed. Probably too much dirt to get on their hands.

"I'm here to heal this prisoner," Merin said. The lie sounded better and better every time she said it. Even Bryce forgot for a minute why they were really there.

"Well, that's fine. He's over there." The guard gestured limply to the shadow hunched over in the corner of the room.

"You can step out now," Merin suggested.

"Little Miss, I'm not going to do that. It's too dangerous to leave a young thing like you alone with a Magic."

"I brought a bodyguard."

"Still, I don't think I should leave," the Watcher said with a laugh.

"Everyone has a right to have a healer without guards present. It's in the law," Merin said. Her father was the head lawyer for the City Council, and she knew her fair share of the rules. Merin turned her back on them and headed toward the boy.

"He hasn't asked for one," the Watcher laughed again, causing Merin to turn. Bryce knew the game. Watchers were obsessed with power and even Merin's influence wasn't enough to let go.

"I doubt that will be a problem," Merin started, but the muffled laughter from the Watcher cut her off.

"I'm sorry little miss, but he hasn't spoken a word since someone reported him. I doubt he's going to start now."

Bryce looked at the small boy in front of him. His clothes were tattered, and Bryce doubted that was only from the fight. The fabric was faded, but he could see remnants of bright colors. Maroon, yellow, cyan. The kind of fabric Kor was always drawn to when they walked through the shops of the city. His skin was a dark olive color like Kor, too. Only the deep brown eyes marked him as something other than Korvo's brother. The boy struggled to move away as Bryce and Merin approached, and he flicked his eyes at them. They burned.

"Hadranian?" Bryce asked. The boy's eyes softened, and he nodded. In Hadran's language, Bryce asked the boy if he wanted the Watchers to stay in the room. He shook his head no.

"See," the Watcher said, letting his thumbs slide into the heavy belt that held his club.

"If you want them to leave," Bryce said in broken and forced Hadranian, "you have to answer 'yes' when I say this so they'll understand." The boy said nothing for a second and then nodded.

"Do you want them to leave while the healer examines you?" Bryce said so the Watchers could understand him.

"Yeas," the boy squeaked out. It may have been rough, but it was clear enough that even the most power-hungry Watcher couldn't deny it now.

"I'll have to ask you to leave," Merin said.

With a grumble, the Watcher moved toward the door.

"You really shouldn't trust Magics that much. It's not good for you."

"Good thing she's a healer," Bryce said with a smirk.

The Watcher did not respond but slammed the door behind him, making the room shake just a little.

"You really have a knack for people," Merin said. Bryce smiled.

"At least I noticed our little friend here is from the South."

"I... I..."

"It's fine. It's not like you speak much Hadranian," Bryce said, sitting opposite the boy. "What is your name?" Bryce asked the boy in Hadranian. He was awfully skinny. His clothes hung loose around him, and they looked like they were hand-me-downs.

"Tiernan," the boy replied. He stared at Bryce as if he were strange-looking. The boy only broke eye contact when Merin reached out to touch his shoulder, and he flinched.

"Will you tell him I'm trying to help?" Merin said. Bryce attempted. The boy struggled against her, even when she used her most soothing words. "You don't know the word for help?" Merin scolded the third time Tiernan pulled out of her grasp.

"What can I say? Help doesn't seem to come up a lot in the discussions I have with Kor about Hadran."

"Could you say it another way?"

Bryce shrugged. Kor had been teaching him Hadranian in the hope that they could use it to code their conversations, and Bryce wondered if Kor hoped one day to help the people back home. He tried a few combinations of words, but nothing seemed to relax Tiernan.

"Then maybe just let me try to work," Merin said as Tiernan pulled himself into a ball.

Bryce gave her space and sat down on the bench bolted to the wall. He crossed his leg over his knee; he was kind of enjoying someone disobeying Merin. It wasn't a sight he was used to.

Suddenly Tiernan relaxed.

"See, I didn't need you," she said, sticking her tongue out at Bryce, but Bryce saw Tiernan's eyes were locked on the Raven tattoo on his ankle. Bryce rolled back the pant leg so it was even more visible and smiled at the little boy. Merin huffed, but got to work on her newly obedient patient.

Bryce watched Merin's fingers dance over the lump on the boy's temple as she let her magic flow through him like healing water. She would be feeling the pressure of the blood trying to get oxygen to somewhere that was hurting. Her shoulders slumped a little. Anything near the brain made her job twice as difficult.

When she finished with Tiernan's head, Merin looked back at Bryce with a small smile, and he couldn't help but smile back. She was soft and refined. She was everything he would never be.

She flicked her hand at him, and he tossed her the small bag of medical supplies she always kept on her. She put gauze around his knee. No use wasting energy on something that would heal up on its own.

"How are we going to get him out of here?" Merin put on the last bandage.

"I was just thinking about that. I was going to suggest you demand he be taken to the hospital for his head injury, but now that you've worked on it, it doesn't look so bad anymore."

"True, but I couldn't leave him like that." She glanced over the boy, and Bryce wondered how much of her power she'd had to use to help him.

"And they just think I'm some brute and not my most charming self," Bryce said as the outline of a plan flashed into his head. He tried to make the quick calculations of risk that Kor did endlessly, but he felt the details getting foggy. Best to wing it. He winked at the boy, who was still sitting on the table looking back and forth between them.

"If you were your normal self, you would have gotten yourself thrown into one of the other rooms here and I would have had to get you out, too," Merin said. Her arms crossed in front of her.

"How likely do you think it is that they checked him for disease before they brought him here?" Bryce asked.

"You mean how likely are the Watchers to actually follow the written law? Not very."

"Watch."

Merin swept her skirts behind her as she sat down on the dirty bench and gestured for Bryce to get on with it. His smile cracked into brilliance. A brilliance that soon faded with a dismal game of charades that ended with Bryce having to take his shirt halfway off for Tiernan to do the same. He didn't have to turn to hear Merin's laughter muffled by her hand.

"Are we supposed to get the guards to faint from the smell?" Merin asked. Bryce could hear the teasing in her voice, but he had to stop from smelling himself.

"Just wait. You'll see," Bryce said.

Bryce stooped to pick up a handful of dirt. Rubbing it back and forth in his palms the dirt became sticky with energy like it did when he walked.

The spots of dirt stuck to the little boy in irregular little spots. When he was satisfied, Bryce turned so Merin could see.

"He looks like he has Bone Fever!" she gasped.

"Told you. Now we get them to let us take him to the hospital," Bryce said, enjoying his handiwork.

Merin nodded and went for the big silver door. She pounded on it. It slid open.

"Had enough?" one of the Watchers asked.

"I need this boy moved to the Kaybrum hospital now," Merin said. Her voice was devoid of any of its normal warmth. Cold authority rang through it now. Even Bryce stiffened.

"That boy is bound for the Refuge. His face don't even look that bad anymore," the taller of the two sneered.

In two quick steps, Merin's long legs had moved her back to Tiernan's side and she lifted his shirt enough for the guards to see the blotches covering his chest.

"Write me a pass to take this child to the hospital and secure transport for the three of us before I report you for failing to check for signs of infection before bringing someone into a government building."

The men scrambled without a word down the hallway, and Bryce stuck his tongue out at them when they were out of sight.

"What if they report to the hospital that we're coming?" Bryce asked suddenly.

"Doubting your own plan?" Merin scoffed.

"Didn't think you were going to scare them so badly," he teased, but really his mind went back to the risk calculations. Kor would have thought this part through.

"I doubt they'll make it official. Those two probably haven't entered any paperwork on Tiernan yet. They'll just let it slip so there is no trace they didn't report an infection. Especially if you're right about there being someone important in the building."

"I don't know if that's all your schooling or the influence you've gotten from hanging with us, but I like it."

"Both," she said. Bryce felt taller than his five-foot-eight frame.

"When the transport lets us off at the hospital, we'll just walk from there to meet up with Kor."

"Do you think he is really the person we were sent to find?" Merin asked as they waited for the transport.

"Does it really matter? Either way, we have to get this kid to Kor."

KORVO:

Bryce and Merin weren't in the garden. No one had seen them for hours.

"Do you think you could find them with the wind?" Korvo asked as they headed toward the Wall District.

"I mean, probably. On their own, no. Bryce smells too much like the garden for the wind to tell the difference. Merin smells too much like the rich. The two of them together ..." She whispered into the wind in a language that sounded like hurricanes and spring breezes. Kor felt an impatient gust of wind whip by him.

"We'll see," she said.

"Do you think they could have already made it to Bethlem's?" The bright colors of the edge of the Wall District came into view.

"You're the one tapping into the future," Aer said.

Kor looked away from her. All day he'd been impatient, checking the cards every few minutes. The cards kept urging him to find Bryce and Merin. All he knew was somehow Hadran was involved. A place he couldn't quite shake.

A cacophony of wind slammed against Kor.

"That was fast," Aer said waving her arms around, calming the wind around her. "I guess you shouldn't worry so much." Aer doubled the pace toward Bethlem's. Kor followed quickly behind her.

Inside Bethlem's, Kor scanned the room for Bryce and Merin, but he didn't see them. The further he walked in, the more his heart sank thinking Aer had been wrong.

"Looking for someone?" Bryce asked, tapping Kor on the shoulder. The two embraced.

"We weren't expecting you until later," Merin said coming from behind the purple silk curtain that cut off the bar from the quieter dining areas.

"Kor was nervous." Aer slid into the corner booth.

Merin slipped back behind the curtain.

"Can we actually talk in there?" Bryce pointed his head toward where Merin had disappeared. His grin dipped a little at the sides.

"Did something bad happen?" Kor asked as they wound through hallways to the farthest room from the bar.

"Depends on your definition of bad." Bryce scratched the back of his head.

"You found the person, right?" Aer asked.

"You'd better see for yourself." Bryce raised the thicker tapestry that acted as the door for the back rooms and disappeared inside.

Kor followed. Bryce leaned against the wall near the door and crossed his arms. Kor noticed the slight twitch in his fingers.

"What is it?" Kor asked before he saw it for himself. A little Hadranian boy stared up at him from where he was cuddled in Merin's lap.

"Meet Tiernan," Bryce said, coming to stand next to Korvo.

"Could he really be ..." Kor turned to Aer. She nodded.

"The wind says so," she said, taking a seat across the table from Merin.

"But ..." Kor looked around. The cards had been so intense. He was expecting an angry teen. Someone like Bryce without the empathy. Someone he would have to contain.

"He only speaks Hadranian," Bryce said, walking over to the table. "I talked to him to get him to come with us."

"It's a good thing you didn't screw up your pronunciation like you normally do," Kor faked levity, while his mind tried to sort everything out into a neat list. No wonder the cards were whispering to him about home. The boy's skin was darker than his own, but the facial features were eerily similar. After spending years with people who didn't look like him, it was strange to see such a familiar face.

"Welcome," Kor said in Hadranian. The thick accent he normally banished from his vernacular came back instantly. He stuck out his right hand to greet the little boy.

Tiernan stuck out his hand cautiously. He eyed Kor's mangled hand.

"F... fire," the boy stuttered, pointing at Kor's hand and jumping up from Merin's lap.

"No, no fire." Kor said. "Acid." He explained in Hadranian. The boy shook his head. He lifted his shirt to show Kor something.

"Fire," he said again pointing. There on his chest, now cleared from the muddy smudges, was a Phoenix emblem.

"What does it mean?" Bryce leaned close. The mark was hardly noticeable if it wasn't pointed out. Hardly the place for something like the Raven tattoo they were branded with.

"It's the Phoenix," Korvo said, resting his hand on the boy's chest. He sighed deeply and stood facing Bryce. "It's given to Magics once they have been declared too dangerous for the world. In Hadran, it is used to mark someone for execution."

"Execution?" Merin shrieked, pulling Tiernan closer to her, startling him. He pulled away from her hand.

"Tiernan?" Kor asked, squatting down from his six-three frame to the boy's eye level. "I have it, too. See?" Kor lifted his shirt enough so the boy could see the mark on Kor's chest. Tiernan's eyes widened.

"Explain this at once," Merin said. Her foot stamped and bumped the chair. When they turned to look at her, she turned red.

"I think what Merin is trying to say," Bryce interrupted, "is that we would all like to know just why the hell you have an execution mark on your chest and none of us knew."

"I knew," Aer said quietly.

"Why does Aer get to know?" Bryce asked. His fingers clenched into fists.

"Bryce, get control of yourself. You're scaring Tiernan," Kor grumbled. Bryce let his hands drop to his sides. He nodded and resumed leaning against the wall, but the flick of anger hadn't left.

"Let's sit," Aer suggested. She stuck her head out into the hallway and flagged down a worker walking from the back to get them some water.

Kor found himself across from Bryce. He recognized the stocky boy's furrow. Kor knew he shouldn't keep secrets from him, but it had seemed like the right idea at the time.

He had never planned to put this on their shoulders, but now it couldn't be helped. He looked around the table with a sigh. Aer sat to Bryce's left. A cold drink found its way into his hand. He looked to see Merin. He gave her a smile. She beamed back at him.

"Where do you want to start?" Kor locked eyes with Bryce.

"What is that mark, exactly?" Bryce asked.

"Magic is illegal in Hadran. I expect you all know that," Kor said looking around the table.

They nodded.

"It is less common knowledge that they were exterminating anyone who posed a threat."

"To the people?" Merin looked at the little boy sitting next to her. Tiernan was playing with some water that had dripped onto the table. He was dragging it around, making little pictures.

"To the people in charge." Aer slammed her glass down on the table. Bryce and Tiernan both jumped.

"Anyway," Kor said once everyone had settled, "Magics had no rights, so it didn't matter if they had decided to kill all of us. Powerful or not."

"But you wouldn't hurt anyone." Merin grasped at the edge of his sleeve. Kor smiled at her and let his left hand rest on hers.

"That wouldn't matter to anyone."

"But you just read cards." Bryce's voice strained.

"Knowing the future can be just as powerful as your vines or Aer's wind." Kor looked off into the corners of the room. "So they branded me with the Phoenix because I posed a problem. A potential problem."

"Why didn't you tell us?" Bryce asked. His fingers tapped the glass.

"I didn't want to scare you." Kor looked down at Tiernan and back at Bryce.

"I'm not a little kid, Kor." Bryce slammed his fist onto the table.

"You were three years ago." Kor kept a straight face. They locked eyes. Bryce looked away. "You had enough on your plate."

"How come Aer knows?" Bryce asked indignantly.

"I know because I saw it. Although, I wasn't sure. I didn't want to ask," she turned away from him. Kor reached out a hand.

"I didn't know you knew what it meant until now."

She nodded, taking his right hand in hers.

A gasp from Merin drew his attention back to the matter at hand. Tiernan had a tiny little flame in his hand. It danced. Unlike the flicker of a candle, it turned and moved like a real dancer. Kor watched.

"I told you. You never read the cards wrong," Aer said softly, breaking him from his concentration.

"Bryce," Kor said, standing up suddenly, still staring at the flame in Tiernan's hand. Everyone turned to look at him. Even the flame in Tiernan's hand stopped. "Tiernan is not to leave your sight. He is not to be left alone. You and any of us who can spare time will be guarding him from now on." Kor repeated himself in Hadranian so that Tiernan could understand.

"But why?" Bryce asked. "I mean I get he needs our help to stay out of the Refuge, but the twenty-four-hours-a-day thing is a little intense."

"Do you know why he referred to this mark as fire?" Kor asked, his brow heavy. His finger pointed directly to the mark on his chest. Bryce didn't answer. He looked down at the table. "It's because originally it was only for people with his power. People they could turn others against."

"But why?" Merin asked, standing.

"Are people afraid of you?" Kor asked the room. Bryce and Merin looked away.

"Well," Merin started. Aer glared at her. She moved closer to Bryce.

"No one likes us, except ..."

"When convenient, right?" Kor said. They all nodded. Aer sang at the club for a reason. And Bryce was tolerated in the gardens. Even Kor had non-Magics asking him to look at their cards.

"Fire is almost never convenient," Kor said. "It might warm you, but it can also burn a house down. Burn the crops. Burn a person."

"What would have happened to him if...?" Merin left the rest unsaid. They knew what that silence meant. They let it sit for a second. Everyone was lost in thought. Kor watched the two younger kids process. Would it have been better to tell them before? It didn't matter now.

"We're lucky that the guards didn't seem to know." Bryce rubbed his brow, "And that they probably never filed any paperwork on him."

"But he's safe now. Right?" Merin asked. "He won't be sent back to Hadran or anything if they did?"

"No." Kor nodded. "He wouldn't be. Too much trouble."

"But," interrupted Bryce, "they don't have to let you out of the Refuge."

Kor placed a hand on his shoulder.

"Or worse," Aer said, "they use fear to turn everyone against us."

"Then they'll never close the Refuge." Merin glanced around the room for someone to say otherwise. Bryce scowled but wouldn't meet anyone's gaze.

"Why me? Wouldn't he be better off with you or Aer?" Bryce still didn't look up.

"I can't bring him to the club. And until we know more, he probably shouldn't be around the council," Aer said. A silence fell over the room.

In the moment of silence, Tiernan asked Kor questions in rapid-fire Hadranian while Kor answered him carefully.

Bryce sighed. "Can I teach him something other than Hadranian? I'm not going to be much help if it takes me twenty minutes to tell him anything."

"If you think you can," Kor laughed. The mood in the room eased. Kor felt the tension begin to seep out from their room through the curtain into the bar. He was happy for the respite, but knew he wouldn't sleep much.

"Kor?" Bryce said suddenly. Kor turned and looked at him. "I don't think we'll be safe if he lives with me in the gardens. And there are too many anti-Magics at the club where Aer sings. And Merin ... can't have us," he paused. "Can we stay with you?"

"We won't be able to stay in the lodging house. Too many people. We'll have to stay somewhere else." Kor began thinking through the possibilities.

"I think I know a place no one will notice us." Bryce picked at the edges of his nails. He swallowed hard. Korvo understood what he meant.

"On top of the Refuge?" Kor asked. Bryce closed his eyes and nodded.

Bryce took a deep breath. The vines from earlier reached out of his pocket and twirled up his arm. "I think it's for the best. Besides, then he has two of us to talk to."

Kor nodded.

"I hate to break up this party, but I need to start getting ready for work." Aer stood up from the table. The rest of them gathered their stuff. Tiernan followed them out of the room, holding on to Merin's skirt again.

"I think he likes you," Bryce whispered in her ear. She giggled.

"Goodnight, Merin," Kor said, reaching for Tiernan's hand. As soon as Tiernan had let go, she waved and disappeared into the hum of the city.

"Kor? Do you think I can keep him safe?"

"Worried about him?" Kor asked.

"Merin would kill me if something happened to him. She gets attached to people pretty quick."

"I know you can."

MERIN:

Her house was dark when she came in through the servant's door. She tiptoed toward the main staircase. Darkened lights throughout the house did not mean that her father wasn't still up working away in his study. She padded along to the bathroom in order to bathe. Her headache, while mild, had not gone away even though it had been hours since she'd worked on Tiernan. It was enough that she had forgotten to ask Korvo how his meeting with the Council had gone. Although if he didn't mention it, it probably didn't go very well.

What a small little boy, she thought, reaching for the handle of the door. His body had caused more trouble for Merin than normal. It wasn't that he was hurt badly, but his tiny frame wasn't rejecting the pain like most people do. She felt like her magic had to pry it away from him. Like he was holding on to it. Like it was part of him. She shuddered. The door squeaked under her palm.

"Merin, is that you?" her father's raspy voice called from his study.

"Yes, Father. I couldn't sleep, so I thought I would take a bath." She smiled. She was getting better at lying. Bryce would be proud.

"Could you come here?" her father said through the ornate wooden door. She sighed. There was only one reason her father would want her to come into the study. At least she might learn something about Korvo's school.

"Father?" She nudged the study door open. His desk was piled high with papers. Her father's greying hair was pushed up on the sides as if he had been holding his head. "Is everything alright?"

"Just lots of hard decisions the Council has been making for the safety of the country. I'm not sure I could make the decisions they have to make," her father said, combining the papers in front of him. Merin followed it with her eyes.

"Is there anything I can do?" Merin leaned down and let tendrils of her power soften the knots in her father's shoulders. She hated using her powers like this, but sometimes when he was relaxed her father would talk to her about Council business.

"A little lower, Merin. It's a tough world outside these walls."

"What's happening, Father?"

"Just promise you'll keep your ... talents hidden."

"But if I can help people—" Merin protested.

"There is nothing one person can do. And not all people with magic are so helpful, so useful to the society at large."

"But it's not their fault. They aren't allowed in public schools, and few people can afford to pay for private ones.

And only your sway in the Council keeps my magic a secret. Couldn't all of them be just like me?"

"Nonsense. That's enough. Go sleep."

"But I just think—"

"Merin, I'll do the thinking for you. Keep your powers hidden and stay away from the other Magics."

"Yes, Father," she said demurely.

"Good girl."

Merin knew she had been dismissed, so she bowed her head slightly and went out through the heavy wooden door. She didn't let the bolt click into place and instead listened at the small crack in the door to see if she could hear anything else.

"Only a few more weeks," her father muttered.

"A few more weeks until what," Merin whispered on the way back to her bedroom, her bath forgotten.

Merin looked around her room. The white comforter was stiff and straight against the bed frame, tucked into the edges of her bed. The dolls she had received over the years from various estranged relatives who were never allowed to come over to their house sat staring down at her. Merin wanted to push them away. Their beaded eyes looked down with a level of disappointment that was normally reserved for her family.

She had to do something. She couldn't let good people like Korvo and Bryce live on the streets while she sat around idly and did nothing. But she couldn't even stand up to her father. She lay across her plush bed and stared at the ceiling. She would help to start Korvo's school even if she was the only one who taught day and night.

She pulled a pillow over her head for just a second before rolling over to try and get some sleep. Her headache would just have to go away on its own. She couldn't heal herself.

CHAPTER 3:

KORVO:

KOR WAITED UNTIL HE HEARD THE BREATH of the two young boys deepen and soften. He tapped the cards in his hand. He was tempted to ask the cards to show him something of the future, give him something to believe in. But Kor couldn't bring himself to lay the cards out in front of him.

He had expected some out-of-control and angry teen when he had read the cards. But now he had a Phoenix and a fire Magic. A young one at that. Someone who couldn't help them. Not yet. Not anytime soon. And time was not something they had a lot of. He shook the negative thoughts from his head. They also had someone young to get started in their school. He was going to make it happen even if he only got permission for the building. He could scrounge up money, supplies, pupils, teachers. He'd done harder things. He smiled a little. Tiernan would show great progress. The Council would see it. Korvo sat a little straighter.

He took a deep breath. Kor gritted his teeth and, with a last look at his charges, made his way down to where Aer would be singing.

A blast of cold air sent the chill of the winter night directly into his mangled hand as he approached the club where

Aer worked. He could hear her singing before he had even turned down the street. The wind carried the notes to him. He stopped for a moment and let the words wash over him. For a second he didn't feel the cold. He didn't feel the ache in his hand. This was Aer's real power: to ease the weight of the world from Kor's shoulders.

He sat in the back by the bar like always. His face was almost hidden in the dark room. Even though his darker features were strong, his olive skin faded into the shadows. His yellow-green eyes caught the subtle reflected lights from behind the bar. Only the occasional stranger would sit and ask for a reading, and Kor would deal cards while Aer sang.

But tonight, no strangers came to ask for their fates to be revealed. He let himself concentrate on the music and forget the rest of the world.

"You knew to send Bryce because he spoke Hadranian, didn't you?" he said when a thin shadow crossed his face.

"Why would that make sense? You're the one who is fluent." Aer sat down at the table. Next to each other, they could both look out into the bar scene. Content to watch the crowd mill around, they sat silently for a minute. Men, who were past drunk, kept losing and then finding their footing enough to carry a drink or two back to their table.

A shouting match started on the other side of the bar. Two men raised their hands, but the limp wrists and uneasy footsteps proved not enough to start a ruckus.

"And *we're* the problem," Aer said, reaching over to take a sip from Kor's glass of water. She held the glass up in the light and swirled it around. The yellowish rust blended with the water, making it almost look like something drinkable.

Kor took the glass from her, mocked a salute, and downed it.

"This place has lots of problems." Kor set the empty glass down on the table.

"Magics aren't one." Aer turned so her back was to him. He moved closer. He reached up a hand to touch her hair but put it down.

"Not yet," he smiled instead. She reached back and put a hand on his knee.

"I bet Merin could make the water in this place drinkable. I wonder how they think the water for the upper class is cleaned. They always welcome our gifts when we're useful," she gestured to the crowd who was eagerly waiting for her to continue.

"Merin could be a big asset when it comes to getting the rich on board. And she is the best educated of all of us. No tattoo and no school ban," Kor said.

Aer breathed deeply as if she was about to say something, but stopped. Her hand dropped to Kor's knee. Kor sat straight up trying not to move. He wanted Aer's hand to stay on his knee, her fingers slowly smoothing the fabric of his pant leg. He didn't want any movement to startle her.

Aer shrugged. "I think she needs the Raven's head."

Kor jerked away from her. He looked at her face for some sort of reaction, but her eyes were focused on the table in front of them, and her lips were calm. She had thought about this.

"Aer, isn't that offense number one in your book?"

She pulled the feathered ruffle close to her neck to cover the dark mark.

"It's just a thought," her voice dropped to a whisper, but her eyes were still focused.

A waiter came and filled Kor's glass. He smiled at him and handed him a few coins. Water may have been free, but any kind of service for Magics always came with a price.

"What would that help?" he asked her when the waiter had cleared away far enough so that he wouldn't hear their conversation.

"Visibility. Respect. Isn't that what we want?" She didn't meet his eye. Her arms were twitching slightly. He moved closer.

"Aer," he sighed after a moment, "truthfully, did you know about his Phoenix?"

She shook her head. Then for a minute let her head rest on Kor's shoulder.

"I knew he was from Hadran, and I..."

The feathers in her hair tickled his ear, but he didn't move. He knew better than to move when Aer was having a moment like this. She was not one for showing her affection.

"I was worried you would run away with him," she said raising her head. The feathers left a trace of prickled skin on his neck. He ran his rough right hand over the little bumps to soothe them.

"There's work to be done here," he said, putting his right hand up to cradle her face for a moment.

"And it needs to be done soon." She stood and straightened the short, pastel blue skirt that revealed her thin legs. Kor looked away. This was no time to be thinking about having her body close to his.

"What have you heard?" He reached for the cards in his pocket. She looked around.

"With the number of kids the Watchers are pulling into the Refuge, I don't think it will be too long before people give up on us. Something is going to happen, and we either watch from the sidelines or we lead the charge before we become less than human to them."

"Sure, they've ignored giving Magics their rights, but you don't think they are going to actually believe we aren't human?" Kor asked. She traced her fingers down from his shoulder to his right hand. The mangled flesh still bristled under her touch.

"Don't you?"

"Hadran is a different place. It's bred into people from the time they're born: Magics are bad. But look at how many people come to hear you sing." Every table at the club had at least two people sitting at it. The buzz of conversation that was drowning out their whispers would fall silent again once she took the stage. Aer shook her head.

"And they would throw me away the second I became anything but convenient. I only pick up so many hours here because they can pay me less." She reached for the glass of water, and then took her hand away. "They can give me crap hours, and I won't walk away. These people are no better than the ones that branded that mark on your chest. They just haven't realized what power they have yet."

"They just need to see. They need to know we aren't dangerous."

"I'm just thinking, Kor, maybe it's time we *were* dangerous. Fight fire with fire."

"No, there is no point in proving them right. That's not fighting the fires. It's only feeding them."

"And if Tiernan gets away from Bryce and accidentally lights every tree in the park ablaze? What happens then?"

"That won't happen."

"We used to talk about making a stand."

"We are." He swallowed hard. "We just can't let kids like them stay in danger."

"Kor, I know you believe Bryce is capable of this—"

"You believed in him this morning."

"That was before I knew Tiernan was a Fire Magic. You have to think past your loyalties. You have to think of the big picture."

"I *am* thinking big picture. You told me yourself that I never read the cards wrong."

"I'm just asking you to stop thinking with this," she laid her hand gently on his heart, "and start thinking about this," she jabbed the point of her finger into the exact spot where he carried what was once his death sentence.

"Aer," he grabbed for her hand, but she pulled away. She was scared. The lines in her forehead were cut deep. Her slim hands trembled slightly. He let her go in silence.

Kor looked at the swirling filth in his water and laid his head against the back of his chair. He knew the difference between people being blind to the hurt they cause, and people being blind to humanity. He rubbed his right hand. He shuffled the cards once more before putting them back into his pocket.

He listened for a minute as Aer started her next set. Her feathers danced in the snappy breeze that surrounded her, but the song was anything but the soothing sounds she normally sang. This one was a call for action, and Kor left before he let it take hold of his thoughts.

He had a plan. He had a plan when he got to Kaybrum. Now that plan was to start the school. End the Refuge. It had to be the plan. Aer would see that.

Kor wandered the streets. It was hours before he needed to convince everyone to give toward the school. He should sleep an hour or two before meeting up with the rest of the resistance, but something about the night wasn't letting him. Maybe he shouldn't have given Tiernan the spot closest to the chimney stack, since the cold seemed to be eating at his bones. Nothing to do but walk through the night and think.

Kor had the vision. He was a planner. He moved the pieces. But lately, it felt like the pieces fought him every time he tried to make a move. Kor felt the sudden urge to go wake up Bryce and bring him to the meeting. Bryce was always ready to fight a battle for him, but that was childish, and Kor knew it. He'd have to face the group alone.

He wandered toward the walls of the city. The closer you got to the walls, the closer to Magics you were going to be. The walls may cover even the brightest days with a shadow, but there were always vibrant colors and plenty of music to make up for it. The doorways opened letting the light spill out onto the street.

"Korvo, how's it going?" Bethlem called from up the street. Kor walked quickly over to him.

"Strange days," Kor said, glancing around him. Bethlem took a step inside the bar and motioned for Kor to follow. He followed the older man through the maze of hanging tapestries in doorways until they came to the same back room where Kor had met Tiernan and where Kor would spend another night trying to convince people of this plan.

"Any news?" Bethlem asked. He leaned toward Kor, and Kor let himself sit on the ruby leather couch.

"Are people restless?" Kor ignored the question.

"More than usual you mean?" Bethlem said. His long frame and the way he leaned against the doorway reminded Korvo of Aer. He sighed thinking about what she had said.

"Yeah," Kor heard the air of impatience within his own voice. He tried to swallow it down.

"Well, the Watchers have started making double the amount of rounds they normally do through these parts. I have to admit that makes people a little jumpy." The creases in Bethlem's dark brown skin usually made him seem friendly and open, a great trait for a barkeep. But now, right before

Kor had to ask everyone for more, it just made Bethlem look as tired as Kor felt.

"You're telling them to play it cool, right? We can't have people taking justice into their own hands." Kor rubbed his forehead. His furrow had deepened well beyond his years. "And we can't lose any more older Magics to the labor camps."

"I know the plan, Kor, I just wish it could come sooner. Us old people, at least the ones still here, we just got to make sure we follow the law. But you kids, them Watchers can get you for just looking wrong."

"Justice is a slow burn." Kor rubbed at his hand as the others made their way into the back room.

AER:

Most of the group had already arrived when Aer snuck into the back. A ragtag group of people she and Kor had been able to cobble together over the last few years. There were few people older than them. Bethlem, of course, and a pair of twins who sold doctored water to the rich. Another few faces that she didn't know well, just well enough to gather information from them. Sometimes it was better not to know too much. She scanned the small crowd again. No Bryce or Merin. Kor must really want to keep Tiernan a secret if he didn't bring Bryce.

She let herself stick to the shadows. Tiernan's arrival had sparked a feeling of necessity in her. It felt like her heart was beating fast enough for her to be running, but her limbs weren't moving. She didn't feel like talking to anyone. Even Kor. Although that meant he was going to be by himself up there.

Kor stood tall at the front of the room. He laughed with a group of people as they came in, but Aer could tell he wasn't at ease. His eyebrows pinched together slightly, and the bags under his eyes seemed a little more pronounced than normal.

"Let's get this started," Bethlem said coming to stand next to Korvo.

"Welcome, friends," Kor said. His melancholy pushed to the edges of his pronounced eyebrows, and his fingers rubbed absentmindedly against his damaged hand. Aer doubted anyone else saw. Kor only let people see what he wanted: strength, resolve, understanding.

The room quieted, and the doors were closed. In the end, not that many people had come. They had lost numbers in the last few months to arrests and people giving up, but there were still more people than they had started with.

She had found Kor on top of the Refuge. His hand was still bandaged then. His face was pained and angry. She had climbed up the tower to practice her singing. No one would notice a little extra lightning around the tallest metal structure during a storm.

Kor had been huddled next to the smokestack. His clothes were tattered and wet, clinging to his body, but he didn't seem to notice that.

"Who are you?" she had asked when she stepped onto the rooftop. She gave herself a wide berth. Strangers were not to be trusted. She had flipped her hair to the side and started braiding it while keeping an eye on him.

Eventually, he spoke. "Magic?" he said. His accent was thick with the flavor of Hadran.

"What of it?" Aer said.

"Me too."

"Sure," Aer said looking him over. There was no Raven's head on him that she could see.

He pointed to the bandages on his hand. She nodded.

"This place. It's evil, isn't it?" Kor said looking down at the metal roof. The pinging of rain surrounded them. Aer nodded her head.

"I'm going to burn it to the ground." His yellow-green eyes caught hers. She was mesmerized in an instant.

How long had she felt the same thing? How long had she wanted justice? And this stranger had put words to her feelings immediately.

"Aer," she said sticking out her hand.

"Korvo," he said looking down at his hand and extending his left.

They shook, and after that, they had become inseparable. They spent nights talking and dreaming of what the world could be like. Slowly, Aer had pulled out some details about his time in Hadran. Some, but she knew it was never all of it. It could never be all of it. There was a deep pain behind his eyes.

And here they were now, she thought, refocusing on the conversation Kor was having.

"If they won't give us any money, Kor, it won't matter," one of the twins said from the side of the room.

The other twin echoed her concerns, "Magics have no money. If anyone gives more to the school, they will have less for taxes, and then it's a one-way ticket to work camps and long stays at the Refuge."

"I know it seems like a big ask," Kor said. His throat was tight, but from the distance, Aer couldn't tell if it was anger or sadness that was beginning to choke his words. "But this is our first real chance. We've been working for years for this."

"I heard that some Watchers are giving a test to the little ones. If they can't read, they're a burden to society," someone called from the corner. Aer didn't need to see who it was to know that what they said was true. It was one of the things she had shown Kor before they had found Tiernan.

"Good thing Magics don't get free schooling," a voice snapped from the other side of the room. The din of the room rose. Aer couldn't track the individual voices anymore.

"Doomed." "Unfair." "Pointless." "Necessary." "Hopeless." All of these words filtered in and out of the tangle of conversations around her. She felt her heart tugging at her to run again. The tug to go do something. Burn it to the ground. Kor's words echoed through her head.

As Kor tried to get everyone back together, Aer slipped from her place in the shadows and moved toward the door. She had heard enough. She gave one last glance back at Kor, and for a second his bright eyes found her in the crowd. He turned his head ever so slightly, as if asking her a question. But she didn't respond. She felt his eyes linger on her as she made her way out into the night.

She should have headed toward the walls, but she needed time to process. She couldn't sit around and play nice anymore. Maybe Kor would see he was too concerned with not rocking the boat, but either way, she had to do something.

KORVO:

Aer had left. He couldn't remember if she had ever left a meeting early before.

"I don't think I can ask my people," piped in someone who worked on the north end of the Wall District.

"Let's focus on books for now," Kor said. "There have to be some around from before the school ban. We'll find those. Anything is better than nothing."

Everyone in the room nodded.

"If you happen to come across some books, however you can, that will be enough for now," Kor said, closing out the meeting.

When the room had emptied to just Kor and Bethlem, Kor felt the tension leak onto his face. Bethlem lightly tapped his shoulder. Kor sat down. His body felt heavy, and getting off his feet didn't seem to help at all.

"There hasn't been any word of any Fire Magic, has there?" Kor asked as Bethlem cleared the tables.

"A Fire Magic? Not for years."

"Good." Kor handed over a small silver coin, "You let me know if you hear any talk. Even if you think it's some rumor I wouldn't care about. Anything about a Fire Magic comes to me."

Bethlem nodded. He took the coin and put it in his front pocket.

"Anything else you need from us?" Bethlem asked.

Kor started to stand, his hands pushing the dark chestnut desk in front of him.

"Actually, there is a small favor."

"Whatever you need," Bethlem said, wiping his hands on his barkeep's apron.

"I..." The words stuck in his throat. "Aer...never mind." He turned to leave. His arm had already begun to part the purple gauze curtain.

"Something needs to happen soon," Bethlem said in almost a whisper.

Kor nodded. "I don't need the cards to know that."

"I'm sure you don't. Be careful, Korvo. You've put your neck on the line."

"Well, if I hadn't made it out of Hadran, I'd be dead anyway."

"That's—I'm just—watch out for yourself. Don't wait for the cards to tell you."

"Thanks, Bethlem."

Kor ducked out underneath the curtain. Then he stuck his head back in, "Remember: anything about a Fire Magic and it comes directly to me."

Bethlem said nothing and let Korvo move out into the chaos of the bar.

Two young messengers nearly toppled Kor on his way out. They gave him a brief nod before realizing who he was. Coming to a complete stop, they circled back and gave him a small salute.

"Where you boys off to at this time of night?"

"Delivering some money to the walls," the smaller one said.

"Well, don't let me stop you," The boys turned and kept running into the dark shadows of the night.

He should go to the walls tonight, too. There would be no sleep waiting for him back at the Refuge. And there would be nothing Bethlem could do about the books for a while. He sighed and headed toward the metal walls twenty feet thick and forty feet high. The metal was welded together in haste near the bottom, but near the top it was graceful and gleaming with the slight dance of light hitting where no buildings clouded the view.

Korvo came to a deep fissure in the metal. The wall peeled away from the massive structure. He breathed in for a count of seven and held his breath. Releasing the captive air through his nose, he headed inside the walls.

His eyes adjusted quickly to the absolute darkness surrounding him. The air felt warm on his face, but the stale smell beat out the brief feeling of warmth. Kor took a tentative step, making sure his foot was placed on something solid before letting his entire weight settle. The walls were busy, but that didn't mean there weren't things to trip on if you didn't know your way around. People weren't supposed to hide in the walls like rats, after all.

The glow of a small lantern made his hand jump to his eyes. He stumbled closer to it, letting his feet drag across the floor, looking for the stops and starts of passageways and stairs that popped out of nowhere.

"The Chosen returns," a voice snaked its way to Korvo.

"Sid," Korvo replied. In the weak light, Korvo could hardly make out Sid's features. Sid was shorter than him even though they were the same age. His eyes were almost black, but Korvo wondered if his pupils were just that way because he lived in the walls.

"What is the fabulous hero doing slumming it in here with us?" Sid sneered.

"It's been a while," Kor replied. His voice was calm and cold. Sid had once come to all of their meetings, but that had stopped some time ago.

"A while? Sure," Sid said, looking at his fingernails.

"Sid ..." Kor started.

"Don't Sid me. Everyone sees you as some savior. The burned-hand martyr come to save us from evil. We don't all need saving."

"I'm not trying to save anyone. I'm just trying to give us a fair shake." Kor sighed. "I just wanted to check in."

"Everyone here is fine. You can go now."

"I'd like to see for myself." Kor brought himself up to his full height, letting his arms drop to his sides to give him some mass.

"Of course. Your Majesty." Sid bowed and moved to the side. Kor ignored him and walked past. It was best not to argue. He would only get mad.

"Kor!" The nearest healer cooed when he walked into a medic wing. He managed a smile despite Sid following in behind him. "We haven't seen you in so long. Where's Aer?"

"Busy. I needed to see for myself." He glanced over the beds lined up along the curve of the wall. The beds stretched for as long as the light held, and he wondered how many more of these wings there were around the miles of the entire wall. Hospitals, after all, could deny Magics help.

He looked around at the makeshift hospital. No fresh air or natural light. No wonder some people never got better even with the best healers. Still, it was safer to be here in the walls with some help than out there with nothing.

Kor looked at the sleeping face in the bed nearest him. It was a kid who looked too much like Bryce for comfort. Kor shut his eyes hard. This was the real reason he stayed away. More than claustrophobia or dealing with Sid. There was nothing he could do for these people lying so helplessly in their beds. Merin would be able to help. Aer and Bryce might be able to soothe them. But Kor could only read them their fate. With their shallow breathing he could barely hear despite such small quarters, he knew it would not be hopeful.

"Had enough?" Sid jibed from behind him. "Tell me how your big plan keeps this from happening. Can you?"

The healer glared at Sid but walked away to the next bed. Kor noticed her silence.

"No one can fix everything overnight, Sid."

"But have you fixed anything?" He tapped his fingers on the metal footboard.

"Sid, that's not fair," the healer said from the other side of the room. She gave Kor a weak smile. He didn't return it.

"And hiding in the walls has made a bigger difference?" Kor felt the blood rushing up to his cheeks. "Kept kids from suffering needlessly in the Refuge?"

"It's time you realized that the Refuge is not the problem. It's them," Sid threw his hand against the wall causing the metal to let out a slow groan that echoed through the hallway. "Out there," he pointed. "Out there, those people would rather see us die than give us help."

"And how do we change their minds? Violence? Doing the same that's been done to us?" Kor's fist balled up, but he refused to raise it. Sid's eyes dropped to Kor's hand.

"Stop them before they can do to us what your people did to you," Sid spat.

"I think you need to spend some time outside. See how much is them and how much is your anger."

"I'm not the only one who's angry. You think little hot-headed Bryce is going to toe the line for you for the rest of his life? The kid can hardly keep himself out of fights. How many times have you kept him from the Refuge? Let him fight for a cause."

"Let him be used for your little war games, you mean," Kor spat.

"Like you aren't using him for your own agenda," Sid said.

"At least I care about him. He believes in the future I promised him. What future can you give him, Sid? Your anger might lead you to your own doom, but twelve gods damn me if I let you lead Bryce into an early grave."

Sid balked. Kor turned and walked out of the light of the lantern. He could feel his heart thundering. He clasped his right hand to his chest and held it like he could calm his heart from there. He took a few breaths and headed toward the fissure in the wall.

From the back of the tunnel, he could hear Sid yell. "Bryce isn't a little kid anymore. You'll see!"

Kor took a deep breath before he stepped out into the fresh air. Sid was wrong. The world outside could learn to coexist with Magics. Bryce could quell his anger.

The night was alive with Magics. People from all districts in the city came to partake in the nightlife. Normal people enjoying the amazements of something they didn't quite understand.

He sat back and watched the non-Magics watch two women making water dance to the music of their flutes. It had nothing to do with the flutes; instead, it was their connection to the elements, but the illusion was there. He smiled to himself.

Sid was wrong. Aer was wrong. The plan would work.

"Kor!" Bethlem called from down the street. "Managed to scrounge up a few."

"Where did you get them so quickly?" Kor asked.

Bethlem winked. He handed Korvo a large brown bag filled with bright-colored paper that was worn gently on the edges.

"Thank you." Kor gave the man a pat on the back.

"It's nothing much, but I hope it'll help," Bethlem said.

"It will."

Bethlem nodded and headed back to his bar. Kor looked up at the clock sitting at the top of the city street signs. He sighed and turned back toward the tall shadow that loomed just outside the merriment. He would need to get some sleep before work in the morning. His revolution wasn't going to pay for itself.

AER:

After she left the meeting, Aer wandered around the city. This tightness in her chest hadn't subsided; really, it was building. The tang of anger filled her stomach, and when she stopped walking it threatened to come up. Over the course of the year, she'd been feeling the anger rise up. She had known her patience was thinning. She could hear it in her voice. She had been pushing Kor away. She had known this was coming. Had he?

She pulled the collar of her jacket close against her neck, covering her jagged Raven's head tattoo from the rest of the world.

When had she stopped believing in Korvo? She shook herself. She still believed in him. She just didn't believe the Council would change their mind as long as they toed the line. Didn't the arrival of Tiernan prove that? That it was possible for people to see them and not see a real person? An innocent child being sentenced to death a country over meant it was just time until Kaybrum did the same thing. Kor had the same mark. Why couldn't he see what she saw? Kor's plan wasn't moving fast enough. They needed to force people to listen to them. The people in the Wall agreed, and she had a meeting with them to get to. She slipped through the night almost carried by the wind.

She headed for the Wall. Kor had been sending her to check in on the people in the Wall for years. It had just become part of the pattern. She talked to the people in the Wall who had walked away from Kor's plans; he spent time around the city trying to make the plans happen. They were a team. At least, they had been a team.

"You just missed your little boyfriend," Sid said after she had stepped into the area behind the medic wing they used for a meeting room.

"Korvo was here?" Aer asked, looking over her shoulder. She knew Kor would find out about this eventually, but she needed time to get him to see that creating the school, ending the Refuge, was never going to be enough.

"The Sunshine Crusader himself." Sid slumped into a chair. "I don't know how you can spend time with him."

"You don't know him," she said. "He's a fighter."

"*You* are a fighter. He's just a hurt dog licking his wounds and hoping for handouts."

"He's seen things you can't understand, Sid."

"I understand the way we are treated here. I understand that needs to change. And I understand that sitting around and playing nice isn't going to help anyone. What do you understand, Aer?"

"Something needs to happen," she agreed.

"Good," he said, folding his hands in front of him. "I was worried that lover boy would get in the way. What news did you bring me today?"

"Korvo and I took in a Fire Magic today."

"Fire Magic. That will make some noise." Sid tapped the table.

"He's just a child. But I think we can still use him. But you have to promise he stays hidden until after."

"Going soft?"

"Children don't need to have their lives ruined. We don't need another person with a hand like Korvo." She paused. Sid scoffed. She pursed her lips. Sid didn't care about sympathy. "Tiernan stays out of the fight."

"Fine," Sid said. "But we move in one week. Get everything ready." He stood and walked out of the room, taking his lantern with him. The light drained away with him. Aer sat alone.

A week didn't give her much time. She would never convince Korvo by then. Merin would be too reluctant to fight. It wasn't her fault she was so naive, growing up being treated like a non-magic. Passing the way she did tinted the world with rose-colored glasses.

Bryce. She could convince Bryce. And through him, she thought as she took a deep breath, building up the resolve, through him she could get to Tiernan.

The sun was halfway in the sky when Aer made her way up the rickety ladder. She hoped she knew Kor well enough to know that even though he desperately needed sleep, he would be out working. When she finally crested the top of the building, she hid herself in the growing shadows behind the pipes and metal work. She waited. Bryce was sleeping soundly, his arms propped up over his head, covering the top half of his face. No need to wake him. Tiernan, however, was fitful in his sleep. This only doubled Aer's resolve. No child should live like their worst nightmares had come to life. She sang under her breath. The wind joined with her. She started with a lullaby, but that was not enough to soothe the frightened child in front of her. Tiernan thrashed to the side. See, she tried to direct her thoughts to Korvo wherever he was, peace won't work when the darkness runs this deep.

"Shouldn't he know that?" she whispered to herself, moving next to the little boy. Then, she sang the only other song she could think of, a song of revolution. Of action. Of war. Tiernan woke immediately.

Aer watched the little boy as he looked her over once or twice. He didn't say anything, just sat with his hands cupped to him. The little flutters of light told Aer he was playing with fire. She let him play and poured some breakfast into a bowl for him from a bag she assumed Korvo had left for them. She pushed it over. Tiernan's eyes scanned her again, but he eventually took the bowl.

Bryce finally woke up. His eyes fluttered heavily, but the metal of the roof caught his eye, and he flailed to a seated position. He grabbed for Tiernan. The little boy raised his eyebrow but kept munching on the granola Aer had mixed with some fruit. Bryce still hadn't noticed her.

Bryce pulled the bag of food Kor had left closer to him, fished around inside, and bit into one of the pears. "I bet this tastes like home," he said. He didn't bother translating it into Hadranian. Aer wasn't sure he could.

Reaching back into the bag of supplies, Bryce pulled out a few thin children's books.

"Jokes on you, Korvo," Bryce said to the air around him. "I can't read these either."

"I think he knew that," Aer said, leaning out of the shadows.

"You must-a just missed him," Bryce said looking down at the books in front of him.

"I knew he wouldn't be here." Aer tried to gauge Bryce's mood. He was well known for the pent-up anger he swung like a club in fights around the city. He would fight anyone who even suggested Magics didn't deserve their rights. That somehow by luck of birth they should be orphaned and ridiculed and jailed. But he was also fiercely loyal to Korvo. Aer had to play this close to the chest. She continued before Bryce had time to ask why she was there. "What are you two going to do today?"

"Find Merin." Bryce grabbed a handful of granola from Tiernan. The little boy glared, but let Bryce eat from his bowl.

"And?" Aer shifted so she was sitting upright. Bryce shrugged and held up the books. Aer nodded.

A silence sat between them.

"Is this doable?" Bryce asked. Aer gave him a pat on the shoulder.

"Reading? Yeah. I mean they teach little kids all the time, right?"

"I meant the school. Keeping him safe. Keeping us safe. Ending the Refuge. Being treated as equals," he said in the lightest of voices. It came out almost like a cry. Aer took a second to compose herself from the shock of seeing Bryce so vulnerable.

"The world isn't listening," she said finally. There was no time like the present. A week was ticking down quickly.

Bryce let his breath rush out. "What do you mean?"

"Right now," she gestured to the city, "they aren't listening." Her face was calm.

Bryce leaned in. "But we need them to listen. Kor's plan needs the Council to listen to us and end this horrific prison." He tapped the metal below their feet.

Aer nodded. "Needing them to listen isn't going to make them listen," she said, letting her eyes close for a moment. Her heart churned in her chest, but a fire burned in her belly. It forced her to continue. "We need a little bit of force."

"How?" He shifted closer to her on the roof.

"First, we have to make them hear." She smiled softly and looked out over the cityscape with her tired eyes. In the early morning with the light still causing the horizon to blossom, the city looked hopeful. It looked like change could come.

Aer began to sing—first under her breath and then louder—the song that had woken Tiernan from his nightmares. She felt her limbs creak underneath her. The strain of using subtle magic all night as she sang was starting to catch up to her. But even if the magic in the words didn't reach Bryce, the ideas would. She saw that hope was starting to waver in him, and the only way to keep it alive was to light it on fire.

CHAPTER 4

BRYCE:

AER'S WORDS WERE PINGING AROUND in his brain. His eyes darted back and forth as if trying to catch someone seeing his thoughts. Tiernan, at least, didn't seem to notice.

The revolution she had talked about sounded so good. Fighting back against the people who had branded him, who let him spend nights cold and alone in the gardens without so much as a passing glance. The people who had ... No. He refused to think back to what happened in the Refuge. He spat on the ground. Tiernan turned to look at him. Bryce shrugged. Tiernan spat. Bryce smiled.

"We should talk it through with Merin," Bryce said, placing his hand on the boy's head.

Tiernan perked up at the mention of Merin's name.

"Can we see Merin?" Tiernan asked in Hadranian.

When Bryce looked at him blankly, he tried it again slowly.

"That's where we go," Bryce stumbled through his sentence in Hadranian before giving Tiernan an encouraging smile. They walked through the city. The building Kor had picked out for the school was directly across the city, forcing Bryce to cross the wealthier districts that circled the center of town.

The farther they got from Kor's space on the Refuge, the more the people passing by looked them up and down before turning away. Bryce was used to it. It happened every time he would go sneak over to Merin's place. But he could feel Tiernan tensing next to him.

Bryce kept himself pinned between him and the street to lessen the likelihood that anyone might accidentally bump into him. Every sound made Tiernan jump, so Bryce kept talking to cover the ticks and tocks of the street. He told him about Korvo, Aer, and Merin, about any plant they happened to pass, and about the time before his parents had known about his powers. He had been happy then. He had been loved. Bryce wondered if Tiernan had ever felt that. Maybe losing it was worse than never having it, though. It was selfish. He knew that. But Bryce couldn't help feeling the gaping hole that had been formed when his past life was ripped away from him.

Still, Tiernan was so concerned about every sound and flash of color that occasionally he would realize Bryce was steps ahead and run to grab the hem of his shirt. Bryce didn't say anything, and it was clear that Tiernan, who may not have understood the language or where they were, understood that Bryce was supposed to keep him safe.

Tiernan's fear felt heavy in Bryce's stomach. It made breakfast feel like sludge. Aer's words of revolution wound around his head. He felt the need to talk to Kor, to bring him back to his fighting spirit. Korvo had fought in Hadran. It wasn't something he talked about a lot, but if Kor had fought once, he might fight with them again. This time the war could be won. Non-magics just needed to listen.

But the sludge was beginning to make it hard to walk. It poked and pinched at his stomach like it was trying to get out. Korvo wouldn't like it. Kor had lectured him after every little fight and scrape he had gotten into. Kor had warned him against fighting. But what Aer proposed wasn't war. It was just making people see what was right in front of them.

A thought popped into his mind as he watched the uniformed schoolchildren walk together, laughing, across the street. They weren't much older than Tiernan. Bryce imagined what it would be like to see Tiernan run over and join them instead of holding on to his pant leg for comfort.

Couldn't they do both? Couldn't Aer get them to listen? To see what they had done to the little kids like Tiernan? Like him? And then show them the light. Show them Kor's ability to forgive and better everyone in the same way. They could do it without telling Kor. Bryce could tolerate Sid long enough. And how happy would Kor be then? Everything would be just like he wanted. Besides, there didn't need to be a war. They could get the city to listen with a little magic. A little flash and bang and people would perk up their heads.

Bryce's steps felt lighter as he walked. He felt so secure in his decision that he decided not to talk it through with Merin. Instead, he just nudged Tiernan's shoulder toward the wealthiest district. He wouldn't wait to meet her at Kor's makeshift school; he was going to pick her up. He turned down the wealthiest street in the district, a place he normally wouldn't go unless it was dark out.

As their reflections shone in the large glass windows, so, too, did the glances that they got. Bryce tried to ignore them, imagining instead what it would be like when everything worked out. But his good mood wasn't transferring to Tiernan.

A Watcher followed them closely for a few blocks before getting distracted by something more suspicious. Tiernan had grabbed Bryce's hand when he saw the uniform reflected. He walked so close that their feet got tangled up more than once. Bryce didn't mind; at least Tiernan seemed to have learned the uniform was bad. Besides, this was the beginning of a better life for Tiernan. He kicked at his pants cuff to roll it up a little more.

Tiernan released his hand once the Watcher had passed. He cupped his hands in front of him, and Bryce knew he was about to produce fire. It seemed to be the only thing that calmed him.

"No fire," Bryce whispered down to the little boy.

Tiernan said nothing, but his hands dropped to his sides. Bryce started to speak, but the words were all muddled. How could he explain? He let his mouth close without uttering a word.

Bryce had never met a Fire Magic. He'd heard about them in fairy tales. They were the ones, along with evil queens and jealous siblings, who were always causing havoc. The heroes would come and right the wrongs of the people. They would save the day and win the princess or defeat the evil. He had imagined himself, somewhere around four years before he was branded, growing up to be one of those heroes.

And wasn't he? He kicked a loose rock down the street. It skipped a few times before finding its way into a private garden. He was trying to help the outcasts, the downtrodden. The world was just a little too confusing for him sometimes. Why was he the bad guy? He scowled. Tiernan looked around and balled his little hands into fists. Bryce took a deep breath and tried to calm himself.

Aer had said they needed to make the people hear. He would help her. Things would change.

When Bryce looked up, they had already reached Merin's house.

Bryce touched a vine that had grown up a tree and onto the edge of the house. It wormed its way through the cracks in the siding and had anchored itself there. With a few strokes and a kind whisper, the plant began growing at a fast pace. When he asked for it to stop, it did, sprouting lush leaves right at the window. He knew Merin would see it. He had done this before.

He leaned against the side of the house, letting Tiernan slowly take in his surroundings. When Merin appeared at the front door a few minutes later, he turned away. The rush of seeing her set the blood in his cheeks on fire. He couldn't let her see him like that. He pretended to watch Tiernan.

"Hey," she said, patting Bryce on the shoulder lightly. Her hand was warm and soft. One touch and it felt like the world was lifted off his shoulders. He shook himself. Sappy was not the impression he was trying to get across.

He slapped on the grin he used when teasing her. "Can you come out to play?" he asked. He leaned toward her without thinking about it. Merin's presence made him forget that she escaped the brand. For a moment she made him forget about his own brand. When it was just them together, she made the world Kor promised seem feasible.

"I called in sick for school today." She straightened her school uniform.

"But you're still in uniform?"

"I didn't want my father to realize I wasn't going to school. He only left a few minutes ago, so there wasn't time to change."

"You lied?" Bryce teased.

"I did not. I said I was going to school. And I am. Just not the one I am supposed to."

"Careful, all this hanging out with criminals is causing you to start lying to your parents," Bryce joked.

"Just because you've been to the Refuge does not mean you are a criminal," Merin said, picking Tiernan up in a hug.

Bryce's body tightened, as if the air in his lungs had been sucked out. "Did you have to talk about the Refuge?" Bryce scowled and spat on the bit of road he could reach. Merin reached for his shoulder.

"You brought it up?" she said as a question. Merin was never going to understand the Refuge. But he couldn't tell her that.

"Right, but we're trying to destroy it," Bryce said, snapping back at her.

Tiernan watched slowly, his eyes darting back and forth between the two.

"I know that. That's why we have the school," she said. Her face was so assured. Her smile was light and full of, not hope, but surety that things would be better. There it was. The difference between them was back. He was more sure than ever that Aer was right.

"Yeah, I know," he said sharply. He thought about taking Tiernan and leaving, but the sight of the books in his hands stopped him. "We've got work to do," he said finally, turning back to Merin. They walked toward the makeshift school building, but Bryce took them on a slight detour to the garden. Being around plants would give him the strength he needed. Merin held Tiernan's hand as they walked.

"What did Kor tell you we needed to do today?" she asked, her voice stepping on eggshells when they reached the garden.

"He left these," he dropped the selection of books he had brought with him into her hands.

"Children's books?"

"Tiernan has got to learn the common tongue. I've only talked about breakfast with him and I'm already exhausted."

"So, why do you need me?" She took a seat on the roots of a gnarled tree and knocked a pebble from her shoe.

"I'll let you think about that for a minute," Bryce said. His cheeks flushed red, and he squatted, letting his hands dangle over the grass.

"I don't know what you ... Bryce, can you read?" Merin said looking up at him.

He shrugged. The grass grew in a circle, tracing the movement of his finger.

"Who would have taught me? I'm a kid from outside the walls. A farmer's kid. A Magic, school-banned, Refuge-bound, kid," he said quietly, watching the figure eight of grass get darker and taller. It sent up shoots, trying to reproduce in the dead of winter. Grass was like that.

"I've never had a chance," he whispered to himself.

"I'm sorry. I should have known," she said.

"It's fine." He rocked back onto his heels, trying to push past his embarrassment and anger. The last person he ever wanted to fight was Merin. "I'm just on edge. I really don't want to disappoint Kor."

"What are you talking about?" Merin scooted toward him. He sat on the darkened grass.

"What if I already failed him, by not being able to read?" His shoulders slumped. The blades laced around his fingers.

"He trusted you to do this." She rested a hand on his knee. He smiled at her. The tiniest bit of warmth flowed from her to him.

"I guess." Bryce scratched his head and called Tiernan over to them from where he had been looking at something on the ground. The boy smiled and ran to Merin and found a way into her lap. She was the only thing he hadn't second-guessed the whole morning.

She opened a book with the picture of blue skies and forests.

"Hadran?" Tiernan pointed at the picture. The lush jungles were so many shades of green that Bryce was already lost in the idea of being among that many plants. Merin just opened the book to the first page and, with her finger pointing at each word, she read over them slowly.

"Deep in the jungle," she read, "there was a lonely lion." She pointed her thin, pale finger toward the lion and repeated the word lion. Bryce wasn't sure how learning the names of animals he was never going to see would help Tiernan, but he trusted Merin knew better.

She continued through the book. Her finger danced a slow waltz over the words as she sounded them out for Bryce and pointed out their meaning for Tiernan.

"Can we read another?" Bryce asked when they had finished the jungle book. She nodded and pulled another book from the pile. She turned and looked at him strangely.

"What?"

"This one is *The Little Fire Prince*," she said.

"Fire Prince?"

Tiernan took the book from her and tapped it with his finger. He said something much too fast in Hadranian that Bryce couldn't even hope to understand.

"I think he likes this book." Merin let Tiernan open to the first page for her.

Tiernan looked at the pictures with such devotion that at times Bryce had to shift his weight to be able to see around him while Merin ran her fingers along the text. The story was about an ancient prince who was the only person who was able to bend fire to his will.

He was a hot-headed prince, and often caused problems for his people. He burned their crops when he was throwing a temper tantrum and scared the deer out of the forest when they were hunting. After speaking to a loyal knight of the realm, the prince realized his power was too overwhelming and could only hurt people. So he made a deal with the gods, and they took his magic and divided it up among all the people of the world so that everyone could control fire a little bit, but no one could bend it to their will like the prince had.

Tiernan frowned when he saw the prince smile at the end of the story. He brought his little hands up to his chest and Bryce could tell from the orange glow that emanated from his fingers that he had fire cupped in that little pocket.

"I don't think he liked the ending," Merin said, looking over her shoulder to make sure no one was near them.

"It was a horrible ending," Bryce said. The darkness percolating through his brain had returned tenfold.

"What do you mean?" Merin shifted so Tiernan wasn't putting all his weight on one of her legs.

"He gave up his powers? He was a rotten kid? I had forgotten how these stories went."

Merin raised an eyebrow. "Stuff like this is pretty common. It's all about how people couldn't get enough control over their powers. They're flawed and therefore shouldn't have the power at all."

"Flawed?" he asked. Anger began taking control of his body. He could feel the adrenaline in his system flooding his veins.

"Everyone has flaws, Bryce." Merin crossed her arms.

"This is why people hate us," Bryce groaned, pressing his eyes on the bottom of his palms.

"It's just a story," Merin said.

"Do you think of me like that? Have you thought of Aer or Korvo like that? What about yourself?"

"Keep your voice down," Merin snapped, once more looking for moving shadows in the garden, "You know people don't know—"

"I think you need to tell people. Just let them see they know someone that is kind and caring and gentle and has magic. That we aren't like the prince in this story."

"And when they turn on me, too? How are we going to keep getting access to the private information coming from the City Council?"

Bryce balked. He didn't know what to say. Who needed the Council when Aer was going to get them to listen?

"I don't think of you like that," Merin said. Her eyes were locked on the ground. "I'm not afraid."

"Let's just get to the school," Bryce spat.

KORVO:

Kor paced through the city. He should have stayed and waited for Bryce to wake up. He stroked his hand before shoving it deep into his pocket. He needed to have a plan before he could talk to Bryce.

Bryce looked up to Korvo, in the same way that Kor had looked up to the resistance fighters he had spent time with in the jungles of Hadran. Ghosts of Hadran seemed to have followed Tiernan to Kaybrum, and Korvo couldn't quite escape them.

He murmured his list out loud.

Get to the school and help Merin set up.

Tell Bryce the truth about what really happened in Hadran.

Protect Tiernan, even if his life depended on it.

His hand throbbed in his pocket. Somehow number two seemed the hardest. But he had felt the anger rising in Bryce, just like he had with Aer. If he didn't tell him the truth, he would be doomed to the same sense of darkness that Korvo had felt all those years in Hadran. Korvo sighed, taking one last look over the city block he had found himself on, and turned briskly to get to the school and help Merin.

When he got there, Merin was already cleaning and straightening things. Bryce was sulking in a corner of the room, picture books spread out on the floor in front of him. Tiernan was playing with a small flame in his hand, the shadows dancing over the pictures in Bryce's books. Bryce scowled at the boy, but Tiernan either didn't notice or didn't care.

"Hello, Korvo," Merin said, coming over to him. Sweat beads had formed on the edges of her temple. She had been working hard.

"What's with Bryce?" Kor asked.

"We had an argument. I think you should talk to him. I only seem to make him angry lately." She looked down at the rag she was wringing in her hands.

"I doubt that. What did you argue about?" Kor took the rag from her hands. She looked up at him. Her eyes were welling with tears.

"I'm not even sure." She looked over at Bryce. Bryce either didn't hear them or didn't feel like offering an explanation.

"It's alright, Merin, go finish setting up. I'll talk to him."

She nodded and went back to her cleaning. Kor grabbed a chair that seemed not to wobble and pulled it over to Bryce. He flipped it backward so he could rest his chin on his arms on the backrest.

"Bryce, I'm sorry I didn't tell you about my Phoenix mark," Kor said finally. Bryce grunted and flipped a page in the book. His brow furrowed even deeper. Kor nudged the book with his toe. Bryce looked up.

"I should tell you about Hadran."

"You've told me lots about it."

"I haven't told you all of the important things. I wasn't trying to keep secrets from you. I was just trying—"

"To protect me," Bryce said with a huff. His eyes rolled, and he looked toward the book in front of him.

"Yes," Kor sighed, "but also to protect myself from having to live through them again. From having to admit them to you."

"Life hasn't been easy for me either, Kor."

"But you've never been to war, Bryce. I have."

"I know. I've seen what they did to you." Without meaning to, they both glanced at Korvo's hand. Kor slid it into his lap.

"Sid wants a war." Kor paused. "Aer, well, it sounds like she does too."

"I just want people to listen to you. I can stop Aer from doing anything crazy."

Korvo nodded. So Bryce already knew about their plans. There was no point in telling him that nothing could stop Aer.

"I just want you to know what war is," Kor said, watching Tiernan for a second.

"What do you mean?"

"Hadran was at war ten years ago."

"I know that."

"I know you know, but do you know any of the details?"

Bryce started to open his mouth but shook his head instead.

"You wouldn't. It was a country away, and you were only five years old. Magics were beginning to hide in the jungles to escape persecution. So, deep in the jungle, a revolution was brewing."

"You were part of the revolution," Bryce said. Excitement jumped to his face. Kor shook his head, paused, and then nodded.

"Yes and no. Not at first. I lived on the beaches on boats; I was a fisherman's son. The jungle was miles away, and our life focused solely on the sea. My father used my power to predict the tides and the migration of the fish."

"Like my father used me for the farm before they couldn't deny who I was anymore." Bryce pulled his feet in closer to him.

"Right." Kor scratched an itch behind his ear. "Anyway, on the beach we weren't a big part of anything. People lived and died on about a square mile of land. But the cards, they felt things deep in the ocean, in the forest, in the hearts of the people far away."

"What did the cards say?"

"They used to say so much more." He looked at his mangled hand. "The images were clear. There was less mist to sift through."

"But if you were at the beach, why would it matter if you saw things happening in a jungle? Why would that land you with a ..." Bryce pointed to his chest.

"It's a long story." He took a deep breath. They were never going to get to the end of it if he kept stalling. He tried to calm his breathing, taking a deep breath that permeated down to the bottom of his chest for a count of seven and then releasing for a second count of seven. He imagined his inner light, his connection to the world and magic. He saw his light as a warm buttercream edged with gold. He breathed in again letting that light fill him.

The whole story. He watched it play out in front of his eyes, the images dancing in and around the buttercream light.

"One winter night, I read the cards saying there was going to be a great storm. Deaths would be huge. No one fished that day, but a storm never came. My father was angry for missing out on a day's worth of profit. He beat me. I was probably ten at the time. It happened again and again that winter. The cards would show me heaps of bodies. All I had known was the beach: the water, the waves, the sand. There was no way I could realize the cards were showing me the war happening in the jungle. I didn't know those people. I couldn't see those people dying in the forest. That was the first revolution that I remember. Those images still haunt me at night sometimes. Piles, Bryce, there were piles of bodies."

"Were they Magics?" Bryce asked.

"Most of them," Kor said.

"But they had powers. How could they lose?" A strange shadow crossed over Bryce's face, and Kor wondered how often his young charge thought about fighting back more than just his bruising and brawling out in the city.

"They were tired. They were hungry. They were disjointed. It was a mess."

"But how does this involve—"

"I'm getting there," Kor shifted on the chair. The words were coming out easier than he had expected. "It kept happening that the men were missing out on fishing. Then finally they decided they would go out anyway. But this time there was a storm. Wind howled through the night. Five of the fishermen died. My father survived. He kicked me until I could hardly walk. He told me to get out. The people I had grown up around, lived with, worked side by side with, refused to give me any food or shelter. I wasn't useful to them anymore. Or more the cards weren't useful to them anymore. Without use, it wasn't worth any of them violating the country-wide magic ban. I had no other choice than to go out into the jungle to try to find some way to survive. I found some of the rebel Magics on my third day in the jungle when I could hardly get up. With my injuries and the burn of hunger in my belly, I was on the brink of death."

"But they took you in."

"Yes, and for a while we were successful. I helped them predict the movements of the Hadranian army. The ban had become even more intense as people from the East pushed into Hadran."

"What do you mean? Hadran is much worse than here."

"But it wasn't always. Magic was something people spoke about in shadows. It was why the people of my village accepted me until I wasn't useful. The war was started by the East pushing their way into the government. Taking over the army."

"I don't understand."

"Another time." Kor shook his head. This was not the time to explain the ramifications of globalized politics. This was about Hadran. "The Magics that found me," he continued, "let me stay at the camp while they went out and fought. But one day, some of the soldiers circled behind our camp to try to trap them. They found me. Alone and unguarded."

"Did they capture you?"

Kor nodded. "Why? I'm not sure. I had the Raven. I was obviously part of their rebel group. It was probably my age, but I was brought back to their camp. The small rebel group I was with was a ragtag group of fifteen. This was the camp of an army. Everywhere there were tents and people. More people than I had seen in my life. Everything felt hopeless then." He stopped for a minute. The ghosts were all trying to come out at once. Korvo took a deep breath. Bryce started to open his mouth. "Twelve Gods, Bryce I'm getting to it."

Bryce mumbled, but let his legs go from scrunched into his stomach to stretch out in front of him.

"They let me keep my cards. I thought for a moment that it was some small comfort, but I was wrong. I was there for maybe a week before the General of the Hadranian army appeared in front of the prison they had set up. The prison was small. The walls were merely five feet from each other. At times I shared the tiny space with as many as five other Magics. All older. They never lasted long. When the General came, there were three other people shoved into the minuscule space. He pointed directly at me. I felt like he was staring into my soul. He had ice-blue eyes. I recognized the color immediately. It was the blue that kept flashing through my mind when I had been seeing the storms. His eyes were the reason that I kept thinking the ocean was going to attack. He said very little to me once he pulled me out of the prison. Just tied a rope around me and pulled me behind him through the entirety of the camp. The soldiers all laughed at me. Called me a dog. One spit on me. It was humiliating, but I wasn't going to say anything. There were so many bodies of Magics out in the forest that I didn't want to join them.

"'Read the cards,' the General said once we got to his tent. There was a table, a chair my feet dangled from, and about four other important-looking men with shiny buttons on their jackets."

"Did you read the cards for them?" Bryce asked, looking up.

Kor looked away. He took a deep breath and nodded. Kor didn't want to see the look on Bryce's face, so he kept talking, staring deep into the grain of the wood building.

"At first, I wanted to lie to them. I was planning on telling them to go to the wrong places, but the General turned right before he left the tent and said that wherever I said they were supposed to attack I would go with them. There was no way I could send them into an ambush now, even if I knew where the rebels were hiding. I was a child. I was scared. I did as I was told."

"I bet that killed you," Bryce said, and Kor could hear the strain in his voice.

"I kept little pieces from them. I tried to make it close to accurate, but not enough that they were successful enough to be victorious. But it did almost kill me when one night the General came in and put a hand on my shoulder and smiled down at me. They'd had a particularly good day. A whole section of the jungle had been cleared because of me. Everything after that starts to blur together. The General kept me a year or two in the camp with all of those soldiers while they hunted for the small groups of stragglers. They weren't all unkind, but they didn't see me as a human. At best I was a useful pet. Somewhere between their horses and their dogs.

"When the war in the jungle ended, the camp was packed up in a couple of days. The soldiers formed a line as long as the beach I had grown up on and started marching back to the capital. I had hoped they would let me go, but they didn't. The General even had the audacity to force the soldiers to march right by my town. I could smell the salt water, my toes begged to be in the sand, in the cool touch of the water, but I was kept with the horses. You might have liked it, it smelled like Earth, but I longed for the salt water. I wanted it to heal the scars that crisscrossed my brain. I wanted it to pull all the hatred that had begun to bulk in my muscles and growing bones. But the General, in all his finery, walked down to my parents' house—"

"Did he tell them you were helpful to the war effort?" Bryce asked.

"He handed them coins and thanked them for their livestock in the war effort. My life was worth less than the cost of dinner." Tears were forming in Kor's eyes. He tilted his head up and tried to blink them back. The hatred was still bottled up underneath his layers of composure. He knew the nightmares would never go away.

For the first time, Bryce was quiet. Kor took a moment before he continued.

"When we got to the capital, I stopped taking orders. There were just too many people suffering. The other Magics I knew, the ones in the jungle, had chosen to be there. They wanted to escape the government. I had known that. I had supported them. But I didn't truly understand what they were running from.

"Every single person living in the street had the Raven mark on them. People ignored them. I saw one old man get trampled by a horse. No one did a thing. That day I just stopped.

"I wouldn't do it. It hurt in that way it hurts when you don't see plants all day, that empty ache, but I refused. I would spend all day meditating to the sound of phantom waves. The General had me whipped, but I would have nothing more to do with it. It was the end, Bryce. I was angry. I was seething. When I saw the General, bile would burn my throat. I was done being scared. I was done helping them murder my people.

"One day the General came to the cell they had thrown me in. Those ice-blue eyes greeted me. All the calm breathing in the world couldn't keep me down. My anger was so fierce it forced me to stand. I charged over and tried to punch the General. He stopped my hand before I even got close. All my anger, and I couldn't even get past his arm.

"He told me it saved him the trouble of having to come into the cell. Still holding my wrist, he dragged me down the hallway without a word. I yelled. You should have heard the names I called him, the curses I threw at him. I think I even invented my own. He didn't even react. He took me to a room that just had a large oven. It was so warm that for a moment my anger relaxed because it felt like lying in the sand of the beach. But that was short-lived. The Phoenix isn't a tattoo, Bryce. It's a brand. A real one. The General pulled out the red-hot poker from the fire. He didn't even remove the thin shirt I was wearing. He just pressed it to my skin. My vision went white. I must have passed out because when I woke up the Phoenix was already on me."

"Why would they brand you? Isn't a tattoo enough?"

"Using the heat would be a horrible joke to a Fire Magic. Their body would actually pull them into the brand. I never said it wasn't anything but sadistic."

"I meant, why you?"

"They needed me out of the way in case I tried to help the revolution reform. I told you. Predicting the future can be just as dangerous as fire."

"But how did you escape?" Bryce asked. He was leaning in now.

"They let me have more freedom once I was marked as a dead man. Well, dead child. I got time to go outside. I watched the guards and made a plan. And one day, I ran. They would have killed me on the spot if they found me. So I ran to the jungle."

"And you ran to Kaybrum?"

"No. I went to start my own war."

"But you're so against Sid? Any time he calls for action you tell him to wait. You're building a school."

"Because Sid is stupid. I was twelve and I was angry. He has no excuse."

Bryce's eyes flicked down to the ground. "But what made you change your mind?"

"Crusades always end poorly." He rubbed his hand. "No one wins. Nothing changes." He sighed and shook his head. "We need to make sure people welcome the changes."

"But sometimes people just hate us. I think about the Watchers that have taken me into the Refuge. They get off on the power. They love it. We need to get rid of them."

"There will always be people like the General, Bryce. Their eyes will show you what they think of us."

"Less than human?"

"Exactly. But the soldiers in the story—"

"The ones that spit at you and called you a dog?"

"Some also brought me food and called me by my name. They shared their sweets from home."

"So what? Kor, they held you captive for years."

"But I was becoming human to them. If a soldier from Hadran can recognize our humanity, think of what we can do here. We can do that on a larger scale. We can show we aren't mistakes of nature, but people just like them. We just have to remain calm."

"Aer was just talking to me about making sure people are listening."

Kor perked up.

"She said that to you?" Kor's mind immediately turned to calculations and risk tables. If they already had a plan in place ...

"Kor?"

Kor looked up from where he had begun staring a hole into the wall in front of him.

"Hey, Korvo, that still doesn't explain what happened to your hand."

Kor shrugged, putting his hand into his pocket.

"I've relived enough nightmares today, and I need to go talk to Aer." Without waiting for a reply, Kor left the dilapidated building in the fastest walk he could without breaking into a run.

MERIN:

She watched Bryce out of the corner of her eye. His anger seemed to have dissipated, but there was something else now on his face. Something she didn't understand. Or maybe, she sighed, she couldn't understand.

"You okay?" Merin moved to stand next to where Bryce sat. He took a deep breath and stood. He was taller than her by an inch or two, but it hardly seemed like it at the moment. He was so deep in thought he seemed like he was hardly there. Like three-quarters of him had walked out when Korvo left.

"I'm fine," he murmured and walked over to Tiernan. The little boy let the flame in his hand die immediately. His control was something masterful. She wondered how he could produce something and never seem to grow tired. Doing anything more than easing pain or doctoring water to help heal left her almost devastated. She wished she had the power that the others seemed to have, but she was forced to hide her powers. Right now it was better her powers weren't something that would get her kicked out of her school. Who would teach the Magics then? Korvo?

"Do you want more help?" She looked down at the book he had loosely grasped in his hand. He shrugged.

"I'm not sure there's a point, Merin."

"You can learn to read, Bryce."

"No, it's not that. It's just … Korvo was telling me about Hadran just now."

"You guys have talked a lot about it." She could see the pain on Bryce's face.

"I think he wanted me to see that there was no point in fighting."

"The school is the best option. You know it's the only way we are ever going to convince the Council to take us seriously. They will never listen to people with no education. It gives them the power to write us off the minute we go in front of them. It's just a different kind of fight."

"I know, Merin, but they aren't listening. Even getting this old building took Kor almost a year."

She felt him getting distant again. How many times could he try to push her away?

"Something big is coming," Merin said, trying to keep Bryce talking to her.

"What kind of thing?" he asked.

"Something to do with Magics. Maybe it's their own plan to accept us. Make it look like it was their idea." She knew she was grasping at straws, but the hurt in Bryce's eyes made her stomach clench.

"While I can see the Council taking credit for all of Kor's work, I highly doubt they are somehow going to reverse public opinion on Magics without apparent reason."

"That's what the school is for."

"Merin. You aren't listening. The school isn't going to be enough. No one is going to notice us. Even if you and Kor work miracles, we're still a dot on their horizon. Something they can sweep under the rug. We have to get them to look at us."

"They see us," she said. Her voice squeaked.

"*Actually* see us, Merin. The rest of us. The ones who can't pretend to be anything but what we are. They look through me, or they see garbage. Something that can be thrown away. They may see you as human, but not me. Not Aer and not Kor. We are nothing."

"You're not nothing to me," she said, holding eye contact with him. Merin heard the contempt in his voice growing. He always did this. He pushed her away. She could see in the arch of his eyebrows that he didn't want to say the things that were coming out of his mouth, but it wasn't that they were untrue. It hurt. Why couldn't he let down this invisible barrier that seemed to come between them? No, not invisible. The black tattoo of a Raven would always come between them, and it was anything but invisible.

Bryce took a deep breath. "When is this big event coming?" He lifted his hand like he was going to place it on her shoulder but stopped halfway.

"Maybe weeks. I haven't picked up a lot of details yet." She knew her answer discounted the school. There would never be enough time to sway public opinion, but she almost hoped Bryce missed the lack of connection. He didn't.

The door opened, casting a beam of sunlight across the room.

"Ms. Merin?" A small girl held the door open, keeping most of her body behind the door. Merin smiled at her.

"Did you come here to learn?" Merin walked over to the door and crouched down to the girl. "Did you bring some friends?" she asked, and the girl nodded. "Well, come in then." Three other children came into the room. They were dressed like Bryce in clothes that had seen better days and were dirty from their playing in the streets. She swallowed, forcing the growing lump in her throat down. "Bryce, will you bring me the books?"

Bryce dumped them on the table. Merin reached out her hand and placed it on his arm. She didn't try to use her magic; she knew he would be able to tell. She'd fixed enough scrapes and bruises for him; he knew what it felt like. She just let her fingers rest on his arm. She could feel his muscles tighten beneath her. She smiled at him. He relaxed.

"I think you and Tiernan should go for a walk," she said with a smile.

"Why?"

"Because you seem like you have a lot on your mind, and being cooped up here isn't going to help. I'll be fine with them on my own."

"It's not like I'm much help," Bryce gestured to the books on the table.

"There are lots of things about being educated that don't come from reading," she said. She knew from the faint smile that barely resembled his normal grin he was only placating her.

"I've got to figure some stuff out," he said, and he gave her arm a brief squeeze before he explained to Tiernan in Hadranian they were leaving, and headed out the door.

"Ms. Merin?" called one of the kids. Merin pulled her eyes from the door.

"Yes?" she said, her smile already there and waiting.

"Can you help us?" a little boy asked.

"Of course," she said sitting down with them and one of the books. "Any time."

CHAPTER 5

AER:

AER WASN'T SURPRISED to see Korvo sitting at the bar at Bethlem's. She was, however, slightly worried that his face was pressed into the wooden grain of the bar.

"You doing alright?" she asked, taking the seat next to him. Across the bar top, papers were strewn about. She recognized them immediately. Arrest warrants. Business closures in the Wall District. Bad news.

"The cards keep showing me disaster, but somehow I always think it's going to be different when I look at them. That somehow having the school open for a day will have curbed these numbers." He drew a heavy breath and picked his head up off the bar.

Aer knew only the empty room allowed Korvo to show such honesty. In front of anyone else, including Merin and Bryce, he would be all hope and no downside.

"Things are getting worse, Kor. You have to admit that to yourself."

"Bad enough for you to be talking the same nonsense as Sid?" he asked, shuffling the papers into order.

Aer started to say something, but Kor waved his hand. "Don't answer that. I'm having a bad day as it is."

"Any more than other days you get the reports?" she asked, glad he had sidestepped the Sid question. It wasn't that she didn't have the conviction she was doing the right thing joining Sid, she just wasn't ready for this, whatever it was between her and Kor, to be over. And, she bet, neither was Kor.

He put a hand on her knee, hesitating only a little before he made contact. He knew she didn't like being touched without permission. She put her hand on top of his to let him know it was okay. His shoulders seemed to relax.

"The Council gave me a slot to talk to them again," Kor said. "Sometime in two weeks. To review the use of their building."

"Bethlem told me on my way in that Merin had students already. It will go fine."

"But I need to prove that it helps more than the Refuge."

"The Refuge doesn't help at all, so that won't be hard."

"I think I need to bring Bryce along, and I'm not sure he can handle that."

"You want to take Bryce into the Council? Will they even let him past the door?" If there was one Magic besides the two of them the Watchers followed, it was Bryce. He was not known for taking things lightly or remaining calm in any given circumstance. Kor was getting desperate if he was willing to gamble on Bryce staying calm with the Council. She could hear him yelling obscenities now.

"You know as well as I do that something has to change."

"I know." She pulled her hand away from Kor's. He looked at his hand on her knee for a moment and then returned his hand to the half-empty glass on the counter. He rotated it around so the liquid inside spun tightly like a miniature tornado. He set it down, and they both watched the vortex slowly dwindle into nothing.

"I'm assuming you're not coming by the school," Kor said without looking at her. She could sense the command in his voice, but she could tell it was also painful for him to say it. He couldn't have her involvement with Sid tarnish the school. She nodded.

"I have other things I'm taking care of for the next few days." The air around them tightened. Aer reached for the papers, and Kor shifted away from her.

"You won't let me read the reports? I helped you get those," she said.

"It's not—"

"Then what is it?" She could already feel the panic begin to surge inside her. There was only one thing Kor ever tried to hide from her. How could she have been so naive? He knew the arrests were going up; he knew people were suffering; that wouldn't have caused him to have his guard up. Only one thing would.

The same thing that had happened to her. Her fingers snapped to her neck where her jagged tattoo shone out to any passerby. It was not the neat lines of Bryce's tattoo. No. Hers was not done by the government in their brisk and impersonal way. She had been held down in an alley by a mob. Sometimes at night, when Kor rolled over and his arm fell on top of her, she would wake up in a sweat. It would take her hours before she could no longer feel the men as they pinned her to the ground and tattooed her across the neck while she kicked and screamed. Her mouth filled with the dirt from the alley, her eyes with her hatred for non-Magics.

"You didn't want me to know," she said when she could finally get her throat to remember she was in Bethlem's and not choking on the dirt of the street. Her words still came out hoarse.

Korvo nodded and handed her the paper, but black dots were filling Aer's vision. She couldn't be sure if they were from panic or anger. Her hands twitched and the paper fluttered in her grasp. She let it fall to the ground.

"Can I stop you?" Kor asked in such a whisper she almost missed hearing it over the sound of her winds coming to her rescue. Her stomach flipped.

"No," she said, letting her cold green eyes match his. She focused on the brightness of his eyes so that her conviction wouldn't fade looking at the worried furrow across his brow. She stood and took a step toward the door. Nothing was more important than this. He'd see.

"Promise me," he said reaching up his hand but letting it drop, "you're just trying to make people hear about the atrocities. You aren't trying to start a war."

Aer walked out without looking back.

BRYCE:

The temperature dropped almost immediately when they entered the garden. The pockets of shade chilled Bryce.

He wasn't ready yet to go back and talk to Merin. He had too many things on his mind, so he decided to teach Tiernan some words.

"Tree." He pointed to the nearest tree.

Tiernan repeated. "Tree."

"Climb," Bryce said, grabbing the lowest-reaching branches and hauling himself up into the tree. They continued this way, learning words in the common tongue until Bryce was satisfied he could give brief commands and Tiernan would know what he wanted. The last thing they needed was for him to have to try to search his limited Hadranian to tell Tiernan he needed to run.

"Tiernan," Bryce mused when they reached the top of the tree. The little boy looked at him. "I think I love her." He pointed to his heart.

Tiernan cocked his head much like a puppy and poked himself in the chest. "Fire?"

"No, no. Love." He took Tiernan's hand and flattened it so that his palm stretched across most of his small ribcage. He could feel the subtle beat of Tiernan's heart too.

"Love?"

"I don't know how to explain love," Bryce said in Hadranian after a minute. He didn't even know the name for love in the language. It was not something that came up a lot when Kor was teaching him. "Love is good. It feels like protection and safety," he attempted to explain. But either his pronunciation was that bad, or Tiernan didn't understand those things either, because the little boy continued to look at him confused. They sat in silence for a while.

"I learned Hadranian." Bryce's confidence bloomed in the presence of so much nature. "Kor taught me Hadranian just speaking about home. Telling me short phrases."

Tiernan nodded, even though his eyes remained blank.

"It's just that if I learned a new language from Kor, I can learn to read from Merin. Then we'll be on equal footing, and maybe I can finally get her to understand what it's been like for me instead of just getting so mad."

Tiernan moved closer to Bryce and put his hand flat against his chest.

"Love?" Tiernan asked.

Bryce laughed. "We should make sure Kor explains before you tell everyone you love them." Tiernan smiled at the mention of Korvo's name. Bryce didn't blame him in the slightest. It couldn't be easy having to follow him around and not being able to communicate easily.

Reverting back to the simplest childhood pleasures that didn't require language, Bryce took a deep breath, letting himself think for a moment about the past. His mother's berry dumplings warm from the oven and cooling on the counters in their farmhouse. The pleasure of getting the scraps of dough, sweet and sticky on his fingertips.

"Come on." Bryce swung down to the lower branches. When they reached the ground, he picked Tiernan up, placed him on his shoulders, and headed toward a bakery near the gardens.

Bryce slid the few coins he'd made from working with the city florists over the counter. The clang they made on the counter was bold, and the warm puffs of pastry sprinkled with sugar with a quick and reckless hand plopped onto the wax paper in front of them. Tiernan's eyes lit up, and he had eaten the first bun completely before Bryce had even taken a bite. There was no trace of the sticky sweetness on Tiernan's lips. He had scarfed the whole thing in one go.

"Slowly. Enjoy." Bryce opened his mouth wide and tore a bite from the bun, smearing the warm sugar glaze across his face. He wiped the back of his hand across his lips. "Enjoy," he repeated and handed Tiernan another warm breath of pastry. Tiernan took it in his hands and looked at it before taking a slow bite just like Bryce. Bryce smiled down at him and took the bag with them as they exited the shop.

Bryce gripped the bag close to him to absorb some of the lovely warmth his purchase had brought him.

"We can't be doing this every day. I don't make a lot of money," Bryce said to Tiernan, who ignored the foreign words that fell flat on his ears. He was still enchanted by his second bun, taking small bites until he had hardly enough room to still hold on to it.

Tiernan reached up and put his hand out to Bryce.

"Another? There are only two left." Again, Tiernan's eyes were empty of understanding anything other than the delicious sugar glaze he had tasted for the first time. "Fine, but the last one is going to Kor." Bryce handed him the larger of the two and licked his fingers clean.

As they walked, Tiernan ventured farther and farther from Bryce, until they turned a corner and Tiernan stuck like glue to the older boy, causing Bryce to get tripped up by Tiernan's feet.

"Why are you walking so close to me all of a sudden?" Bryce asked, aware it made very little sense to ask. He sighed and repeated the questions in the best Hadranian he could manage.

Tiernan simply pointed around them.

A Watcher was glaring at them from across the street even though they were back on the poorer side of town.

"Watch it, Magic," a man bumped into Bryce crossing the street.

"Excuse me?" Bryce said with a little more sass than was ultimately required.

"You heard him. You and your little Hadranian rat better not think you're trying anything on my beat," a Watcher said coming to join the conversation. His baton was already drawn.

"I'm just trying to get home," Bryce said, flashing his most charming smile, trying to hide the anger starting to boil in his chest. Without Tiernan he might have tried to fight this out, but now he just wanted to escape.

"I can take you where you belong. The Refuge is always taking riffraff like you." The Watcher took a step closer.

"Now, I'm not sure what is going on here, officer," Bryce said putting his hands up in front of him. "But I'm sure we can work it out."

"That's just the thing with you Magics," the man who bumped into him chimed in, "you think you get a say, but you don't."

The Watcher smiled a toothy grin.

"Tiernan," Bryce whispered, "Run. Find Bethlem." The little boy looked up at him and nodded. Bryce stepped in between him and the Watcher, and Tiernan took off.

"He's too young for the Refuge," Bryce said as pleasantly as he could, but his eyes were locked onto the baton in the Watcher's hand. Usually, Bryce was pretty clear when his anger got the better of him in a situation, but he wasn't even sure what had started all of this. And he was very sure that it wasn't his fault. That didn't mean he had any more plans on going to the Refuge.

"And what about you?" The Watcher took a step toward him.

"I'm too smart," he let the ground rumble beneath him. Roots from any nearby plant rushed to him now. It was a gamble. The magic would drain him of most of his energy. If he couldn't get far enough away, he was a dead man running. This was too much magic for him to really try, but he wasn't going to the Refuge, and he wasn't going to fail to protect Tiernan. That left him with this one option.

The Watcher fell to the ground with a grunt, and Bryce ran. He heard the Watcher get up and run after him. Bryce's legs were turning to mush. The rumbling ground didn't make it any easier to keep his footing as he ran.

The roots broke through the hard-packed dirt of the street between the cobblestones. He was running out of magic, and he wasn't close to anywhere he could hide. The school was blocks away, and Aer's house was too close to the Refuge for comfort in a situation like this. He was too tired to fight now, too. He would only get one good punch in before he could barely stand. He had to find somewhere quickly. The footsteps of the Watcher closed in. Bryce braced himself for the blow from the baton. He's going to hit me in the shoulder, right at the neck, Bryce thought. But the blow didn't come.

He chanced a glance behind him and found the Watcher's feet tangled in the little roots that had come for him. The Watcher pulled at the roots, but they just tightened around his boots, holding him in place. Bryce said a silent prayer to any of the Twelve Gods that were listening, thanking them for plants and their strong roots. Now he had time to hide.

He slowly worked his way through shadows, leaning heavily on the sides of buildings, in order to reach the closest safe space: the friendly florists who worked in this part of town. A smile and some help to bring out the most brilliant colors of the flora gained him a lot of favors here.

Behind the shop, Bryce could feel his energy dropping. His hands were shaking, and he let his back slump against the brick wall. He wasn't even sure he had enough energy to turn the doorknob.

He could wait behind the crates in the back of the shop. In an hour or so, he'd have enough energy to keep moving. He buried himself a little deeper. At first glance, no one would see him from the road. Once settled, Bryce stared at the road. No one was going to sneak up on him.

Leaves fluttered down onto Bryce.

"What are you doing?" Vycky asked, her hands full of clippings. "You better get out here and explain yourself, Bryce."

"I could use a little help," Bryce said. Vycky was his favorite. She was young, barely older than Korvo, slender, almost vine-like. Her hands were always stained with some sort of color. Her apron always had twigs and leaves sticking out of the pockets. Bryce liked that she didn't try to look like anything other than someone who played in the dirt throughout the day. Too many of the other florists in the marketplace tried to dress fancy. They presented flowers like jewels. Something only the rich could afford. Vycky took the time to nurture the flowers herself, and didn't buy them from far-off greenhouses or outside the city in order to make quick cash.

"You're in a garbage pile. I think that goes without saying." Vycky pulled him up by the hand. Bryce almost fell back down when she let go.

"You've been using magic?" she said, ushering him into the back of her shop.

"I was just protecting myself."

"From whom?"

"Some Watcher who tried to pick a fight. I didn't do anything. I swear, Vycky."

"I believe you. Been too many Watchers in town. It's like they're looking for trouble," she looked at him. "And they found you. Can you walk?"

"Not far."

"Help me finish these bouquets, and when I drop them off, I'll drop you at Bethlem's."

They didn't talk much for the next twenty minutes. Bryce just handed her flowers as they worked. He didn't have the energy to cut the stems or perk up the flowers. Even his mind was blank.

"Last one. Ready?" Vycky said, shaking Bryce from his nothingness. "Grab whatever is in your little bag, and let's go."

Bryce was glad no one was in the alley to watch him tumble into the delivery cart. Even Vycky pretended not to see, but he caught a smile on her face that sold her out.

Nestled among the roses, Bryce felt safe as they cruised through town. He peeked into the bag, the pastry was a little worse for wear, but Korvo would still appreciate it.

After dropping him at Bethlem's back door, she waved as the cart bounced away. Bryce raised his hand in salute, and then slowly and carefully made his way into the bar.

Tiernan nearly pounced on him when he lifted the cloth door of the back room above his head.

"This little one get away from you?" Bethlem said, following in behind the staggering Bryce. Bryce tried to smile, but the effort was too much. Bethlem's face softened. "He seemed rather worried, but it looks like you got yourself out of trouble." Bethlem set a tall glass of clean water in front of Bryce. He chugged it without responding. It would take him some time before anything other than tasks of basic survival were beyond him.

Bethlem left them in the back room, and Bryce slumped in the padded chair. Tiernan ran around poking him places, lifting his arms and legs to check for bruises or blood. Satisfied, he sat making small fires in his hands and letting the fire walk from finger to finger. Bryce watched, mesmerized by the flames and the Tiernan's control.

"I bet you had to have good control. Otherwise, they would have found you earlier. Me, I came from a farm. It's a pretty easy place to hide my power. I was ten when they finally decided plants crawling into my room at night was not normal. It really broke my parents when they had to face the truth," he mumbled with his cheek pushed against the table. He hadn't even told Merin about his past. It was too painful.

He closed his eyes and suddenly he was only a few years older than Tiernan, running back from the fields. There was a man in a Watcher's uniform standing on their back porch. Bryce hadn't feared him then. He stopped just short of the little wood stairs, looking past the man to his mother, who was weeping in his older sister's arms.

"This him?" the man asked. His mother only wept harder. His older sister nodded. The man reached down and grabbed his wrist.

"Mom. Mom? Mommy!" Bryce reached for his mother. She turned and sank, her feet giving out, and his older sister stared out into the fields with blank eyes.

The man took Bryce to a group of other men in fancier suits. Their buttons gleamed in the sunlight, as did the large needle the tallest man had in his hand. Bryce's cries pierced the afternoon autumn air. And when Bryce kicked, the other two Watchers held him down. One for his wrists, the other for his leg while the last carved with the needle and inked a Raven's head into his leg.

He struggled, but there was nothing his little body, as strong as he was from working the fields day in and day out, could do against three grown men with batons at their waists. The pain was seared into his mind. Some nights, when he closed his eyes, he could feel the needle raking across his skin. It felt like fire and bee stings combined into something purposefully malicious and horrendous. Tears streamed down his face onto the field below him.

He could still feel the pain now, the humiliation, and fear. Then the only thing to do was to start throwing punches until it stopped hurting. It rarely stopped hurting.

"Run home," the first man had said when they'd finished. Bryce had stared at him blankly.

"Get out of here, Magic," said the man with the needle. Bryce turned and looked down at the painful red and black smudged mess that had taken over his ankle and hobbled back to his house. It took him nearly an hour to walk with his sore leg pulling behind him. Even though the dirt and leaves clung to him, he could still see the inflamed mess. It was like his leg stopped, or something about himself stopped, where that tattoo covered his ankle.

He could hear the sobs before he had even gotten on the porch. Not wanting to hear his mother cry anymore, he put the weight onto his foot the best he could. He plastered on the smile that normally got him cuddles and kisses. The grin his dad called "the lady killer." He would show them that grin, and everything would be okay.

"Momma, I'm okay," Bryce said bursting through the door. The sobbing had only gotten louder.

"How will this look to the neighbors?" his older sister said to no one in particular.

"The men did something, and it hurts. But I'm okay," Bryce said again. No one looked at him.

"Magics ..." his father said under his breath and headed back to the field. "Should've taken him to the Refuge." The door closed.

Those were the last words his father ever spoke in his direction.

"When were you given the Raven?" Bryce asked when his head had recovered enough to translate into Hadranian.

"Don't remember," Tiernan mused.

"You don't remember?" How could he forget? Bryce would give anything to forget that day. The tattoo itself had become part of him, but the memory of that searing pain was something he would rather forget.

"I was a baby," Tiernan said.

"Baby?" Bryce repeated just to make sure he had heard him right. Tiernan nodded and made a rocking motion with his hands.

"Baby."

KORVO:

Kor came running. As soon as the word made it through to him that Bryce was incapacitated in the back of Bethlem's bar, he knew he needed to get there as soon as possible.

"Is Tiernan okay?" he said as soon as his eyes saw Bryce sitting at the table with four empty glasses in front of him.

"Don't worry. I just nearly died today," Bryce said, saluting Kor and handing him a bag.

"Are you drunk?" Kor asked.

Bryce stuck out his tongue. "Just tired. Tiernan is in the corner. I told him to stay out of sight," he took another sip of water. "Or at least I think that's what I told him."

Kor moved to the boy and gave him a once-over. He seemed perfectly content and healthy. Bryce, on the other hand, looked like sludge. Kor came over and sniffed the glasses next to Bryce. There was no smell. He'd been telling the truth. Bryce's eyes tracked his movements but said nothing.

"What happened?" Kor asked, finally taking a seat. "A fight?"

"Your guess is as good as mine." Bryce tried to sit all the way up. He finally seemed to decide on some sort of elbow lean on the table.

"What do you mean?" Kor curved his back so he was at the same level as the slouching Bryce.

"We were just walking. And this man and some Watcher tried to start a fight," Bryce gestured.

"Bryce, you're supposed to be protecting Tiernan," Kor said.

"I was. I got him out of there. I didn't start this fight, Kor. I swear on my life. I didn't even throw a punch."

"And you're sure you did nothing?"

Bryce nodded. "I even tried to be nice. Ask the kid."

"This is worse than I thought," Kor let his body slump against the chair. He picked up a water glass that had a little liquid remaining. Wishing something much stronger was inside, he swallowed it in one swig.

"If you're going to be alright, I think I'll leave you two here for now." Kor got up. Bryce started to speak, but then stopped.

On his way out of the bar, he dropped a handful of small coins for Bethlem. Without moving closer or stopping from washing the glass in his hand, Bethlem nodded. Kor knew he would take care of Bryce. They wouldn't have gotten this far without Bethlem. Not without the gossip he pulled in by the glass during the night. Not without the safety of his backroom. Not without his stash of healing drinks. And not without his friendship. Kor would have considered Bethlem like a father if he felt fathers were worth caring about.

He followed his feet while he let his mind wander to the day's events. He tapped the soft edges of the cards against his finger. The warmth of their power calmed him. He looked down at the bag Bryce had handed him. He hadn't even noticed it was still clenched in his fingers. One lone pastry sat squished in the bottom.

He had to protect Bryce.

When he was back on the top of the Refuge, out in the open air, he could finally think. He pulled the cards out in front of him. He needed details. He shuffled until they felt right in his hands and swept any dirt away with his arm before putting them down on the metal roof. He needed room to be able to do a reading this complicated.

For something this hard he had to see the pictures. Had to know what side up the cards were. He massaged his right hand hoping for some clarity.

He turned over card after card, his face drooping with every one. His simple readings had been sending him bad tidings, but this could only get worse.

There was the tower.

There was the card of justice.

The moon. A lone wolf howling into the night.

The hanged man. A Raven dangling from one foot, its one crazed eye open and staring into Korvo's soul.

His skin prickled with goosebumps. Things were going from bad to worse. There was one last card. Lovers in reverse. He shoved the cards back into his pocket.

CHAPTER 6:

BRYCE:

"MERIN STOP. If you do any more work on me, it's going to put you in the same state," Bryce growled as Merin flitted about poking and prodding here and there. It would kill him to have to sit and watch Merin suffer the same exhaustion he was feeling. Although he had to admit her helping had given him the power to at least remain sitting up.

"It's not my fault you overextended yourself. You know you could die, right?" She huffed and sat next to him.

"I could also die in the Refuge," he said.

She frowned. He shook his head. He should be trying to make her laugh. She'd come all this way just to help him. "Besides, I had to think of Tiernan."

Merin pulled some of the children's books out of her bag. Bryce noticed none of them seemed to feature Magics.

"For Tiernan?"

"Upset you're not the baby anymore?" she teased.

"I wasn't the baby before," he grumbled, letting his head flop back onto the chair.

"Sure, you weren't," she paused, sliding the books over to Bryce. "But these are for you."

"For me?"

"Yeah, I went through my house after I left the school and found some that you wouldn't hate as much. I figured if I could help you, it will be another person helping at the school." She slapped him lightly on the shoulder.

"About that..." he paused, trying to find a good way to tell her that he wasn't sure it mattered. Before the events of the afternoon, he would have beamed at her, but now it had just confirmed his suspicions. People didn't see him as anything other than a worthless Magic. He sighed. There was no reason to tell her; they would only argue. As much as he wanted her to show everyone she was a Magic, he couldn't stand the idea of her being put anywhere near the Refuge. It was always a fight with him. And fights landed you in the dark and dreary Refuge.

"I know."

"You do?" he asked. He stared at her. Her face gave nothing away. She had been quiet and calm. She lifted her serious blue eyes to his soft grey ones and put a light hand on his arm.

"I know you're embarrassed you can't read when that's part of Kor's plan. You feel useless."

"Right, yeah." He settled down into his seat. It was best to keep what was burning inside him a secret. It benefited her. Besides, he'd ask Aer how to talk to Merin. How to get her to understand how much he needed her and how little she understood what it meant to be him.

When Kor still wasn't back after a few hours, Bryce left Tiernan in Merin's care. His head was woozy before the hours of reading practice Merin had insisted on, and now, after, he was probably not the best person to look after him. Besides, Merin would take over teaching the poor boy some common tongue so they could all communicate better. Merin was a good teacher. Even now Tiernan couldn't seem to stop himself from sounding out the signs around him. So much of his world had changed now that the letters made sounds and words and sentences. But maybe that was also because he hung on to every word, every syllable, every letter that she said. Bryce kicked a loose pebble on the ground. Did any of it matter?

He wandered through the Wall District. Being around other Magics would do him some good.

He felt the most himself here. He rolled up the cuffs on his pants and let the earth stick to his shoes even though it caused him that lurching sort of swagger. In the Wall District, he was among his own people. His plan had been to track down Aer before she left for her gig at the club five blocks over from the Wall District. He wanted to talk to her about Merin, and to be perfectly honest, he didn't know who else to talk to.

Even in the Wall District, though, Bryce's head was on a swivel today. The threat of the Refuge had been too much. He never wanted to go back there. He'd been there too much already.

He smoothed the lines on his shirt as if he could shake off today. His thoughts were tangled all together into a knot he had no hope to untie. Merin, magic, Kor, anger, mistreatment, pride, reading, they all wrestled for control inside his mind. Bryce wasn't one for making the pieces line up. A little smile and some fancy footwork around the problem and most of the time things were resolved. When that didn't work, he wasn't afraid to use his fists. But he doubted that would help him dissolve the riddle that kept growing in his head.

"Plant boy," a nasal voice said behind him. Bryce turned slowly to see Sid standing in the middle of the street, staring at him.

"Wall rat," Bryce said, giving him an overzealous salute.

"I'm going to make a difference."

"Shut up, Sid." Bryce turned back to the world ahead of him.

"Are you going to follow in Korvo's footsteps for the rest of your life? Or are you going to stand up for what you believe?"

"I believe in Korvo," Bryce said simply, giving the older boy the most serious face he could muster.

"How many times have you seen the inside of the Refuge?" Sid asked. Bryce shrugged. He knew perfectly well it was five. But Sid was an idiot, and there was no point in talking to him. He waved at Sid and took a step away. Bryce might have been behind Aer, but that didn't make him like Sid any better. Best to ignore him until he got everything straightened out in his mind.

"Does it bother you that things are getting worse?" Sid asked Bryce's back. "I heard you got roughed up a bit today." Sid slid over to put his arm around Bryce's neck. "Took a few Watchers out with you."

"There was only one." Bryce moved away from Sid's arm.

"Still. I bet it felt good. Using your gift."

"Actually, I still have a headache. Too much power hurts. But I guess you wouldn't know since you hide in the walls like the rat you are," Bryce said with a sneer.

"I know plenty about power. And these fools will know about my power soon enough," Sid returned the nasty tone.

"And when that fails, Kor will pick up the pieces and make some real change." While he defended Kor, the knotted lump clogging up his brain began to throb.

"You think you can change people by knowing what the legislature is going to do? By presenting information to the Council? By showing them we are human through some sort of legal means? Wake up, Bryce. We look human. Without these marks there would be nothing to tell us apart from them. They know we're human. They just refuse to believe it." It was like a mirror reflecting the dark places in Bryce's mind. The anger, the injustice. Sid had taken hold of one end of the knot and pulled. Bryce could feel himself unraveling.

"And so what? What is the master plan here, Sid?"

"Come to the market tomorrow, and you'll see." A smile returned to Sid's lips.

"No." Bryce couldn't let go just yet. The image of Kor sitting in the schoolhouse telling him about the dangers he faced in Hadran lingered in his mind. He would be so disappointed if Bryce turned his back now. Kor didn't deserve it. But, voiced an incessant whisper in Bryce's mind, Bryce hadn't deserved the way he had been treated either. The whirlpool of his thoughts sucked him in deeper. He felt like he was choking on decisions.

"Just don't forget what it feels like to use your powers against the people who are unjust to you. Don't forget we need people like you on our side. Making people hear."

Sid walked away, fading slowly into the milling crowd.

Bryce walked past the nightclub where Aer worked. He stuck his head in, but the nice waitress near the door told him she wasn't in yet. He nodded and continued on his way. He would take a moment to slip into the garden area before trying again.

The garden was dark now, lit only by the occasional lantern post throughout the whole district. But Bryce didn't need to see in order to find his way around. He had lived among these plants for years now. Besides, he had to thank them for coming to his aid. He walked through, meticulously putting his hands on the trunks of the trees and letting his fingers trace over each leaf that moved toward him as he went. Even though it was the dead of winter these plants were always doing well. The trees dropped their leaves, but with his hands on the bark Bryce could feel the energy of new growth churning inside of them, waiting to become something new.

That was the thing about plants; they could take the harsh winds and cold weather, but they found ways to come back in the spring. To come back seasons if not years later, when the conditions were better.

"We're not all that lucky," he said to his favorite old tree near the center of the garden pathway. "Some of us are stuck in the conditions we have now. We can't wait," he mused, sitting in the dip on the lowest branch that fit him perfectly.

"I thought I would find you here," Merin called from the circle of light made by a lantern. Tiernan was still holding her skirt and glancing all around. Even the shadows made him jumpy.

"You brought Tiernan out here on your own?" There didn't seem to be any immediate danger, but it still made him feel uneasy.

"It's alright, Bryce," Kor said, stepping into the light. "Besides, Merin could handle herself if needed."

"I know that," Bryce said, getting down from the tree.

"Ready to go home?" Korvo asked.

Bryce let his hand gently fall from the rough bark of the tree and nodded. Merin smiled and waved, turning to walk the few blocks to her house where her window looked over the East side of town. The side where the Refuge was far from sight and mind. He watched her go until he couldn't see her anymore.

"I talked to Sid today," he said finally.

"You did? And?" Kor said with so little inflection that Bryce couldn't read him.

He paused, not quite ready to tell Kor everything, but feeling enough guilt he had to say something. "He's right about something."

"About what?"

"It felt good. It felt good to use my powers today. I mean, I felt like garbage afterward, but it felt … right. Those roots rushing to me. I felt power."

"Power? While you were running from the Watchers? Power comes, Bryce, when you don't need to run."

"People are being mistreated."

"Our plan will work." There was an edge to his voice. "We will teach all the young Magics how to read. We will continue finding out the secrets behind the scenes in order to find an ear that will listen. Change takes time."

"Do you think Hadran will ever change?" Bryce looked up at Kor.

"Someday," Kor said, but he stared down at his hands.

The three of them walked silently the rest of the way to the Refuge. They approached from the side where the fire escape was slowly being forgotten about. Bryce hesitated on the first step. Kor turned and opened his mouth to say something. Bryce ignored him and scooped some dirt into his pockets before climbing the rest of the way up.

At the top of the building, the muscles in Bryce's arms buzzed and sweated, but with nothing but sky above him, for the first time he could understand why Kor came here. There was something about being free from the shadow of the Refuge that made him feel like he had gotten his first real breath of air in three years.

He sank his head down and shut his eyes. He tried to focus on the sound of the wind around him, but he couldn't hear voices like Aer. So, instead, he strained his ears and his limited Hadranian to listen to Korvo talk to Tiernan in the softest tones about what was happening and what was below them. He didn't need to know much Hadran to understand what Korvo said about the Refuge.

"Death," Korvo said again pointing down. Bryce wished he hadn't heard. But more, he wished he didn't understand the truth in those words. This was exactly why, Bryce thought, this was exactly why he had to go see what Sid was doing tomorrow. It felt like utter betrayal of Korvo, the person who had watched over him for years, but he had made up his mind on the walk to the Refuge. The people had to listen.

"Stay with Bryce. He'll keep you safe. I'll keep you both safe," Kor said.

Bryce wished he hadn't heard that either.

AER:

"Everything is set for tomorrow," Aer said, sitting for the first time in three hours.

"I talked to the plant boy." Sid sneered from his position at the head of the table. Aer jerked up.

"Did you tell him about tomorrow?" Ever since she had talked to Kor, she was having second thoughts about bringing Bryce into this. Sid swore they needed Tiernan if they were going to make a big enough statement. But it didn't have to be on day one.

"It helped us out that the Watchers decided to bother him." Sid cleaned some dirt from underneath his rough fingernails. Aer cringed.

"And what would have happened if something worse had happened to him?" she asked. The preparations for tomorrow weighed heavily on her, and she couldn't get up her usual amount of gusto for a fight.

"Everyone loves a martyr," Sid said, standing and crossing the dimly lit room. Aer stiffened. He placed his hands on her shoulders. Her heartbeat raced. The room seemed to slip into utter darkness.

"Get off," she stammered.

"See you in the morning, Aer." He let his hand brush her lower back. She recoiled and pushed him away. "And don't go sneaking off to Korvo and losing your nerve." He walked out of the room, and she picked up a file to throw after him but she didn't have the energy.

He isn't worth it, she thought, sliding down into a more comfortable position. She hummed to herself. In the confines of the walls, her songs were even stronger. The magic language of the winds reverberated off the metal and came back toward her stronger than before. She sang to herself until she felt calm enough to read the folder in front of her.

Sid was getting lazy. With his big demonstration looming, he was delegating more and more tasks, which meant she was finally getting access to his information. Most of it was worse than Korvo's. Sid only had the information he could gather through the walls, and Korvo had his net spread wide throughout the city, but there were some things Sid seemed to have that Kor didn't.

For instance, this folder contained quite a few references to the Ice Man. Aer didn't know anyone who had ice magic, and she wasn't sure why the person's name was being kept a secret, but it intrigued her. She knew better than to ask Sid for more information; he would only lord it over her. He was power-hungry. But Sid was a means to an end, an end that she very much needed.

If tomorrow went well, the Ice Man was going to meet with Sid tomorrow night. If it didn't go well, Aer stopped for a minute to think about all the ways things could go sideways, he would wait a day or two before showing up in the walls. Cautious. Smart. Aer planned on being there to meet him no matter what happened.

But first, she had to make it through tomorrow. The plan was simple. She could almost hear Korvo listing the things they needed to do. He loved making lists. For a moment, she longed for him to be there while she made this one. But instead of sitting in Bethlem's or in her apartment, she was in the dimly lit and cramped spaces hidden in the walls. She took a deep breath and recited the plan to herself.

1. Gather a large crowd of Magics in the market

2. Use her powers to keep shop owners and patrons in the market

3. Give the preplanned demands

4. Leave a charred mark of the Raven on the market square

5. Disappear into the crowd before the Watchers arrived

When she was satisfied she had thought through her entrance and exit strategy, she willed herself away from the table and into the makeshift closet of a room she was staying in. It felt lonely in a single bed by herself, but she was undeterred. Things would be fine.

BRYCE:

Bryce woke determined to join whatever plan Sid had for the marketplace. He had told Korvo he needed a break from Tiernan. Bryce mentioned something about getting used to talking to himself. Korvo didn't pry, he just accepted what Bryce had said. That only added to the guilt competing with anger for the majority of Bryce's mind.

There was, however, a third contender for the emotion driving his every move. It had struck Bryce somewhere in a nighttime fit that if something were to go wrong today, if he was sent back to the Refuge, he wouldn't have told Merin how he felt. So before the market, before anything bad could happen, he had to figure out what to say.

In his head he understood it. When his eyes were closed, he could hear the words coming out of his mouth, but whenever he was with her it just came out all wrong.

"I mean, maybe there isn't a point. I'm going to get rejected. Look at me." Maybe there was some truth to the idea that he had made a habit of talking to himself. He shook his head and scuffed his boot against the road.

"What's got you in a huff?" Aer said, popping out of the opening in the wall. She was dressed in her leather jacket and there were no traces of her makeup from the club.

"Merin," he said looking down at the ground.

"Did you guys have another little spat?"

Bryce scratched his neck. "No, I just can't seem to tell her anything."

"You mean like how you worship the ground she walks on?"

Bryce snapped to attention. Aer smiled.

"I do not."

"You do so. Literally, flowers wilt when she walks away." Aer started walking down the road, and Bryce jogged a few steps to catch up to her.

"When I go to say anything, it comes out like mud. Could you help?"

"With Merin? Sure. What is it you want to tell her?" Aer glanced up and down the street.

"Tiernan and I were attacked yesterday. I was almost sent to the Refuge again. I can't have that happen to her."

"And? What is it you really want to say?" Aer stopped and crossed her arms. Bryce took a deep breath.

"Her laugh makes my insides feel like spring, and her smile makes my knees feel weak. How do I tell her that I want her to tell everyone she has magic? The most beautiful magic that feels like liquid silver finding all of my broken spots and mending them. And that I am so happy there isn't a black Raven on her beautiful skin. That her intelligence is something I make fun of because I know it's something I will never be able to get—"

"Just say that. Look, I got to go." Aer's eyes stared straight ahead. She started walking away, Then she turned and looked at Bryce for a minute. She opened her mouth a few times but didn't say anything. Then finally, "Sid moved the demonstration to tomorrow."

With that, she turned on her heel and jogged into the distance. Bryce felt the rush of the cool winter breezes chasing after her.

"Why?" Bryce asked, but she was already far away from them. He had told Kor he would be gone all day. It dawned on him that this was the first actual confirmation he had gotten that Aer and Sid were working together. If Aer was involved, then he felt a little more comfortable. Aer could get anything done.

Kor was always giving her things to do. She was just as well-known as Kor. And she could be a little more forceful in getting things done. She was the one Kor had sent when the Council members were having a hard time with passing a law delaying the marking of children with the Raven's head until they were at least eleven. It wasn't a large victory. Bryce would have only gotten one more year before that moment in the field, but, he sighed. For a kid like Tiernan, it would have been like a lifetime.

"But if he doesn't even remember it, maybe that's better?" Bryce sighed as he made his way to the garden. Kor knew what he was doing. Little victories, he would say, end up with a lot of progress. The next victory had to be getting rid of the Refuge, the worst thing Bryce had ever known.

The air inside the Refuge was stale. It was recycled through hundreds of kids. Most of them were sick from the conditions and the lack of sunlight and fresh food. The rats outnumbered the people, but nothing was ever done about it. Kids were forced to share a cot between two of them with only one blanket, full of rips and holes.

He had been there five times. The first time was when he'd first gotten to the city, three years after they tattooed him. When he'd run from his parents, he didn't have anywhere to go. They'd caught him sleeping in the garden curled under one of the rose bushes.

Before he had even been awake, they were dragging him onto his feet and pulling him into holding to be processed into the Refuge. At first, when he saw the building he thought they were helping him. But the minute the door closed behind him, he knew he would rather endure a million nights of his father not talking to him, his sister eyeing him suspiciously, and his mother's frequent outbursts of tears than spend another minute in that hellhole.

That first time it was just for a few nights. Kor had found him not too long after that and worked out a deal with the head gardener and the florists for Bryce to help out in conjunction with their allowing him places to sleep where there were growing things. Kor had done a lot for him.

The second and third time, he had been thrown into the Refuge for fighting. Once he had been labeled as a menace to society. That was a mandatory two-week sentence. Another time he had been sent in for re-education, as if they had given him any education at all. Magics "didn't have the control to be at school."

"As if we were going to burn the place down," Bryce had told Kor when they had been going over the plan after his last trip to the Refuge. He had been angry. Too angry to sit. He had paced back and forth, his hands waving. Now he thought of Tiernan. But Tiernan had such amazing control he wouldn't burn tissue paper unless he wanted to.

His fingers brushed the rough stems that had hardened to get through the winter. He felt the life buried inside them. It was the same green light he saw inside himself. His connection to the elements and the plants. He took a deep breath and tried to concentrate on his light as Kor had taught him.

It jumped and fizzled whenever he reached out to it. At least he had another day to figure out what to say to Merin. Maybe that would help relax his inner light. The growing headache he had since talking to Aer had been no help.

He could sneak over to Merin's house tonight and let her know once he had all the words. Maybe he could even write something simple. She'd be impressed by that.

He walked the length of the garden and found himself among the roses quickly.

"Maybe by the time you're blooming next year, she'll know how I feel. Maybe I'll give her one of your flowers." He let a finger trace the hardened thorns. "With your permission of course."

"Bryce," Vycky called from behind him. "You are just the person I was hoping to run into."

"I am?" He looked at her.

"I was having some trouble with the camellias this morning, and I have a large order for them coming up."

"You want me to come take a look?" Bryce let his fingers drop the rose leaves in his hands.

"If you don't mind. A dose of that charming smile of yours and they all seem to perk up immediately," she said, smiling. Bryce couldn't help but blush a little.

"Well, I do have a pretty distinct advantage." He crossed the little cobblestone path to be next to her.

"You do indeed. So, you'll help?"

"Of course. You saved me the other day." They walked together, pointing out the little plants they noticed in the gardens. Bryce almost always won this game now. He never forgot the name of a plant once he had heard it. If only the letters and words Merin had been teaching him would do the same.

"Vycky? If someone was going to tell you that they love you, how would you want them to do it?"

"I was just about to ask where your shadow was. How is Merin?"

"Can we just focus on the question?" The red across his cheeks felt scalding. If Aer had been more help, he could have spared himself this embarrassment. He stopped walking, wondering if it was worth this feeling congealing in his stomach. Vycky stopped and walked the three steps back to him.

"Decided you'd just keep pining after her?" Vycky said.

Bryce shook his head. "Sorry for asking, but Aer was no help this morning."

"Oh, what does Aer know about expressing her love?"

"What do you mean?" Bryce asked, surprised by Vycky's tone.

"I live near her, you know. I see Korvo coming and going. But that girl is as frigid as they come," Vycky said.

"Kor and Aer aren't together. They're probably just working,"

"You're not that little, and you shouldn't be that naive, Bryce. Kor and Aer have been sleeping together for the last two years at least."

"They have not. They have the missions."

"They also have needs," Vycky looked at him. "I know you know what I mean by that."

Bryce could not have turned a deeper red if he tried. He looked away.

"Telling Merin you love her can't be the only thing you think about when you go to sleep," she said.

"Well, nothing comes of anything if I don't figure out how to tell her," Bryce mumbled. He kept his eyes down, avoiding looking at Vycky. She laughed and touched him on the top of his head. He couldn't help but notice she would be about the same age as his older sister.

"I can see how you wouldn't know they were together. It's not like they ever touch. But you can see the way Kor looks at her, the same way I can see the way you look at Merin."

Bryce looked away and tried to find something else to focus on.

The marketplace was extra crowded today. Bryce wondered what the occasion was. There weren't usually this many people here during working hours, but it wasn't like he troubled himself with holidays. Holidays were for family, and except for Kor, Aer, and Merin, he didn't have any. Merin spent holidays with her family; Kor celebrated his own from Hadran, and Aer hated them with a passion. Everything Aer did she did with a passion.

Vycky led Bryce to the back of her shop. It smelled like fresh cuttings, water, and earth. He took a deep breath.

"You should really think about coming to work for me full-time," Vycky said, handing him a pair of clippers. They were just the right size for his hands and made a lot cleaner cut for the plants than ripping dead growth off with his fingers.

"Maybe once the Refuge is gone." Bryce was already nose deep in the camellias. "Right now there is too much darkness with that thing in the world."

"You are just like my plants, Bryce." Vycky's tone drifted to somewhere soft.

"Beautiful and worth a ton of money?" he grinned up at her.

"You need sunshine and fresh air."

"It's in my blood," he said, still smiling.

"I'd pay you a full salary," Vycky said. Bryce frowned and turned back to the greenery. It shouldn't be up to the mark on his ankle if he got paid as much as the other employees Vycky had to train for weeks to do what Bryce could do by instinct. He should be getting paid *more*.

He let his power flow through the plants, looking for anything that was disturbing them. When he found leaves with even a hint of sickness he clipped them with the clippers. He moved from plant to plant.

"Maybe you should give Merin a plant? When Sylvia first told me she loved me, she gave me that orchid over there," Vycky said, taking the seat next to him. She started arranging bouquets, skillfully mixing the different flowers and greenery to make them look both random and perfect.

"I was thinking I would give her a rose from the bush you saw me with earlier," Bryce said.

"You were going to wait till spring?"

"No. I want to tell her tonight."

"Tonight? Why tonight?"

The question needled at Bryce. He trusted her, but he couldn't tell her about Sid's plan. The pounding in his head reverberated. He stared down at the flowers in his hands.

"None of my business, I get it. I didn't mean to pry." Vycky pulled the flowers out of his grip.

Bryce let all the air escape from his lungs. "I might as well wait. Everything comes out wrong. I snap at her, and it's all my fault. Besides, maybe then we'll have the Refuge figured out, and I can work on building my life." He let the clippers rest on the table. Vycky laughed.

"You shouldn't ever wait on something like that."

"So, what kind of flower would you give someone?" He looked around at the shop. Winter was full of flowers if you knew where to look, but Bryce preferred the brightness of spring.

"Not a flower silly, a plant."

"I don't think Merin is ready for something as picky as an orchid."

"Something easy to take care of, then."

"Why a plant, anyway?"

"If you want someone to know that you love them, and you give them a flower, when it dies there is no reminder of how you feel. But a plant, that's a living thing. Like love. Every time I see the orchid bloom, I think of Sylvia. Besides, with your skills, you could keep it alive forever."

"Isn't that cheesy?" Bryce asked. He wasn't sure he could imagine saying any of that to Merin. She would probably laugh at him, which would only make him frustrated.

"I'd like it," Vycky said, looking down at the plants in front of them.

A sound like a thousand limbs breaking screamed through the air. Both Bryce and Vycky jumped.

"Get behind me," Bryce said.

"The hell? This is my shop. You stay behind me." Vycky headed from the back room to the front office. Bryce followed closely behind.

"The windows," Bryce said. The glass was shattered. Little pieces fell into the arrangements of flowers like crystals. They sparkled with the light dancing across the sky. Even though the day had been cold before, there hadn't been any clouds. Now the sky was dark, and thunder crashed over their heads.

"It was just lightning," Vycky said, looking for a broom. "It will pass soon. If we stay in here we'll be fine." She turned to the customers in the front of the store, "Everyone, why don't we make our way to the back room to avoid all the glass." Both the employees and the customers mumbled their support for her idea. Vycky swept a clear path to the back of the building and returned. Bryce was halfway out the window.

"Get inside," she snapped.

"I don't think this is normal lightning." Bryce said. The clouds weren't moving. Enough time with Aer had taught him how to watch the weather. Enough time with Aer told him that only someone like her could build this type of storm and hold it here. After enough time with Aer, he would have thought, kicking himself, he would know by now when she was lying. The demonstration was today.

"It's safer in the back," Vycky gestured again, but Bryce ignored her.

"She lied to me..." Bryce said as he knocked out the last few pieces of the windowpane.

"Who?" Vycky asked.

"Aer. The one making this happen."

"Bryce! Get in—"

But Bryce was already out the window and halfway down the street. Windows were busted in almost every shop.

"Aer?" he called, but there was no one in this area. Despite all the people who had been milling around earlier, now the streets were deserted. He saw a few people huddled in the buildings covered with glass. A few had cuts on their faces and hands, but no one looked seriously hurt. Another rumble sounded. This time it wasn't lightning, it was people.

He ducked down the alleyway that would get him to the other side of the market the fastest. He climbed a stack of wooden crates to drop over into the other side of the market, but when he got to the top he froze.

"At least I found the rest of the people," he said, staring at the large crowd that had mobbed together. They filled the entire main square of the marketplace. He could barely even see the street below. He looked again.

This wasn't a mob. This was a fight.

People were punching and kicking at Watchers who held their batons and large shields in front of them. Bryce had been knocked by one of those before. It left a welt the size of a grapefruit.

Bryce looked around. He was far from the florist shops that all sat in a neat row next to each other. It'd be hard to get anything growing fast enough to protect people. Maybe he could at least get some roots like he had before.

On his second glance over the middle of the market, he saw people weren't just throwing punches. Magic attacks were on full display as well. Sid had taken control of some rope and, using magic, he had the ropes whipping anyone who came close. Aer, of course, was standing to the side. Bryce could see her chanting under her breath. She had to concentrate to control the weather. Even with the help of the wind, this was probably taking everything in her.

"Aer," he yelled again and started to move toward her.

"Protect the Magics," Aer said, momentarily breaking her concentration. The cloud trembled but held firm when she started chanting again. Bryce's heart beat faster. They were in danger. More danger than anything he had been involved with before.

He tried to calm himself with the deep breaths Kor had taught him to quell his nightmares, but nothing was working. Every time he closed his eyes there was an explosion, the crack of one of Sid's ropes, or a desperate cry from someone in the crowd. Bryce didn't know where to look.

The Watchers began to fall back. People were cheering, but up on top of the crates, Bryce could see what was happening. There were Watchers in full combat suits coming. They were coming with weapons.

"Get out!" he screamed, but no one could hear him over the din of the crowd. He called to the plants he could muster. Build a wall. Build a wall, he thought down to the roots and the leaves and the vines. Build a wall. He could feel the plants respond. They were closer this time, but some of them were listening to other Magics. They pulled toward him, but Bryce wasn't sure it was fast enough. There would never be time. Lightning cracked overhead. Aer had seen it, too. The Watchers had only slowed for a moment to collect themselves. Now the real fight would start.

Sid found his way to the top of a cart someone had left outside their shop.

"We will make them hear," he yelled.

The crowd answered. "We will not be afraid."

He turned then and faced the Watchers. He pounded his chest and yelled.

Then, before he even had a chance to move, something whizzed by and caught him in the mouth. He spun as he fell. His legs and arms crumpled beneath him. The ropes he used went limp.

Bryce couldn't even hear himself yelling for Sid to get up over the fizzle of the lightning that struck the group of Watchers. Bryce might have hated Sid. Bryce might have told him to crawl into a hole and die. But he had never expected him to die in front of him.

The blood was oozing out of Sid. Bryce could stop the bleeding. Merin had shown him how to use non-magic techniques.

Bryce frantically called the plants. Grow. Grow. Grow. Protect us. He poured his magic into the ground. He felt it rushing through his veins, his inner light filling every corner of his body. His steps were getting weaker. The lightning crackled around him, but he could tell Aer was losing her strength. Plants were starting to sprout out of the ground. The vines grew the fastest, winding themselves around the light poles and carts, following the lines of buildings. Wooden roots sprouted and intertwined, making a barrier three feet from the ground.

Bullets flew everywhere now. The crowd had increased their fury. Rocks whizzed through the air, and Aer's winds howled. Water from nearby cracked as it whipped the closest Watchers.

People were scrambling. Bryce was still half a courtyard away. He ducked into shadows and behind carts. Bullets buried themselves in the wood. He could feel the heat coming off of them and the stink of gunpowder was thick in the air.

Working his way slowly across the road, he pulled roots from his makeshift wall and had them curl over wounded people in the street. He could feel himself slowing. His legs were shaky, and he needed to find cover and stay hidden for a moment longer before he could make the jump to the next hiding place.

Finally, he got to where Sid's body was lying. The blood was already starting to coagulate in the cold air. His eyes were open, but the rest of his face was unrecognizable. Bryce stooped down to close Sid's eyes.

"You dumb son of a bitch," Bryce said. "Go well and rest easy."

"Bryce!" Aer's voice called. She was behind his wall of roots. The bullets chipped away at the wood, but it didn't give.

"Aer, don't move; I'm coming!" His knees buckled beneath him. He had to release the plants. They would probably stay where they were for a little while. But plants were plants and didn't normally form walls. They couldn't grow rapidly without him. He let go. Immediately he felt empty. When he connected with the plants like that, he felt whole. He felt part of something larger. Now he was just Bryce. All alone again, scared, but somehow still standing.

"Bryce," Aer stood right as one of the smaller roots began to fall. Without Bryce's support, it lost the ability to stand on its own. A bullet whizzed by and struck him. He spun.

He tried to get up, but he couldn't keep his balance. He scrambled on his hands and knees for some stability. The plants curled over him. His arm was bleeding. He ripped his shirt after three tries. If only he were stronger ... He looked up. The clouds were starting to part.

"We have to get out of here," Bryce said, wrapping the cloth around his arm and calling out to Aer.

"I know where to go," Aer said, coming close.

He nodded. He put his good arm around her shoulders.

Despite the hammering of the pain in his arm, and the weakness from using so much magic, anger and fear drummed out all other things.

As they ran, Bryce's anger grew, while his ability to stay awake began to falter. The Watchers had done this. People had done this. They had hurt him just because he was a Magic. His blood boiled, but his eyes wouldn't stay open.

He felt Aer lay him down on something hard. A table most likely. His eyes shut. He couldn't will them open. But at least it was quiet. Finally quiet. The screams and the explosions of the guns were finally just an echo in his mind.

He heard Aer's footsteps falter as she moved around the school, trying to find things that would help him. She heard her whisper things to someone, and he heard whomever it was rush off. Then he heard the door open one more time.

"Aer?" he called.

And he heard what he thought was "I'm sorry," as wind whipped through his clothing.

KORVO:

Bryce was sleeping back at the school with Merin and Tiernan both hovering over him. He hadn't been able to get any information from Bryce. By the time he'd run over after the messenger Aer sent finally reached him, Bryce was already so deeply asleep that they couldn't wake him.

Kor excused himself, even though he wasn't sure Merin could hear him, and made a break for the outside world.

Hadn't he known it would come to this? His mind whirled with possible outcomes. Just like his plan for the Magics, Kor tried as many times as he could to run the possible scenarios of what would happen when he found Aer.

Three of the proposed scenarios ended with Aer throwing a glass of water in his face. He'd rather avoid those. Two had him punching Sid, and while he enjoyed those immensely, it wasn't what he needed.

He needed to talk to Aer. Alone. It was the only scenario in which he thought he might actually get the truth. He needed to know what happened.

Of course, the truth was also why he kept trying to think of a new outcome for the entire eleven blocks to get to her apartment.

But when he found himself face to face with the door, he still only had the one plan. He sighed, waiting for a breeze underneath the crack to let him know she was there. He didn't have to wait long before air was coming out from the door, rattling around the edges of his clothing. He took a deep breath and knocked.

The door opened.

"I wondered when you'd show up," Aer said from deep within the darkness of her apartment. Ground floor meant there wasn't a lot of sunlight streaming into the windows, and with half of them blocked with blankets to allow her to sleep during the day, it took Kor a minute to adjust to the dark.

"What happened?" Kor said. He didn't sit across from her. He just stayed leaning against the framework of the door. He needed distance.

"You want to know if we started it?" she asked. In the darkness, he wondered if she could even see him shrug.

"We didn't. It was supposed to be day one. Get the message across. Show some resistance. Tell them we wouldn't let them walk all over us."

"And?"

"The Watchers came. A fight broke out."

His shoulders slumped. He could feel his face go limp. She rose from her chair and quietly opened one of the shades to let light bounce all over the small room. Kor blinked. In the light, he could see her in front of him. Tall and lanky, covered with nicks and dirt. Hair a mess. Graceful and airy, though, like a dream he could never quite hold onto in the morning. His Aer. No. Aer on her own.

"We both knew this was coming. I got tired of waiting. Tiernan was the last straw. He is a child, Kor."

"But he's not even from here. He wasn't tortured by the people of Kaybrum."

"But that is what humanity is capable of. Without batting an eye. We are no different than the people of Hadran. There is nothing keeping them from doing that to us," she said. Her voice and eyes pleaded for Kor to understand, to realize. He sighed.

"And what happens when people attack Magics for changing things too quickly? Bryce is lying bleeding on my school desks." Kor moved from the doorway. The anger in his blood was making his body stiff as a board.

"Is he all right?" she asked, taking a step towards him. Her eyes softened.

"He's fine. For now. Merin is with him. But next time he might not be." His arms crossed reflexively over his chest. Aer was silent for a few minutes. Her eyes darted everywhere over her apartment.

"Sacrifices might need to be made," she said, wincing.

"You'd sacrifice Bryce?" The words came out cold.

"No," she countered, "not on purpose. But there are casualties in war. And he chose to be there."

"You're waging war now? You're Sid's little general?" Heat flashed across the bridge of his nose and into his cheeks.

"Sid's dead."

There was a moment of silence.

"Playing nice on the playground isn't going to get you what you want, Kor. It's time you see that if you want anything to change people have to listen. It's not enough to talk to them. They have to actually hear what you're saying."

"And you're doing that by declaring war. By saying we need to fight. I am fighting. I'm just doing it in a way that doesn't get any of us killed!" Kor said. His right fist slammed into the doorway. A silence fell as the sound reverberated throughout the small space.

"I'm just doing it in a way that will work." Aer turned her back to him.

"If you think I'll believe that, then …" he trailed off, afraid of what might come out next.

"Then what? I don't know you? Because I'm not sure I do. The Korvo I met had fire in his belly to make things right. The Kor I knew wouldn't back down from a fight. The Kor I loved was changing the world."

"Loved? Past tense?" Kor said. Aer didn't answer. Even the breezes that had been whipping up around them were quiet.

"Sid knew nothing about the real world. He hid in the walls and saw the world as he wanted to see it. Sid rejected the people of Kaybrum. Not the other way around. I thought you would see things differently. But it looks like you've rejected us, too," Kor said finally.

"And you know the hearts of the people here better?" She wouldn't look at him. Kor wondered if that was better for both of them.

"I know revolutions like this. I know those sacrifices you're talking about. I've seen them." His eyes rested on his hand. The skin caught the thin rays of light, causing the rough edges to look even more sinister and covered in shadows.

"Because you've seen, I thought you would understand."

Her eyes were also fixed on his hand. The depth of his feelings pooled together into a swirling mass of rage.

"I hope you didn't think of me as some martyr ready for the pyre."

Aer winced and turned her head to look out the window.

"And I sure hope that wasn't why you let me close to you. Why you let me into your life, your house, your bed."

"Kor ..."

"I don't need to hear it, Aer. Be happy with what you chose. But I won't fight this war with you. I won't stop Bryce or Merin or anyone else, but I'm not giving up all the work we've done these last few years for a fight you will lose. A fight that's only going to make things worse."

"Together, Kor..."

Kor put his hand out and shook his head. "There is no together. Not on this foolhardy suicide mission."

"We're two sides of the same coin," she whispered. He wanted to move to her. To be next to her. But she was right. They were two sides that wouldn't meet.

"Goodbye, Aer." Kor turned to leave. He could still feel the winds around him blustering until he was a long way away. Despite his anger, he couldn't help thinking that with all of that wind, Aer would need to take a nap. She always slept best if she could stick one leg out from beneath the blanket, and she snored less if she let her head prop up against his chest. But that was no more.

He never read the cards wrong. No matter how many scenarios he had run through, he'd known this would be the conclusion.

He walked around the city. The crowds were still frenzied, and everyone was on high alert. He stalked through the shadows to stay out of sight. The last thing he needed was for the people to demand his opinion. His thoughts. His guidance. He just needed a drink.

He found himself at Bethlem's.

Sid was dead. He deserved it, Kor thought, pacing through the main part of the bar. He didn't bother waiting in one of the back rooms. There was hardly anyone out since the city had declared a curfew that he was about an hour from hitting.

"Do you think it's over now?" Bethlem asked, still cleaning glasses like the regular crowd was about to stream in at any moment. Kor sat down.

"Hardly. People will be scared, but they spilled blood." Kor thought about the disaster in the marketplace. He had pieced together the details after he left Aer. Five people were dead and who knows how many were injured. "People will want revenge. They'll want justice."

Kor shook his head and gave the drink in his hand a swirl. Bethlem had handed it to him with a wink, but so far he hadn't taken a sip. The brown liquid swirled easily enough in his glass, giving him something to think about. A couple walked into the bar and sat silently at one of the tables behind Kor. He turned a little to hear their conversation better. He needed all the intel he could get.

"It was scarier than anything I'd ever seen," said the man accepting a glass from Bethlem.

"I heard the poor Sid kid didn't make it home," Bethlem said with a sigh. Bethlem had a way of getting people to talk about what Kor needed to hear.

"It got him right in the face," the man said with a shudder.

"They weren't expecting the bullets, I reckon," the woman said. Kor cringed. This was bringing back too many memories.

"Do you think they're done?" Bethlem asked, heading back to the bar. "With Sid gone and all. He was the leader."

"That girl, Aer, seems like she's taken the lead. She's back in the Wall getting the medics busy with the wounded," the man said, taking a drink from his glass. Bethlem shot a glance at Kor. He closed his eyes, sighed, and downed the drink in front of him in one fluid movement. The fire of the drink raced down his throat, but it was nothing compared to the fire in his soul.

If Aer was in charge there would be no stopping her until she was dead, which, if today were any indication, would not be that far off for all of them.

"I just wish they'd lay low. It's going to be hard on all of us for a while," the woman said. Kor got up, careful not to show them his face. It was probably only the shock of the day that had kept them from recognizing him from the back. Because with recognition would come questions about Aer. Questions he didn't know and didn't want to know the answers to.

He placed some coins on the counter and found Tiernan asleep on the couch where Merin had dropped him off in the last few minutes. Kor scooped him up and headed back for the Refuge. It might have seemed like the most dangerous spot in the city, but above the Refuge, he could think clearly. And it was always good to have a high vantage point.

"The smokestack is cold," Kor said, touching it when they finally reached the top. He bit his lips to hold back a scream. Of course, they were punishing those in the Refuge for what Sid and Aer had done. It would be cold in there tonight.

"Tiernan," Kor said. The boy jumped. Kor gave him a smile. "I need you to drop some fire down into the smokestack and light the fires down below. Can you do that?" Tiernan nodded.

A ball of fire appeared on his hand like an orange. Tiernan slipped one after another into the smokestack. Kor half expected to hear a *thunk* when they landed, but he didn't. After an hour of Tiernan's fires burning below, the metal at the top was beginning to warm. Tiernan let a larger ball of fire drip off his hand like molten metal and carefully warmed them without making any changes to the world around him.

"Is Bryce alright?" Tiernan asked, looking directly into the blaze.

"I'm sure he's going to be okay," Kor said.

"Are we going to have to leave Kaybrum?" Tiernan asked, pointing to his chest.

"No, I'm still going to make things better here. I have to make things better here. Where would we go? Outside the capital walls things aren't any better," he said, flicking Tiernan in the ear. The little boy frowned.

"I don't like it here," Tiernan said watching the fire in front of him.

"It's only because you have trouble communicating. You like Bryce and Merin," Kor said. Tiernan nodded. Kor fiddled with the cards. Finally, he laid them out in front of him. Tiernan came over and looked over his shoulder.

"Strength," Kor said pointing to the lion etched into the card face. "Right now, it's reminding us we need to keep our heads in this situation. We can't let our emotions get the better of us."

"What's that one?" Tiernan asked. He pointed to the picture of the dove with an arrow through its chest.

"That one is death."

"Is it 'cause that guy you don't like died?" Tiernan asked. Kor shook his head.

"The cards aren't that simple." Kor let his hand rest on it for a while. Death was always a hard card for him. Too many memories of things that had ended came floating back to him every time he touched it. His last conversation with his father, the day he ran from Hadran, and now his conversation with Aer haunted the card like a phantom. He took a breath and touched it lightly with his fingertips. The burnt smell of lightning overwhelmed him. He saw Aer's eyes flash with anger. Reflected in them he saw flags and fists. Things from today were far from over.

"Four of cups." Growing discontent, he drew the next card. He didn't even need to touch the card to feel the intensity behind it. He could hear the rumble of the whispered conversations going on in houses across the city. He could feel the heartbeats of the people frantic with fear and frustration.

He pushed the cards away from him and let his fingers be warmed by the fire Tiernan was now playing with. He was drawing strands out of it like cotton candy and spinning them around his fingers.

"Does the fire feel hot to you?" Korvo asked.

"Hot?"

"Like the sun on your face? If I touched the fire, it would hurt me," Kor said, trying to explain.

"Fire doesn't hurt. It feels like people. Like when Merin hugs me."

"Even fire you don't create?" Kor asked, looking out across the city. With curfew forcing the city to be inside, he could see all the lights and fires through the windows across Kaybrum. Tiernan nodded.

"I am fire," Tiernan said, looking at the flames curling around his fingers like tiny snakes.

"What do you mean? I'm not the cards. They just help me see."

"When I look inside myself, I see a flame," Tiernan said. Kor thought about the inner light he always pictured when he was trying to calm himself. He wondered if that was what Tiernan meant. He let the conversation stop and float out onto the wind.

"How did you get out of Hadran?" he said finally.

"I ran."

"I know that. But how did you escape?"

Tiernan shrugged. His brown eyes turned cold, and he looked away. The fire around his hands grew white.

"I don't want to talk about Hadran."

"I can understand that," Kor said and leaned back against the now-warm stove pipe. The amount of power and control for creating all of that fire from nothing was probably beginning to drain the poor boy. At least they, and the rest of the Refuge, wouldn't freeze that night.

Kor stared off over the city. The usual bustling nightlife was quiet. Kor thought for a minute about how Aer would react if she were sitting with them now.

"First night off in years and I have to spend it sitting on top of the Refuge?" He could hear the words rolling off her tongue. Kor closed his eyes. He reset the situation. No Tiernan. No worries over how Bryce was. He let the tape in his head roll again.

"First night off in years," he heard Aer saying, but now they were in her apartment. She was already under the covers of her bed. He knew beneath those covers she was only wearing one of his shirts. "And you're going to take that long to come to bed."

He let that tape play in his head a while longer.

"One day they left the gate open," Tiernan said, poking at the ashes of his fireball.

"Huh?" Kor said snapping back to the reality in front of him.

"That's how I escaped. One day they left the gate to the prison I was in unlocked." Tiernan was drawing pictures in the ash before it was blown away by the little wisps of wind that swarmed around the tower.

"Did they mean to do that?" Kor asked. Tiernan shrugged.

"I set it on fire after I left," Tiernan explained coolly. He looked up at Kor like he expected him to reach out and strike him. Kor smiled.

"Why didn't you set it on fire beforehand?"

"The inside was all metal. The outside had wood."

"Were you all by yourself?" Kor asked, inching over to the boy.

"Most of the time. People came sometimes for a night or two, but they were always gone by morning." No wonder the kid's speech could be so awkward even in his native language.

"How long were you in that cage?"

"Since I was three, I think," Tiernan said counting on his fingers. Kor let his head thump against the smokestack. Three years. He had hardly survived two. Tiernan's behavior made a lot more sense now. Of course he jumped at every sound and glared at everyone around him. It had been years since he even knew he could trust someone. Probably four since he really had someone to talk to.

"It was a nightmare," Kor said, lifting his finger to streak it across the silver ash. He looked at it closely. He didn't need to ask Tiernan to describe it anymore.

"Is Bryce coming home tonight?" Tiernan asked as the lights around the city began going out one by one.

"He's sleeping at the school." *At least he's safe as the world starts to burn*, Kor thought. He looked at Tiernan. *Or maybe people's hearts have just begun to ice over.* A chill ran through him despite Tiernan's fire.

CHAPTER 7

AER:

AER MADE HER WAY BACK TO THE WALLS. She checked all the medic wings for the healers and had just gone and gotten the last things she needed from her apartment. She doubted today could have been classified as going "well," but she wasn't about to miss a chance to meet with the Ice Man just in case.

Aer knew her own day couldn't be called anything near fine. She knew a reckoning was bound to happen between her and Korvo. But, why had the words come out so poorly? How could she not tell him she had tried to keep Bryce out of it? That she wouldn't sacrifice him. But somewhere in the darkness as she walked toward the opening in the wall, she wondered if she would have.

Curfew had settled over the city, and Aer felt like there were still too many things that were making noise. Her ragged breath and her crazy heartbeat were the two biggest culprits.

The gash in the Wall that served as an entrance was dark. She felt around with her feet for the first twenty steps or so without lighting the lantern, but after that, she figured there was enough space and metal between her and the outside world. There was, after all, a curfew in place. Still, she let the lantern burn low, and she kept it down near her feet to light only what was needed. Within minutes that felt like hours, she found herself in the same meeting room she had been in twenty-four hours before. She looked over the seats arranged around the large table, and with a moment of hesitation took the seat where Sid had sat. The head of the table. They had asked her to lead now that Sid was gone. She wondered if Kor felt the weight she felt now.

Aer sat alone. Her winds fluttered around her, but she was so tired only the weakest of breezes would listen to her. It felt suffocating sitting there waiting.

"Was Kor right?" she asked the little wind as it danced around her, playing with the edges of the papers that had been left on the table, completely oblivious to the concern in Aer's voice.

"I'm sure there's another option," a voice sounded from outside the door. It was muffled, but it was clear and authoritative. Aer stumbled to her feet. The door creaked open.

"There's no need for you to stand, Aer."

Instinct told her to stand, hands raised in fists. No one was safe. A large man filled the doorway and then came to lean against a chair on the far side of the room.

"How do you know my name?" She leaned close, careful to keep herself out of range of the tall, lanky man's reach.

"It's a murmur on the people's lips. And all of those murmurs get back to me. You'll find I know about a great many things. Including your friend Korvo." Slightly stronger winds swept around Aer, causing her hair to lift. They must have followed him in. She felt sturdier with them around her. Braver.

"You know Kor?"

"Longer than you have, I suppose."

Aer looked at him then. The man wasn't dark like Kor or Tiernan. He wore no uniform, but the straight back, and the close-cut facial hair, screamed soldier. His face was full of hard lines, as if they were all there from years of practice. Even the smile he wore felt routine, like part of a drill he had perfected in the mirror. When she finally looked up from his plastered smile, she took a step back. His eyes were bright blue. The color of ice. They flickered and shone in the light, and it made him seem even more out of place.

"You're from Hadran?" She gave him another once over. Nothing about him reminded her of Kor. Kor was the warmth of wood that had sat in the sun. He was comfortable silence and faith that things would get better. The man before her felt like winter.

"You don't seem convinced." The man leaned closer to her. She dropped her fists, but the gusts of wind stayed tightly packed around her.

"You don't look like you are from Hadran," was the best she could manage.

"You don't really look like you belong alone in a revolution, but here we find ourselves." The man removed a speck of dirt from his shoulder and flicked it toward the empty corner of the room.

"How do you know Kor?" She shifted now to a seated position. She tried to make it casual, as if she had power in the situation, but really she was just tired. Besides, if the man were going to attack her, he'd already had his opportunity.

"He helped me during the war in Hadran."

"You knew him in the revolution?" This man had fought with Kor, she thought. Why didn't he go talk to him?

"For years. He's grown into quite a leader."

Aer didn't know how to respond. The blue-eyed man was right. Kor was a great leader. Everyone valued his opinion, his vision, his faith. They followed him because he was clear. They followed her because she was angry. She was filled with deep anger that even Korvo couldn't control.

"Still," the man continued, "there isn't always a time for peace and talking. Sometimes actions need to be taken." He said it quietly, like he was simply thinking out loud.

"Well, currently *this* is where action gets you. Five dead and more wounded."

"Only because you tried to save them."

"Most of them are just kids."

"Sacrifices sometimes need to be made, Aer." The familiar line grated on her. She had hated herself for saying it to Korvo, she had hated when Sid had said it, and she realized now it all stemmed from this man.

"Besides, the deaths of kids make headlines." There was no change in his facial expression. Aer shuddered.

"Who are you?" Aer asked.

"A friend."

"How did you get past the Watchers?"

"You've made your way around the city tonight with the curfew in place."

"Well, yeah, but..."

"Anything is possible with enough of the right stuff." He plucked at his sleeves, straightening them. In the dim light, Aer could only barely make out a blur of black lines on the man's wrist. It had to be the Raven's head. She let her shoulders relax.

"So, what's the next move?" Aer asked. She rapped her knuckles on the table in front of her.

"Today went better than expected," the man said.

"Better? People died." Her voice rose until it echoed through the room.

"You want change, don't you?" The man's expression never faltered. His face stayed in its practiced perfection.

She wanted change more than anything. It burned so fiercely in her that it was hard not to agree on principle with everything the man was saying.

"I don't want a war," she said finally.

"You do," the man said. There was no hint of a question. It was like he could see into the very nightmares that kept her awake. Kept her from being close to other people. It's like he could see the anger projected outside of her. She did want a war.

"War never worked in Hadran." She tried to match his calm demeanor.

"Didn't have the resources then."

"What resources?"

"Sid claimed there was a Fire Magic he could get in our service."

Aer balked. Tiernan. She knew Sid wanted him. But the way this man talked about him seemed sinister. Calculated.

"He's only a little boy." Aer scooted back her chair. She stood again, realizing the man with the blue eyes had never sat. He stood straight and tall with perfect posture.

"I'm sure his youth hasn't helped him escape a lifetime of tragedy," the man took a moment now to pull out a chair and sit.

Aer sat, too. "Tiernan has suffered enough."

"Haven't we all? People need to see Magics as powerful," the man said. "They need to see that Magics are not just for convenient use when non-Magics have a need."

"So, what is the plan?" she asked again, tapping the contents of the folder in front of her. She needed some illusion of control.

"Show your power. That boy with the plants today, will he recover?"

The abrupt change to Bryce threw Aer off track.

"He should be fine." She hoped. She had just left him and sent messengers for Kor and Merin. Kor had said he would be fine, but she had wanted to check on him. Even thought about doing it after this meeting was over, but she knew she was too tired to avoid the Watchers patrolling for curfew.

"Good. We'll want him there, too," the man said. His answers were so brief Aer was chasing after him for every scrap of information. It was not a feeling she liked.

"Where? If I'm to lead people into a revolution, I damn well better know where the hell it is I'm going." Her voice admitted her frustration with his cryptic nature.

"The Council Building."

"And what, pray tell, are we going to do at the Council Building?" She had spent hours in the marble halls of the Council Building with Kor. She had sat through fifteen of his speeches. She had given three of her own. The place reeked of injustice and rich fabric. She had no intention of going back anytime soon. The time for talking to the Council was over. That was Korvo's route. Today had blocked her from ever attempting that again.

"Surprise them with power. Show them control and mastery. Show them you will not stand down to live as second-class citizens anymore."

"And how do we make sure the Watchers don't know we're coming like they did today?"

"Sid, Twelve Gods guide him, had a bit of a mouth. He told too many people. Which we needed then. But this is now. Now you work with only those who will come through. The people who have the conviction."

"The anger," Aer interrupted.

"The power," he continued without acknowledging her, "to see this through."

She thought of the people who had been in the marketplace today. Most of them did not fit that bill. They were angry, sure, but most of them were scared. She knew a few. The ones that took up the battle cry when Sid had died. Bryce. She knew deep in her soul Tiernan should be the angriest, but she left him off her mental list. She hadn't lied to Kor when she told him that Tiernan had pushed her over the edge. The injustice and torture he had faced—to be sentenced to death as a child—was the final straw. The fear that something like that could happen here, that it felt like they were getting close, was forcing her to act. Forcing her to stay in the room with this stranger.

"And what are you going to be doing during all of this? I didn't see you at the marketplace today."

"I was there." The man smiled now.

"And you didn't help?" Aer asked. She hadn't gone a single minute of today where she wasn't trying to get the winds to stop bringing her the screams of the marketplace.

"I had to make sure it would work. That there were people in Kaybrum who could stand up and fight."

"And now that you've seen it?" she asked.

"I am ready to back this campaign financially."

"But not fight? Not take the same risks you're asking us to take?"

"Years of war in Hadran leave you a little tired. This is the best way. You know as well as I do that revolutions take money."

Aer gritted her teeth. She knew that all too well. "And what will your financial support get for us?" she asked.

"You are wise to ask. Our late friend Sid never did. I'm glad you're in charge now, Aer." He rose from the table. Aer watched him move to a box at the edge of the room that had been put there a few days earlier. Aer was pretty sure no one had touched it in all that time.

"What's in there?"

"These," he held up what looked in the dim light to be woven gray suits, "are a technology that has been perfected in Hadran."

"Something that helps Magics is coming from Hadran?" She was skeptical of what a garment could possibly do.

"As if you and Korvo haven't gotten smarter when you've had to hide from the world. There is still resistance in Hadran," the man scoffed. He gingerly tossed her the jacket. She felt the weight in her hand.

"Is it supposed to be armor? A uniform so they know who to shoot at? This isn't going to protect from any bullets," she said, laying it down on the table in front of her.

"If you're wearing this, you won't need to worry about bullets," the man said, coming back to lean against the chair.

"Because we'll be too fashionable to shoot? You have to give me something to go on here. I need to know what to tell my people."

"Are you tired tonight?"

"Is that a real question? Of course I am. I used the wind to call weather from thirty miles away." She could barely move her arms, her head was swimming, and it was taking more concentration than she'd like to admit to follow this conversation.

"You could pull weather from one hundred miles away with this and be no more tired."

Aer held the jacket in her hands. Something that could increase their abilities without the risk of draining away their life force. That would be an immeasurable help in something like what happened today.

She thought for a second and pulled it on. Immediately the small breezes that had come into the room were growing. She put her hand on the papers in front of her, but the wind was hungry and pulled at them. She didn't know how, but the jacket seemed to work.

"When can you get enough of these?"

"Three days," the man said. "I'll have them delivered here."

"I assume I won't see you again before then."

"You assume correctly."

"Our business is done?" She couldn't help but feel on guard. This was someone who was giving her a huge advantage, someone who wanted to help, someone who knew Kor, but she couldn't let herself fully relax. Maybe it was just the events of the day or his overbearing sharpness, but she was ready to have him gone so she could get some sleep.

"Goodnight, Aer." He turned and slid back into the darkness of the hallway from which he came. Aer slipped the jacket off, but couldn't quite put it down yet.

She carried it into the makeshift bedroom and placed it next to the bed.

When she woke from a nightmare, she found she had pulled the coat around her.

MERIN:

Merin had watched over Bryce until she could hardly keep her eyes open. When she had enough strength to get up and take Tiernan to Korvo, she decided she was coming back and sleeping in the school. Even if a Watcher had seen her, she would just plead ignorance. Nothing on her marked her as a Magic. They would let her through.

It was cold during the night, but she was too exhausted to really notice. When the sun peeked in through the windows, she jolted upright. It was the first time in her life she had spent the night outside of her parents' house. Her back ached, and she stood to stretch before checking on Bryce. Bryce, who slept like this every night. Who spent most nights, even those in the winter, outside in the garden. Bryce, who had slept with a grimace on his face.

The wound was healing well. She had spent most of her energy on that. It would take another day or two, but he would be okay. His clothes were still drenched with blood. She ran a finger across the furrow in his brow, and it softened beneath her touch.

"Merin?" Bryce said. His eyes fluttered open.

"How did you know it was me?" She smiled at him.

"You smell good." He tried to laugh but he grabbed his side.

"What's wrong? You shouldn't have any broken bones." Merin moved toward him.

"Just sore. Used a lot of magic." He struggled into a seated position. He looked down at the little blanket nest she had made with some of the old furniture coverings. "Did you sleep here?"

She nodded. "Are you feeling okay?" She put her palm to his forehead like she was feeling a fever, but if she had to be honest, she just wanted to be closer to him.

"I'm just sore. It'll take me a while to get up," he said with a groan. He looked down at his clothes and sighed.

"I can get you some more when I go home," she said. She was going to have to get home soon anyway. Her parents would be furious with her for not being there, but the curfew gave her an excuse. Her plan was to say that she stayed with a friend because of the curfew. It was best to come up with a half-truth.

Merin started to gather her things. She had brought her medical supplies with her. Aer had sent a messenger and all they had said was that Bryce was at the school and he needed help. Her medical bag had already been packed. Her house was far from the marketplace, but not far enough that she didn't know something big had gone on, and she was smart enough to know that, based on how distant he had been the day before, Bryce had been involved.

"Could you stay for another minute?" Bryce asked. His gray eyes looked scared and small. She set down her things.

"Of course."

"I ... I had something I wanted to tell you. And I wanted to tell you before anything went haywire, but it's too late for that now. But since I still can, I want to tell you."

"What is it?" She leaned closer to him.

"Well, my mom used to bake these little cream puffs all the time when I was little."

Merin squinted a little, and Bryce hurried on.

"This was before, of course, they knew what I was. Those were the good years. Those cream puffs made me feel special. They made me feel like I could grow up to be someone successful. They just filled my belly with warmth and confidence. And... you... you make me feel like that. Like the good times."

"I do?" The smile that forced its way onto her lips betrayed her happiness.

"It's just, there have been bad times, too. So many bad times. And I never got cream puffs again, so it's hard to not want to make sure that feeling won't go away again. And I know it isn't your fault that your family has been able to keep you from all the horrible things out in the world. But sometimes it makes me feel like the cream puffs are going to be taken away again. That, one day, you'd rather not spend time on the streets with someone who sleeps in the dirt and whose only pair of clothes is covered in his own blood. Someone who has been labeled a criminal, a nuisance to society. That someday you're going to choose to walk away because you can. And I'm sorry I take that out on you. And I'm sorry I push you away. I just want you to understand that I'm not sure I can handle the good times going away. That's why I want to help Aer. I need to help Aer. So they never have to." He stopped for a minute, and she tried not to move toward him.

"I love Kor," he said finally, "but I can't keep waiting and hoping. I have to do something so I can make sure the good times stay. That *you* stay."

"I understand that," Merin said looking at him. "At least I think I do. I can try."

"I get it if you don't feel the same way," Bryce said. His fingers rubbed his wound as if he was ashamed of it. "About me and about the revolution, but I had to tell you how I felt. Just in case..." he tapered off. She let it remain unsaid.

"I can't say I feel the same way about the revolution brewing. But, Bryce, I do feel the same way about you."

His eyes met hers.

She didn't have far to lean down so her face was next to his, and she kissed him. She felt him tense and then relax. His arms went around her. She felt his strong muscles against her back. His lips were rough and salty, but she didn't mind. She liked it. It was exactly how she thought it would be. Warm and safe.

He pulled away from her for a second. She didn't want to let him go.

"I'm going to hang out here today," he said, resting his forehead against hers. "I'll even practice my reading like a good boy."

She laughed. It was a giddy laugh she hadn't realized she could produce.

"I need to run home and get you new clothes and make sure my parents don't kill me for being gone all night, but I'll be back as soon as I can."

"Take your time," he said with his spectacular grin, "I'm not going anywhere fast today."

She leaned in and kissed him again, and then reluctantly pulled herself away to get home.

When she was outside, she let herself pause for the moment sink in. Then, once she had pulled herself together, she checked herself all over to make sure she hadn't gotten any blood on her clothes. That would be difficult to explain to her parents.

When she stepped into the house, no one was around. She wandered the halls for a bit but didn't see her mother in her normal chair by the window. She also didn't see any of the help bustling about. She hoped they weren't sent looking for her.

Merin tiptoed through the house, expecting to see her mother's angry face at any point. It wasn't until she had gone by her parents' bedroom that she noticed the door was open. She stuck her head inside, ready for the hysterics.

"Oh, there you are, Merin. Your father could use some assistance in the study," her mother said, without any indication that Merin had been missing up until that point. Maybe her mother was just choosing to ignore it so she would be useful, or maybe she didn't know.

Merin stopped by her room before heading to her father's study. She changed clothes. Her clothes were wrinkled and sweaty, and she also couldn't get over the fear that there was some of Bryce's blood on them. She stood at the closet, thinking about what Bryce had said about his one change of clothes. She had plenty. She could choose to spend an hour trying on outfits and pick the one Bryce would like her in the most, but she couldn't bring herself to take out the light blue dress she had planned on wearing. Instead, she grabbed a simple brown dress and a jacket to match.

She had to get clothes for him. She wasn't sure how she could get into her parents' room without them knowing.

"Ms. Merin. I hope you had a pleasant evening."

Merin turned to see Rachael, the person who had helped raise her most of her life. She was a thin woman, but she always looked pressed and clean. Her hair was mostly silver now, but it had been chestnut when Merin was little. Rachael had always been there for her.

When Merin didn't respond right away, Rachael began placing Merin's dirty laundry into her basket. "I don't suppose that mess yesterday and that little Bryce boy had anything to do with you not coming home last night?" she asked nonchalantly.

"Do my parents know?"

"Ever since yesterday afternoon, your father's been locked in his study. He was getting a stream of messengers all last night. He even gave most of the staff some time off so he didn't have any noise about the house while he worked."

"And my mother?" Merin asked.

"She's been holed up in their room. She was quite scared. 'Attacking us next,' she kept saying. But I'm sure she didn't know you were out."

"Rachael, thank you for not saying anything to them."

"Oh, but I'll say something to you. Staying out all night with that Bryce fella ... He's trouble. I know he's got a grin that makes ya feel like melting, but his eyes are troubled. Best not happen again on my watch."

"It's not like that. He was hurt yesterday at the marketplace. I was just helping him feel better."

"I'm sure ya were. I saw you taking your time picking out an outfit before I came in."

"Rachael."

"But them marketplace people is dangerous. If Bryce has gotten himself involved, you are going to want to stay away from him."

"Why? Bryce isn't dangerous."

"Not him sweetie, but the world. While you were snoozing away somewhere, the world was buzzing. Things are on the edge now. Just talk to your father, and you'll see the Council is up in arms. And I'm old enough to know that when things become unstable it's people like your friend Bryce that pay the price."

"Because he's a Magic? So am I."

"Not because of that, dearie. People with anger in their hearts … It'll consume them. They can't rise against the Council. They'll just tear themselves apart."

"So you're saying there's no point in them fighting?"

"The world is the way it is. I just don't want you going down in flames with it. Your parents worked hard for you to remain unmarked. Don't let that boy's anger drag you down."

"But I should be able to let people know about my magic. I help people. Why should I have to keep that hidden?" Her voice rose to a squeak.

"I know it's hard, sweetie," Rachael smoothed the hair around her face, "but people with powers make others feel uncomfortable. And when people feel uncomfortable they get defensive, and you know how an animal is when they get backed into a corner."

"So what if it makes them uncomfortable?" Merin asked. She was having a hard time keeping her voice level.

"Aww, sweets. You'll understand someday." Rachael patted her arm. "Just promise me, you won't get yourself involved. You'll stay hidden while all of this blows through."

Merin didn't respond. She had no intention of fighting, but hearing Rachael tell her to stay hidden didn't sit right.

"Rachael, will you do one more favor for me? Just let me see something through."

"Of course."

"Will you get a couple changes of clothes out of Father's dresser? Things he won't miss."

"Things that might fit young Bryce?"

Merin nodded.

"Have it to you in an hour," Rachel said, picking up her basket and placing it square on her hip.

Merin took another look around her room and headed into her father's study. There was only one reason she was ever asked to come in there. He wanted her to use her powers, but maybe she could use him, too. She knocked quietly.

"My sweet." Her father didn't look up from the paperwork in front of him.

"Hello, Father. Mother said you had something you wanted me to take care of."

"Just a bit of back pain." He tapped the top of his left shoulder, still looking at his work. Merin moved into her familiar place. She took a moment and spread her fingers wide over the edges of her father's shoulders. She glanced over him at the type covering the pages in front of him.

The pages were a blur of writing. Clearly, things were happening fast. Whatever it was, despite being a week or more away, looked like it would be happening in a matter of days.

"What is the Council saying?" She added a little fear to her voice to try to coax her father to give her some information. She found important men like her father almost always fell for the damsel in distress routine.

"A little to the left, please, Merin dear," her father responded. She shifted her fingers a few inches to the left. Her magic jolted over a few knots in her father's back before returning to the nice, even, steady flow she was giving out.

She wondered if she should ask again. She needed time to work out what was in front of her. If she could get information to Kor, then maybe whatever it was that Aer was going to do next, that Bryce was going to do next, she could stop. She could bring them back to the idea that the school would work.

Her desire to try to understand Bryce filtered through her mind, and her power wavered.

Shifting the papers in front of him, he sighed. "That's enough, Merin. No need to tire you out."

"I have a lot more—" she said restarting the flow of warmth through her father's tight muscles.

"Run along, child."

She had been dismissed. There was no more arguing that would get her any more information.

"Yes, Father." She stole one last look at the papers on the desk. His shuffling had caused the cover page to come into clear view. 'Operation Fire Bird' was in clear black letters along the top of the page. Merin's mouth opened, and she was about to ask, but she knew she would just get reprimanded for not knowing her place. Better to find out on her own.

Rachael had left clothes bundled up in Merin's bag. They were sturdy, plain clothes that her father never chose over his wardrobe of elaborate fabrics and bright colors. But they would fit Bryce, and he wouldn't have to walk around in his own blood. She hoped he would take them.

She shifted the clothes aside so she could fit more medical supplies inside. She figured by now more people were going to need help. She would go check on Bryce and then maybe see about heading over to the Wall to see if she could help. Maybe Bryce would even come with her.

Bryce. Her cheeks flushed with color. She had been waiting for Bryce to say something to her about his feelings, but she hadn't expected how little anything else seemed to matter when they kissed. Her bones had ceased wanting to hold her up. But that had been fine because his arms were around her. Her stomach dropped. It was too much to think about in more than small spurts.

She shook her head. She had places to be. Why spend the day dreaming when she could be reliving it instead?

"Mother?" Merin called, as she headed into their bedroom. Her mother sat, but she didn't have a book with her like usual. Instead, she just stared out into the city. Her tea sat untouched on the table next to her.

"Mother?"

Her mother finally turned to look at her. She had worry lines Merin had never seen etched into her face. Merin wondered how much of what had happened in the marketplace had affected her.

"Is everything okay?" Merin asked, sitting next to her mother.

"Promise me you won't get mixed up with any of these rebel Magics," her mother said. Again with the promises. Merin felt like bile was burning the edge of her stomach.

"I'm sure they don't want to hurt anyone." Merin tried to keep her voice pleasant. If her mother caught any hint that she was helping someone who was there yesterday, she knew there wouldn't be a second night when no one seemed to miss her.

"People should just be happy with what they have," her mother said. "Wanting more than what you have always gets you into trouble."

Merin couldn't help herself.

"What they have? Most Magics live on the streets. Some of them are abandoned as children just for being Magic. They just want to be able to live."

"That's why we have the Refuge. For those less fortunate. Somewhere to live, to be educated among their own kind."

"That horrid place?" Merin's voice rose an octave.

"Surely, you don't think now is the time to take this tone with me, young lady. Your father has been up all night helping the Council because some people aren't happy with what they have. You of all people should understand when it's best to keep your mouth shut."

Merin wanted to scream, but she used the training her parents had purchased for her in private schools for years and bit her tongue.

"I was hoping to go over to a school friend's to study since they seemed to have canceled school." She wasn't sure that was true, but it was a safe bet her mother didn't know either way. "Maybe they will be able to help me remember my place."

"Very well dear, just remember that when you come back, I expect that you will have stopped with this nonsense."

"No more of the nonsense, Mother," Merin said. And she meant it. She just didn't quite agree with her mother on what part the nonsense was.

"Run along." Her mother looked back out the window.

Merin had never run faster out of her house. She quickly made her way to the dilapidated school building. Bryce was waiting for her and so was Kor.

"Good morning, Merin," Kor said. The same deep lines of worry were etched onto his face. He looked old at that moment. His features were heavy.

"We'll finish our conversation later, Bryce. I have to go finish preparing for the Council."

"The Council?" asked Merin.

"Yes, they moved up my meeting with them. I think they're trying to catch me off guard while everyone is still dealing with yesterday."

"Something is happening with the Council," she said trying to remember all the little details that she had seen in her father's study. "I told Bryce that something was happening in a week, but now it looks like they have something big planned in just a couple of days. Something they're calling 'Operation Fire Bird.' My father has been working on it all night. They need him to get all the legal permissions."

"Do you know anything else?" Kor asked. There was something in his yellow-green eyes, and it certainly wasn't hope.

"No. My father wouldn't give me any details."

"That's okay," he sighed. "At least I'm going in with something. Take it easy, you two. I'll take Tiernan to Bethlem's so Bryce can rest." He left then, his shoulders square, but Merin knew he was forcing it.

"I'm feeling a lot better," Bryce said. She turned to smile at him.

"But I could use some more care, just to make sure." He smiled. Merin was happy to see him smile again. He hadn't done it much since Aer had sent them out to find Tiernan. That felt like it was years ago.

Bryce pulled her into a hug, and she let him. There was nothing she wanted more than to spend all day wrapped up in his arms.

"I brought you clothes," she said letting the tip of her nose rest on his. They were so close she was sure he could feel her heart beating.

"How was your house?" Bryce let his hand glide across the edge of her face.

"Same as always. My parents seemed pretty rattled about the marketplace, but other than that, nothing has changed." She wasn't sure how to tell him what her mother had said without bringing back the anger. She wanted a few more minutes with calm and happy Bryce.

While he changed, Merin told him she wanted to go see if she could help anyone who was hurt yesterday and was in the medic wards in the walls. Merin had never been inside the Wall. That was always an errand for Bryce or Aer. People in the Wall District didn't trust her much.

Bryce smiled.

"I was hoping you'd want to do that. I want to go over and check on Aer, now that she's staying in the Wall. It's been driving me nuts all morning not knowing how she's doing, and Kor won't even mention her name."

"He's that mad? He didn't seem mad at you."

Bryce shrugged.

At the Wall everything was bustling. Lanterns bobbed up and down throughout the tunnels, and Merin was glad Bryce was holding her hand. She didn't want to lose him in the chaos.

Bryce led her to the medic ward. There were beds crammed together. People were everywhere.

"Will you be alright if I leave you here for a minute?" He leaned in so he spoke directly into her ear. His breath made all the hairs on her body stand up.

She nodded. "I'll be busy here."

"I just saw Aer outside. I'll only be gone a minute."

He gave her hand a squeeze and threaded his way through the healers walking around. Merin stopped one of them and they immediately put her to work. It was mostly soothing bruises and small cuts, but a few people had broken arms from when everyone tried to escape the bullets. She was busy enough that she didn't miss Bryce until she heard his voice as she passed by the door.

"Two days. I'll be there," he said. She imagined he spoke to Aer, but the dark prevented her from seeing.

Was two days all she was going to get before he went back to something that had put all these people in the hospital? She'd have to enjoy it while she could.

KORVO:

Before this whole mess with Aer, he had been getting somewhere with the Council. Merin had been bringing inside information from the rich districts; Bryce was running all the errands, and—even in his thoughts he struggled with her name—Aer was helping him with the recruiting process. He wondered when she had stopped doing it for him and started doing it for herself.

He had wanted to bring Bryce, had been planning on bringing him, but it was too much of a gamble to put someone who was at the marketplace in front of the Council today. It would have to wait. He would have to hope for another chance.

He ran through the possible scenarios. His hand subconsciously found the edge of the cards in his pocket and riffled the edges without him even knowing.

Scenario 1: They would ask him for a peace offering to make everything go away as quickly as possible. He would tell them to end the Refuge. This was the best option.

Scenario 2: They would refuse to see him completely, having invited him only as a show of their power.

Scenario 3: The Council would declare Magics enemies of the state. This was obviously the worst.

Scenario 4: He would be a puppet for their press releases. He would talk. They would flaunt the fact that they were in open discussion with a Magic leader no matter which leader it was.

Scenario 5: They would ask him to talk to Aer. His stomach plummeted. What would he even say to her? He'd been avoiding her name, but not for the reason Bryce kept implying. He didn't hate her. He couldn't blame her for what she was doing. And dammit if she wasn't better than Sid. It just hurt. She was his first friend in Kaybrum. She was... he couldn't finish that thought and still make himself presentable to the Council.

He ran through about ten more scenarios in his head, but he had no clarity for what was going to happen when he got to the Council. Even the cards weren't helping make anything clearer. He rubbed his right hand.

The Council building was the second tallest building in the city next to the Refuge. On the side of the building with the least windows, someone had painted the Raven's head in dark, black paint still wet enough that it was dripping down the stone. Kor couldn't help but smile a little, even if its presence made his job harder for him. But at least the

Council was still standing; that got one of the worst of the possible situations out of the way.

He took a deep breath before he opened the door and went up to see the Council.

"And why should we believe a word he says," the Council member behind Kor asked. He was surrounded by council members who all sat in their large, ornately-carved seats high above him. Currently, they were just talking over him. They hadn't offered a peace offering.

"If I may," Korvo interjected. His voice was lost among the clatter of Council members arguing about him as if he weren't there. He knew them all. Not personally. Very few Council members would be seen with a lowlife like him outside of this room. But he knew them from the intel he had gathered. The pieces he had moved. It was all supposed to lead up to this moment.

"Why are we even talking to him?"

"Let's just hear what he has to say. What can it hurt?" The Council member closest to Kor's right hand spoke now. Kor couldn't hide his smile. Out of everything they had researched and done, they hadn't had to do anything for Councilman Jacqui. He was the youngest member of the Council and the only one who fully supported the rights of Magics.

Kor had still done his research. Jacqui's youngest brother was a Magic. He moved earth. Something had happened in a bar one night that led the brother to a labor camp. Kor sighed. Magic was preferred only when useful.

Kor stood as straight and tall as he could. He tried to let the events of the past age his face as much as they had aged his soul. He would not give them vapid reasons like his age to shoot him down. He had to make them really listen to the problem, and not find a reason to sweep it under the rug.

He used the deep voice he often used to order Bryce to calm down.

"Your esteemed Council," he said. The men stopped and looked down at him, and Kor cleared his throat. "If I may? I know I was not there at the marketplace. But I know their concerns. I know their feelings, and I know their plight."

"So, you sympathize with them," someone off to his left said. Kor ignored the comment. Of course he sympathized with them.

"Show them you are listening, and their fears can ease. Show them you care about them and not the destruction they cause, and it may stop."

"May stop, or will stop?" someone else asked.

Kor took a deep breath, letting things come out as calmly as possible.

"Right now they won't stop."

"Are you threatening us?" The head of the council stood up from his chair so he could lean down and stare at Korvo.

"No sir, I came here today for the same reason I've been coming for years. I have been asking for a chance to meet with you all about the Refuge. It is time we find a new way to help our young people. The school I started will—"

"The Refuge is a re-education program," the bald Council member said, sitting back in his chair.

"No offense sir, but it is not. It's crowded and infested with rats. It is no place for a child. Just last night they turned off the furnace."

"I saw smoke coming from the Refuge last night," the Council member said. Korvo hesitated. He couldn't tell them Tiernan had lit the fires without exposing him.

"Eventually," added Korvo.

"There is a reason each of those children gets placed in the Refuge—"

"Because they are Magic," Kor said. His voice was cold and flat.

"They're on the street causing trouble," another man cried. Kor wasn't bothering trying to keep them straight.

"Because there is no one to care for them. Adult Magics more often than not end up in your work camps or have to work three jobs to support their children due to the low wages they take home. Or if a Magic has the immense misfortune of being born to a non-Magic family, their parents kick them out because of the stigma and there is no one to watch them during the day. Without school—"

"Magics can't be at school. They don't have control. That's why the Refuge is..."

"Correct me if I'm wrong, but no Watchers were killed at the marketplace. No random passersby were harmed by magic." The Council members said nothing. "That's the definition of control. We can control our powers, but you want control over us." He didn't care that his skin was turning red, or that his bad hand was clenched into a fist. They would hear him. Aer wasn't the only one who had that deep need in their soul.

"And what would you suggest?" Jacqui asked.

Korvo opened his mouth, but before he could say anything a Council member slammed his hand onto the desk. The sound reverberated through the round room. Even Kor jumped a little, his shoulders tightening up around his head.

"Why are you listening to some kid, Jacqui?"

"Listening to ourselves hasn't made this get better," Jacqui replied calmly. The other man turned away.

"First, I would suggest you go and visit the Refuge unannounced and see if it truly is a 'reeducation' center for lost children. Then, when you realize it's not that at all, I want you to disband it."

"I've heard enough," the head of the Council said, and Kor knew he had been dismissed. Already the Council members had turned to each other and the plans for lunch floated down to him.

"Korvo," Jacqui called out to him. Kor looked up. The robes the Council wore looked even sillier when they weren't seated on almost identical thrones. The man had stuck out his hand. Kor shook it. Jacqui looked down at his mangled hand for a moment, then the man stared up at him. Kor shrugged. He was used to people being put off by his hand. It was just a fact of life.

"I appreciate the time," Kor said, turning to go again, but Jacqui held him. His eyes fixated on Kor's hand.

"I would like to take you up on it. I want to see the Refuge."

Kor nodded.

"It won't be pretty," Kor said.

"I can imagine."

"I can't go in with you," Kor said after a moment.

"I would never expect you to, but company on the walk over would be nice."

Kor smiled and shook the man's hand again.

"Wait just a minute for me to change," Jacqui said, heading for the large red door at the end of the room. Kor waited patiently in the foyer.

"Jacqui is too young to understand," a voice said, drifting through the empty hallways to Kor's ears.

"It's pointless. We've already made our decision. Operation Fire Bird is necessary to deal with this problem once and for all. They'll see that eventually." Kor strained to see if he could tell who was talking, but the echoes of the marble walls distorted the voices too much.

"The only reason I agreed to see that dirty child was the hope he would implicate himself and make it easier on Jacqui."

"Easier?" whispered Kor to himself. He didn't like the sound of any of this. He would need to get more information from Merin and to check in with Bethlem on his way to her.

Jacqui appeared to Kor's left with a big smile.

"So you really think this will change anything?" he asked. Kor took a second to realize he was talking to him.

"Getting rid of the Refuge? Getting rid of the marks on our skin? Yes. Anything to make us feel human," Kor said, wondering if he should just ask the Council member about Operation Fire Bird.

Jacqui nodded. Kor didn't want to blow his opportunity to show this man the Refuge. Out of his robe, he looked like the typical rich person in Kaybrum. Kor couldn't see any difference between him and someone from Merin's family.

"If we end the Refuge, what's going to happen to those kids?" Jacqui asked. Something in his tone made it obvious he was testing how far Kor had thought this through. Kor smiled.

"I've already started the school I was asking for help with for months. Students come every day."

"But some of these kids have no education. How will you get them caught up?"

"Any education will be better than the Refuge."

The Council member cocked his eyebrow.

"You'll see."

"But what about food and shelter?"

"That's part two of the plan. And honestly, anything is better than the Refuge," Kor said.

The rest of the walk went quickly. There wasn't much traffic in the streets when you were worried another brawl might start at any moment.

The Refuge came into view.

"There it is," Kor said. "And this is where I leave you." Jacqui shook his hand one more time and crossed the courtyard by himself. Kor stayed long enough to watch him demand entrance from the guards. After that, he figured, it was up to him to see.

He headed straight for Bethlem's. Tiernan and, hopefully information, were waiting for him.

"Kor," Bethlem beckoned from the front of his bar. Kor walked over to him. The bar was filled to capacity.

"What is it?" Kor asked once Bethlem led him to the back.

"You told me to tell you if I heard anything about a Fire Magic," Bethlem said. His forehead was creased.

"What did you hear?"

"Not much, just rumors that one is around. It's really stirring those who are on Aer's side."

"But nothing specific," Kor said. He could feel beads of sweat forming at the edge of his hairline. "Right?"

"I just heard snippets of conversations, but you made it clear you wanted any information."

"Thanks, Bethlem."

"How did the Council go?" Bethlem pulled up a chair.

Kor sighed and rubbed a hand through his hair. "Not well. Not horrible. Jacqui is still on our side. But Aer and Sid did some serious damage."

"You have to admit that people here are feeling more empowered." Bethlem nodded toward the tight-knit groups of people whispering up a storm. Kor sighed.

"Until they catch Aer and drag her screaming away to a prison camp."

"You think that will happen?" Bethlem's eyes searched Kor's face.

"She won't scream. She'll be as stoic as ever, but yes, at some point this will catch up with her."

"What's your next move?"

"See how Jacqui reacts to the Refuge, I guess. And hope he can convince someone of something," Kor turned to go and stopped. "Have you heard anything about an 'Operation Fire Bird?'" Kor asked.

"No. But I'll keep my ears listening like always."

Kor nodded.

"I haven't seen Bryce today," Bethlem said before the moment could turn to an awkward silence.

"He should be with Merin, resting."

"How did Bryce get caught up in this? He's your biggest follower. That boy looks up to you." Bethlem reached out his hand for Kor's shoulder. "He's grown a lot, too, since you first brought him here. I could barely tell there was a boy under all that dirt," Bethlem said with a small laugh.

"Yeah," said Kor. He remembered the Bryce from three years ago, too: a bundle of pine needles and resentment. "But he's still angry inside. And anger can cause almost any thought process to be lost."

"Speaking from experience?" Bethlem's eyebrows were slightly raised, his forehead soft.

"There is a reason Bryce likes me. Just like there was a reason Aer did." He rubbed at his hand.

"Because of that hand? Because of some horrible life you lived a lifetime ago, a country ago?"

Kor didn't respond. He stared at the tapestry. The whirls of color called to him.

"Korvo, you know that is ridiculous, right?"

Kor continued to look at the door.

"They don't care for you because you are some sort of war hero."

"I don't know if Aer would agree with you."

"Kor, I have known you for over three years now. And I've known Aer since she could barely walk. They care because you care about them. You see them. You care about their struggles. You give them the space to safely worry and complain."

"Well, worrying and complaining aren't going to make the world a better place," Kor said. He was done with this conversation and just wanted to go home. There was nothing more Bethlem could tell him.

"You can try not to believe me. But I've got a few years on you, kid. You may have a better mind for strategy and politics, but I've seen enough people come through this bar to know what I am talking about."

Korvo nodded, but his heart wasn't in it. Bethlem rapped the table with his knuckles. He patted Korvo on the shoulder one more time, and then he went back into the crowded bar.

"I hope you're right," Kor said to the empty room. "I really do."

CHAPTER 8

BRYCE:

HIS ARM HAD COMPLETELY HEALED in only two days. He wasn't surprised; Merin was a miracle worker. And maybe, he thought, heading over to Bethlem's to collect Tiernan from Kor, she had healed him in other ways, too.

But today there was a job to do. He had to watch Tiernan closely. There had started to be a murmur that a Fire Magic was in Kaybrum, and Bryce knew it would only end badly for Tiernan if people found out about him. Everyone would have an opinion about the poor boy. Later, when Aer gave the signal, he would leave Tiernan with Merin, safe in the walls.

Merin hadn't openly said she was supporting his decision to keep helping Aer, but she hadn't balked at his plan when he had told her the night before.

Bryce had gotten used to being inside the wall, but he wasn't sure how Tiernan would react. He typically didn't like any enclosed spaces that were smaller than Bethlem's bar, but Bryce hoped the allure of seeing Merin would pull the small boy in after him.

As they neared the Wall, Tiernan gripped Bryce's hand, but he didn't say anything.

"Merin's in there," Bryce said when Tiernan slowed down half a step. The boy nodded and sped back up.

The fissure in this part of the wall was hidden now by ivy. Bryce had put it there himself. A very limited precautionary measure, but it was what he could do when he wasn't at full strength.

A cool breeze met Bryce and Tiernan when they stepped into the twilight of the wall. Merin was here.

"TIERNAN!"

Bryce didn't even have time to look before Merin grabbed the little boy. Tiernan cried out in a mixture of excited Hadranian and the few words he knew in their common tongue. Merin had successfully wrapped her arms around Tiernan and had him snuggled close to her. Bryce was only a little jealous. He could wait his turn.

"Hey," Bryce said, walking up and putting a hand on her arm.

"Look, look," Tiernan interrupted and before Bryce could stop him the little boy's hand had blossomed into a flower made out of flame. Each tendril of light formed a petal. Bryce couldn't even be mad. It was beautiful. Merin's eyes sparkled.

"Love?" Tiernan asked her. She smiled without letting her eyes leave the flower.

"Love," she said. Tiernan smiled. The flower began to lose shape and turned into one glowing mass. Bryce finally felt he could pull his eyes away from the fire.

"Fire stays hidden," Bryce managed in Hadranian. Tiernan stuck out his tongue, but the fire disappeared into thin air. His ability to make it appear and disappear was something Bryce couldn't quite understand.

"The rumors are still just rumors," Merin said, "and there's no one else here. It should be okay for him to be himself."

"I want him to be who he is, but I also want him to stay alive," Bryce said, running a hand through his hair.

Merin hugged Tiernan close to her. Bryce scowled. He didn't like arguing over Tiernan when the poor boy could only understand bits and pieces of the conversation.

Tiernan followed behind Bryce as he let himself into one of the rooms they used for planning.

"Here you can play with fire," Bryce said, turning to Tiernan. Tiernan smiled. His little teeth didn't quite meet each other. Bryce sat in one of the chairs and put his feet up on the table, letting the chair lean on its back legs. Merin sat next to him.

"You're still going today?" Merin asked in a whisper. Bryce nodded. Aer asked him personally, so he was going to go. It shouldn't be that he had to hide. That Merin or Tiernan had to hide. They shouldn't have to live like this.

"How's Kor?" Bryce asked.

"Jacqui still hasn't convinced the Council to even look at the Refuge. They are convinced that the filth he described must have been some misunderstanding," Merin explained.

"Did he go beyond the first floor?"

Merin shook her head. Bryce let out a deep sigh.

"There is nothing else I can think of to do. I need to do this," he said.

"You'll keep everyone safe," she leaned her head against his shoulder. He looked down at her soft hair, and her soft blue eyes looked up to meet his. She leaned over and kissed him on the cheek. He turned to kiss her, but something caught his eye.

Tiernan had created a Raven out of fire. Orange flame rippled like feathers. The bird moved its wings, spreading them wider than Tiernan. Its eyes glowed red. It opened its beak as if it was going to caw, but only the small sound of flames crackling filled the room. It walked off of Tiernan's hand and flew around the room. Bryce watched the bird, mesmerized.

Merin gripped his hand tight. Her fingers laced between his, her warmth, not her magic, flowing through him.

A siren went off.

Tiernan looked at Bryce with a sense of panic. His eyes trembled and the whites of his eyes were visible. The bird disappeared in a dramatic flash. Bryce could feel his heart racing, but his feet were moving faster than his brain. In two steps he already had his hands around Tiernan. Merin stood slowly, shaking.

"It's time to go?" she asked.

"You'll be okay here," Bryce whispered to Tiernan. "Stay with Merin." The little boy's look of horror made Bryce's voice catch in his throat. He felt like his body was trying to run even while his head was still trying to gather information.

"Stay safe," he said.

"Stay safe," she repeated, squeezing his hand. Her eyes were pleading. Tiernan was trembling behind him. Bryce kneeled down.

"Tiernan. You have to stay here. And if things start going badly, you are to protect Merin." Tiernan nodded, but the boy's eyes were still large. Bryce put his hand down, and Tiernan grabbed hold of it with both hands. Bryce squeezed the little boy's hands and turned to go.

Bryce walked out to meet Aer. The image of Sid's face kept flashing through his mind, except each time it was Aer; then, it was Merin, Tiernan, and Korvo. It was worse than the nightmares of the Refuge because he could always leave the Refuge. But he wouldn't be able to bring them back.

He took a minute out in the hallway to collect himself. He could hear Aer giving commands, addressing the group, and explaining the plan. He figured she'd catch him up. He needed a second to breathe.

"We attack the Council Building," Aer said, handing Bryce a gray jacket when he came into the room.

"The Council?" Bryce slid his arms into the jacket. Everyone else was already wearing one.

"They didn't listen, so now we make a louder statement."

Bryce recoiled a little from the ferocity in Aer's voice. He believed in her, and maybe it was just the sound of the siren that was making him jumpy, but he couldn't help feeling like he wanted to run back to Merin.

Kor had taught Aer how to move around the shadows. The group moved in silence. Aer led the way. The next few people flanked her on either side. Bryce's legs felt like jelly underneath him.

It didn't take long for them to reach the Council Building. When they got there, Watchers were already waiting for them. They lowered their rifles and began taking shots. Bryce immediately reached down into the ground to find roots while the vines he now kept in his pockets began digging down into the soil. It was easier now. The plants all the way in the garden were listening to him. Everything green in the city was craving to be with him.

Bryce let his mind fall away. He needed to almost lose consciousness in order to deal with this many plants. He had to become one with the plants. He lost himself in the green. There was no difference now between the green of his inner light and that of the plants. The only thing he could think was grow. Grow. Grow. Grow.

Only the slightest amount of what was happening trickled into his conscience. He heard explosions. They were muted, as if he was hearing them from below ground. A fire ripped through him. He wasn't sure if something had hit him or the plants he was so connected to. Yelling broke through to his consciousness. It was Aer's voice.

The roots he had called to the surface were being shredded with bullets. Bryce pulled himself from the roots. He shook himself. Somehow he had found himself on his knees. He rubbed his hands over his arms and didn't find anything bleeding. He was about to go back into the plants, when a scream rang out.

Another familiar voice. He turned. Tiernan was standing fifty yards from him.

"Tiernan, run!" Bryce yelled, trying to keep control of his barriers. "Run!"

Aer screamed.

"Aer!" Bryce yelled, trying to bring the vines with him as he went. Then the air became orange. The plants shriveled in the flame. Bryce was still connected enough that the fire felt like it was going right through his veins. Bryce fell on the ground writhing. He saw Tiernan holding his hands up. His small face concentrated. Merin was coming up behind him.

Bryce tried to stand, but he couldn't move. With the amount of power he had used, and remnants of the plants still echoing in his nerves, he couldn't get up.

"Merin," Bryce said getting her to make eye contact with him. "You need to get Tiernan out of here." Merin nodded. She grabbed the little boy's hand and pulled him toward where they had come. He wouldn't move.

Merin hesitated. Bryce could see her waiting on the edge.

"Merin run. Find Korvo."

With a last look, she pulled Tiernan, who was sagging a little, behind her, and she ran.

"Bryce, you need to run," Aer said. She was also on the ground. Bryce reached for her. But there was too much space between them.

Bryce attempted to stand again, but the world became a blur of colors, and he sagged back down to the ground. He could hear the boots of the Watchers approaching them and he shut his eyes waiting for the blows. Wind screamed by him. His hair stood on end, the sound of electricity hummed in his ear.

"Aer. Don't waste your energy," he called without opening his eyes. But the hands never grabbed him, and the boots didn't make contact with his ribs. The wind continued to whip through his hair.

"Bryce," Aer's voice insisted. "Run."

He tried to stand again. This time he got to his feet. The sky around them was dark. The clouds bumped and collided with each other, threatening the electricity hidden in them. He took a step, found it held beneath him, and with one last look toward Aer, he ran. He didn't look back. He couldn't. The wind died as soon as he turned the corner.

KORVO:

Kor saw Merin coming in the cards. As soon as he saw orange fire streak across the sky, he had pulled the cards from his pocket. He laid them out with shaking hands. He saw his friends in the future, and Merin running to him. He ran to the Refuge as fast as he could, trying to meet her.

"Korvo! I need to talk to you," Jacqui called when he reached the courtyard of the Refuge.

"Councilman?" Kor said, coming to a stop.

"Do you know what's happening?" The man jogged over to Korvo.

"The resistance group of Magics ran into some Watchers over at the Council."

Jacqui's eyes widened.

"How do you know?" The councilman took a step back and looked over Korvo like he was seeing him for the first time.

"I read it in the cards, just now," Kor looked around the man for any trace of Merin. Jacqui eyed him suspiciously. "I didn't lie to you about the conditions in the refuge, and I'm not lying now."

"Where are you going?" the man asked.

"I know you may not understand, but I have to find my friends and make sure they're okay."

"The people who attacked the Council?"

"I don't think they did the right thing, but they are still my friends. I need to see if they need help."

Jacqui nodded, but his brow was creased. Kor turned. Merin had come into view. There was no time to worry about him now.

"Merin." He ran to her side. Her cheekbones were streaked with dirt, which was disturbed by lines from her tears. "Merin, is everyone okay? Is Bryce..."

Merin just sobbed into his arms. With a last look at the Councilman, he steered her away from the open area.

Safe in Aer's apartment—he wondered for a moment if she knew he still had a key—Merin finally stopped sobbing.

"Where is Bryce?" he asked.

Merin wiped her eyes, but the tears continued to smear across her face.

"I ... I don't know."

"What do you mean? What happened?"

Merin, with a fresh stream of tears, began to explain how the Watchers had advanced. They had brought artillery and gas. The bullets had torn into the people at the front and Tiernan had run after Bryce once he heard the commotion; she couldn't hold on to him. She had to stop for a second before she explained how Bryce had been writhing on the ground with Tiernan trying to help him.

Kor had known, in the deep pit of his stomach, that the orange light he had seen had been caused by Tiernan.

"Tiernan is safe back at the school. I got him there before I came to get you. He's tired and scared, but he should be okay. But Bryce..."

"I saw Bryce in the cards. In the future." He patted her on the shoulder. She seemed to relax. He went and grabbed a glass of water for her. He didn't tell her how many times he had seen people who had turned out to be bodies. For now, it was still time to hope.

Neither of them spoke for a while.

"Aer?" Merin asked finally. "Did you see Aer in the future?"

Kor bit his lip and took another lap around the small room. He let his hand rest on the edge of the blanket Aer had haphazardly left when she moved into the Wall full-time. His fingers caressed the frayed edge.

"She's alive. But other than that ... I couldn't see." Merin nodded and stood. She walked to the bathroom and splashed cold water on her face.

"Do you hate them? Bryce thinks you won't forgive them," Merin said, once the color had returned to her face. Kor shook his head.

"I thought the Council would continue to listen if we kept being nice and polite. I was scared." Kor turned his head away from her.

"Because you've seen things like this before," Merin said. There was no hint of a question in her voice. Kor rubbed his hand.

"I just wanted to protect you. I wanted you to have lives where you wouldn't see the things that I've seen. But I was wrong."

"But the school?"

Kor shook his head. "The school is a good thing," he said hanging his head, "But Aer was right, I was too concerned with being the model Magics. That if we just behaved, somehow things would get better, but that's just another form of prison."

"But?" Merin sputtered.

"I couldn't keep you all from the reality of what life is when you are born Magic. Maybe if I had listened to Aer. We wouldn't be..." Kor trailed off.

"I was wrong, too."

"It's not your fault," Kor said looking Merin in the eye. He had been the one to tell her what the next steps were.

Merin shook her head. "I was wrong because I thought I was doing enough. Bringing you information from my father. Supporting the school. Loving Bryce. But love wasn't enough. The thoughts inside my head weren't enough. Bryce knew that. He knew I didn't understand, and he loved me anyway. I needed to do more."

"Loves. Present tense," Kor said without thinking. The silence crept over them. Kor was lost in his own guilt, and he was sure Merin was lost in her own shortcomings. Kor felt the desire to smooth the worry off her face by telling her they had done what they could. But he knew he'd be lying.

"Can we go get Tiernan?" Merin asked. Kor took a deep breath and tried to fill his lungs with the scent and memories from Aer's apartment before he nodded.

BRYCE:

Bryce watched from one of the big magnolia trees in the garden of a neighboring house. It took the last bit of strength he had not to throw the large cone pods down at the

Watchers who were coming in and out of the station. He was not going to abandon Aer.

She might have known what she was doing and what the risks were, but that didn't mean he had to abandon her. He watched carefully as all the people he had failed to protect were paraded one by one into the station.

Most of them had a few cuts and bruises. A few had rags tied to their arms or legs that already showed blood coming through. Bryce wanted to scream, but he stayed hidden. It didn't do them any good for him to get caught.

Watchers streamed in and out with and without Magics in their hands. Some of the Magics he saw go in weren't at the Council Building with them. The Watchers were just using it as an excuse to round them up.

"Why did I let you talk me into this big of an attack, Aer," he whispered when two kids were pulled into the station. They were younger than Bryce and usually ran messages out in the Wall District. Aer wouldn't have let them come on something like this; they were innocent.

"Finally," he whispered when he spotted Aer. She looked bad. She was barely picking up her feet. The Watchers on either side of her had fingers digging into her arms so hard that her skin was turning white below their fingertips. The space around her eyes was already a garish purple, and she was favoring one side as if she had been kicked in the ribs. Her hands were tied behind her back, and a cloth was tied around her mouth. She lashed out every once in a while.

"Give it a rest," one of the Watchers said and jerked her shoulder. She grimaced but continued to walk. Bryce admired her. Her face was angry, but there was no hint of fear.

"I hope you're happy with your little rebellion," the other said with a laugh, "because it's over."

Aer didn't react. Not even a muscle on her face twitched.

"We're raiding those nasty walls you rats call home," the first spat. They laughed. Bryce's heart sank. Even if they didn't find all the secret rooms in the Wall, the Wall District still had most of the Magics in the city. And the hospital beds.

They had passed him now, and Bryce could see Aer's fists clenched so tightly her knuckles were white.

"Have anything to say for yourself?" one of the Watchers asked, poking Aer in the side. She stumbled. Her eyes flashed hatred. "Well, little lady?" The Watchers lifted the gag from her mouth.

"You think you can stop the people?" she asked, looking straight forward. "The people will always rise."

"Not when we turn them against you. You may have played on the hearts of the people, but that ends today." They yanked the gag back into place. Aer said nothing but began to hum as best she could. The Watchers hesitated. Their hands came off her arms. But they quickly shook the power of the song off. The gag was too much even for Aer.

They pulled her through the door, and Bryce knew he needed to get to Korvo. He'd know what to do.

KORVO:

When they got to the school, all that was left was a smoldering pile of ash.

Kor's stomach sank. He felt like he wanted to throw up. Merin had started running through the neighborhood screaming for Tiernan, but Korvo couldn't move. He tried to center himself, but the light that normally seemed to fill his inner thoughts was missing.

"Tiernan, Tiernan," Merin sobbed. Kor looked away. He didn't need to put any more guilt onto her shoulders. He needed to find answers. He finally moved from the spot to look for more clues. The soot showed heavy footprints from large boots. Lots of them. Going in different directions.

"Watchers," Kor said to himself. He heard Merin's breath stop in her throat. At least, from the looks of it, Tiernan had put up a fight.

"They would have taken him to the Refuge?" Merin said, letting her inflection turn her statement into a weak question.

"I would hope so, but..." he trailed off.

"But what, Kor?" she demanded in between her sobs.

"There is a possibility that they would take him somewhere else. He's a Fire Magic, after all."

"How do we get him?" A sob caught in the back of her throat.

"Tiernan? Merin?" Bryce's voice came from the edge of the clearing.

"We're okay," called Merin. Bryce stumbled toward them. His legs were weak, and Kor could see his eyelids drooping, how his breath was ragged and uneven. Flashes of Kor's time in the jungle overtook him. His chest clenched tight. He reached for the cards to help him make sure Bryce wasn't an illusion, and that everything else was just ghosts from the past.

With his hand in his pocket, the feeling of the ragged edge of the cards made him relax enough to see only Bryce and Merin in front of him. They were both worse for wear, but they were alive. Merin was sending the most minor streams of power toward Bryce, but only the lines around his mouth seemed to release. His eyes still looked dark and haunted.

"They took Tiernan," Merin said, looking up at Bryce. He scowled and spit on the ground.

"Refuge?" he asked.

"Probably," Kor said.

"I'll go," Bryce said, and he turned around before Kor could stop him. Kor hurried after him. He barely caught the boy's shoulder.

"I know you're going to tell me I don't have to go," Bryce said, keeping his face staring in the direction of the Refuge, "but Tiernan was my responsibility. I let him down. I let you down."

"We're not certain he's there," Kor said in a last-ditch effort to keep Bryce in front of him.

"But if he is there," Bryce took a deep breath, "I need to make it right." Then he shrugged Korvo's hand off his shoulder and headed toward the Refuge.

"He'll be alright," Kor said to Merin, who had come to stand next to him. But he couldn't bring himself to put any real meaning into the words. They hung hollow and flat in the still air around them.

CHAPTER 9

BRYCE:

THE REFUGE LOOMED AHEAD of Bryce, and the contents of his stomach churned. He wouldn't have been brave enough to volunteer for this if Merin hadn't given him a little strength just standing there.

When the door to the Refuge was visible, he thought about his options. He could get thrown in and hope for a short sentence in the 're-education' center, or he could try to sneak in. There would be no records of him, so he could leave when he could, but there also would be no one coming to find him when his time was up. It might take weeks to find an opening to get out, especially when he would need to take out Tiernan.

The Watchers would switch their guard soon. That was something he had learned living with Kor on the roof.

He waited; the first set of guards left their posts a few minutes early. This was his chance. He scooped a bit of dirt up into his pockets, patted the vines in his pockets from the fight at the Council Building, and took a final breath of fresh air. He closed his eyes and walked into the building.

The smell of unwashed bodies in varying stages of adolescence hit him before anything else. Bryce ditched the jacket from Aer. At least the sweat and dirt from earlier would help him blend in. The light from the dirty windows filtered an amber glow through the empty area. The desk where they would normally check him in and remind him of his sentence, his "opportunity to change" as they called it, was empty. They must have changed shifts as well. He walked quickly past the places any staff member might be and headed straight back to where he might find Tiernan. This was much better than his original plan, which was to fight his way in.

The dining hall was empty except for a few little kids. Bryce scanned over them to see if he knew any of them well enough to ask about Tiernan. There was only one.

"Hey," Bryce said, sliding into the rusted seat next to him.

"Bryce?" the boy asked, surprised. Bryce flashed a smile. "When did you ..."

Bryce put his finger to his lips. The boy stared at him.

"Have you seen the little boy who's normally with me?"

The boy shook his head.

"He would have come in today."

"About fifty kids came in today," the boy said. "That's why I'm down here. Some biggin' took my bed from me. Can I come sleep with you?"

"I don't have a bed. And if anyone asks, you didn't see me here," Bryce said looking around.

"You snuck in?" the boy whispered.

Bryce nodded. Talking to the boy was beginning to boost his confidence, but he could feel the panic building behind the lump in his throat. He stood, wanting to get out of there before he lost it in front of this kid.

"Will you save me some food at mealtime?" Bryce asked, turning back to the boy.

He nodded. Bryce looked at the little boy. Food was sacred enough as is in the refuge.

"Actually, just eat it yourself. I'm not really feeling that hungry."

Bryce found his way to the staircase that would bring him to the rest of the Refuge. He didn't even have to look. Every piece of the place was burned into his memory. The stairs wound around the central smokestack that kept them warm on the roof. If Tiernan was free to wander around, Bryce would find him closest to the warmth, but something was wrong. Bryce reached out his hand. The smokestack was cold.

So much for his plan on finding Tiernan easily. He took a left when he hit the first landing. These were the first beds. They belonged to the larger kids.

One of the girls nodded to Bryce, and he dipped his head in acknowledgment. Respect was important in the Refuge. It meant little outside of these walls, but there was only so much that kids could handle when they were locked up. Bryce moved on. Tiernan wouldn't be here.

There was a reason the older kids tried to stay as close to the ground floor as possible. They knew what went on in the rooms above. Bryce's arms sprouted goose bumps as he went up the stairs. He hadn't even told Kor about these rooms. Kor had probably seen them when he read his cards, but Bryce couldn't bring himself to talk about them.

"Re-education my ass," Bryce said as he got closer to the first door on the right. He peeked inside, his chest thumping hard enough that he figured anyone near him would be able to hear it.

"At least they won't have me on the schedule for this," he said, getting brave and flicking the leather strap that would have kept his wrists bound to the board. He could feel them even now biting into his skin.

For a moment his vision went white. He could hear a man's voice. He could smell a metallic tang floating into his nostrils, and the tightness around his wrists extended to one around his middle and a long flat belt across his shins. They felt real. He curled his fingers to see if he could feel the leather biting into him, but there was nothing but his skin. He moved one hand tentatively to fully check the other. There was nothing there.

His vision slowly returned. He was in an empty room. With an empty chair. There were no men in white coats or Watchers ready to punch you in the stomach when no one was looking. He took a deep breath. He couldn't be afraid of an empty room. If he was, he'd never survive the night.

He came out of the room and sneaked toward the filthy windows. Except for a rat running across the sill, there wasn't much to see. The light was falling quickly. He wanted to find Tiernan before it was too dark, but that was looking less and less possible. A night in the Refuge was looking more and more likely.

KORVO:

Korvo paced back and forth in Aer's apartment. Merin had gone home to check in with her parents. It was probably the safest place for her to be. Kor kept waiting for the boot coming through the door, but if they had gotten Aer, maybe this would be a safe place to hide for a while.

He ran through possibilities as fast as his mind could think them up:

1: Bryce brought back Tiernan. They ran. Merin would be alright. But the three of them were another story. They could make it to the Northern Border in the span of a few days if Bryce and Tiernan were in good shape. If they weren't

... they would be out in the world through the harshest part of winter.

2: If Tiernan wasn't there, Bryce would be stuck in the Refuge. Kor would have to go after him.

3: The Council declared an all-out war. No one would be safe.

None of those scenarios gave him any hope.

He shuffled the cards in his hand, then dealt them one at a time. He turned them over slowly. Kor first looked over the cards. It let him see patterns he might lose when he got the flashes of images. There was something strange about the way these cards were lying.

He shuffled again, but the same cards came up in a different order.

Their faces were as familiar to him as Bryce's or Aer's. Maybe more. The cards had been with him longer. He stared at them now with a crease in his brow.

He took a deep breath and let his hand run over the cards. Each finger dragged over the divots made by the artist as they scratched in the pictures. In that space, sparks of energy piled up and shocked his fingertips as he gave each their due. Each card took a minute. This was no time to rush.

After he finished, he went back over them again. They were taking him all over the place. It was like they were trying to tell him something other than their normal meanings. Images flashed in his mind for each card, but none of them pieced together like a puzzle.

He went back and sorted them. The tower stood tall in the middle of the stack of cards. That made sense. His whole world had been uprooted almost overnight. But it wasn't the tower that made him confused; it was the images he got when he touched it.

Bryce was there, cast in amber light, but the window he was staring out was glowing orange. Flames lapped at the window's edges, but Bryce wasn't moving. Kor caught himself before he yelled out to the magical illusion in front of him.

Kor had to rest for a second after taking his hand off the tower. Ambiguous images took a lot more out of him than the ones that showed clearly what was going to happen. He sat on the edge of Aer's bed and took a breath, gathering a pillow into his arms. He rested his cheek against the pillow's cool edge.

"Aer would tell you to get it together and go to the next one," he said burying his head into her lingering scent. "So get up."

He took a deep breath and went back to the table where the cards were laid out.

"If the tower is the Refuge," he said laying a finger on the very edge of the card, "Bryce makes sense." He talked it out like he would if Aer were there with him. She often sat on the chair across from him, sipping her tea with honey. She wouldn't make any suggestions, just ask questions now and then, and mutter sounds of affirmation. If he got too lost, she would sing under her breath until he felt his way through the message.

He touched the card that always reminded him of her. The chariot represented strength of will. Aer had that in spades. It's probably why she was missing from her apartment and Kor was still there. When he touched her card, he just got anger. Blacked out anger rimmed with fire.

He let his head rest on the table. He was ashamed. He was hiding. He had been hiding the whole time he had been in Kaybrum. He reached out for the card that represented himself. The Five of Cups. Sorrow. Lost Friends.

He touched it now hesitantly. The card was always the clearest despite everything being fuzzy with his hand the way it was. The images took over.

It was dark. Ashes surrounded him. The cards fluttered around him. Half of them were burned, flames sputtering out as they fell to the ground. He jerked his hand away.

"What do we see in common?" he asked the ghosts of his friends around the table. "Fire. Tiernan? Darkness. The Refuge?" He shoved the cards away from him. "Or they're all dead, and there is nothing I can do." He tapped his fingers against the table to keep himself from losing it.

He had made the table for Aer at work. Working with wood was always a break from the cards. Wood only ever spoke to him of sunlight and rain. It had taken him a week or so to get the grooves right to make it look how he imagined the wind. Now, without his friends around him, it just echoed the darkness he felt in his heart.

"Maybe I start with what I know." He hastily gathered the cards and shoved them back into his pocket before he peeked out the door. The sun had gone down. He shrugged his hood over his head and he walked to the Refuge. He could at least try to get a hold of Bryce.

BRYCE:

Nighttime in the Refuge changed everything. Boys who were ready to take your lunch or give you the stink eye were just as likely to put an arm around you once the lights went out. Bryce waited until the first round of bed checks was complete before he made his way to the beds on the third story.

The little boy from earlier was huddled in a corner. There were always kids without beds who slept on the other furniture. Multiple kids smashed into small beds. Anything was better than the floor. The floor was for rats and garbage.

"I can't have you on the floor," Bryce said, pulling the little boy from the corner.

"But all the beds are full, and no one will share with me."

"Someone will let you share," Bryce said, dusting the boy's thin jacket as best he could. He gnashed his teeth when he saw the tell-tale marks around the boy's wrists.

Bryce looked around. The beds on this floor were pretty full. There was only one small cot left underneath the window, so dirty he couldn't see outside. The cot's legs were broken, and it hung awkwardly, but it was free. Unusable, but free.

"Come on," Bryce said tilting his head to the cot. The little boy followed obediently. It was strange having someone follow him that wasn't Tiernan. The boy with him now looked almost exactly like Tiernan had when he last saw him. Eyes terrified of everything around him.

"It's broken," the little boy said, hiding behind Bryce's leg as if that would somehow change the situation.

"Broken? Hardly. It just needs a little face lift." Bryce had watched Kor work enough to understand the basics of how to lodge the pieces of the wood back together. The bed wobbled, and he bet even if he put just the small boy on it, it would collapse again.

"Bryce…"

Bryce waved him off.

"Give me a minute," he said, reaching into his pocket for the vines. He let them grow, circling and weaving throughout the cot, holding the pieces together. He stepped onto the mattress to test it. It didn't give. The little boy stared up at him. Bryce jumped to make sure he believed him.

"We're... we're not supposed to use magic in here," the boy said. Despite being Tiernan's age, the boy's hand went in his mouth.

"They won't notice. If they cared to look, they might have already seen the rats by now." He patted the boy on the head. He continued to stare helplessly at the leaves on the side of the bed.

"We could get in trouble," the boy said, backing away from the cot. Bryce sighed, sitting on the edge.

"Come here," Bryce said. The boy got closer to him. Bryce wondered if after all of this he could ask this kid to be Tiernan's friend. They probably both needed somebody. Bryce patted the half of the bed closest to the wall. "If they come, I'll protect you."

The little boy relented and was soon fast asleep. His small breath drifted over Bryce's chest. Bryce placed his hands behind his head. He didn't need a pillow. He wasn't going to sleep. Bryce lay staring at the darkening ceiling.

"I'll protect you," he said to the sleeping boy, "more than I protected Tiernan and Merin. More than I protected Aer," he said in a mantra that soothed him.

A knock on the window had Bryce's fists clenched ready to fight in less than a second. The knock came again. Fingers rapped on the dirty glass. Tapped twice slowly and once fast. Bryce grinned. Korvo. He pried open the window the best he could. There was only a sliver of fresh air escaping between them. Bryce scraped his finger, making himself bleed.

"Do you know Bryce?" Korvo asked the stale air leaking through the crack in the window.

"Kor, it's me," Bryce said, sucking on the tip of his finger. The blood was still coming.

"That was lucky," Kor said. Bryce heard the soft thump of a body resting on the glass.

"I haven't found him yet," Bryce said turning away from the window to hide the shame across his face even though there was no way Kor could see it.

"I doubted any of us could have found him that quickly."

"Kor, I need to," Bryce started.

"Find him? I know. I'm looking out here for him too. But the cards aren't helping."

"No," Bryce said, taking a deep breath, "I need to apologize. I went behind your back. I couldn't handle the thing you asked me to do. After everything you told me."

"I need to apologize too. I was trying too hard to keep you from seeing what I had seen, but I was ignoring what you felt. How I had felt. I was ignoring the truth."

There was silence. But Bryce could see the tiny puffs of Kor's breath, even if he couldn't see his face.

"Everything has changed. Now we have to focus on protecting Tiernan," Bryce said, rubbing at his eyes. He knew Kor wouldn't have cared if he cried, but tears felt like hot memories running down his face.

"Do you know what happened to Aer?" Kor asked.

"The Watchers have her. She was pretty banged up."

"And she hasn't been brought here?"

"She was the last one in. Maybe they're keeping her in a holding cell overnight. That might be where Tiernan is, too."

"I'll check in the morning."

Bryce heard slight hesitation in Kor's voice. It wasn't much, but it was there. Bryce knew Kor was probably rubbing his hand. He always did that when he was nervous.

"What about the Council?"

"The Council is not going to listen after what happened today. Even Jacqui looked at me like he was second-guessing everything I said, and the only people that got hurt were Magics."

Bryce pushed at the knot forming at the back of his neck. He had known all along that Aer's plans would put Korvo's in jeopardy, but he hadn't thought their closest ally in the Council might turn against them.

"It's all my fault. I could have said no."

"You could have. There is no denying that. But Aer would have done it whether you were there or not. Sometimes the cause becomes more important than the people you're fighting for. That's the thing I wouldn't forgive you for," Kor said. His voice had dropped almost to a whisper. "You wanted to know what happened to my hand," he said.

Bryce strained to hear him. His voice was barely making it the few inches between them.

"When I started my own army, my own revenge, I had followers. They were like Aer. Hungry for revenge. I told them about the General, and what he had done. I wanted to push them forward.

"We gathered more people around us. We used the city as our battleground. I'll be honest, it was more about revenge than anything. After every attack, more Magics would come to us. Young, and angry like Sid. I had perfected my speech about the General, about what he had done to me. But one of the recruits, he was probably about your age when we first met, didn't see it as a tale of inspiration. He saw it as a warning, and," Kor stopped for a minute. Bryce leaned in, his ear almost on the glass, making sure Kor hadn't just dropped his volume again. But there was nothing. A silence only interrupted by the ragged breathing of the kids in the refuge.

Kor cleared his throat. "Bryce, that boy was the one who dumped the acid on me. My own man. My own friend."

"But Kor—" Bryce started. He didn't know what to say.

"Just like the General feared I could help the Magics, my friend had feared I might help the General again."

"But you were leading them? You wouldn't."

"Sometimes we can't see the forest for all of the trees," Kor said. Bryce heard him take a deep breath.

"Kor ..."

"I've hung on to these ghosts for too long," Kor said. There was a waver in his voice so foreign Bryce almost couldn't believe it was Korvo on the other side of the dirty glass. Bryce placed his forehead against the glass, guessing his friend was rubbing at his right hand again.

Footsteps sounded in the hallway. Bryce jumped. Guards on night rounds were making their way through the halls.

"Kor, I have to go," Bryce whispered. He didn't shut the window. The guards would hardly notice a little fresh air in the stench of the Refuge. Kor knocked quietly on the window to show his acknowledgement, and Bryce watched the shadow his body made against the glass disappear down the fire escape. Bryce wished he could follow. But he had a promise to keep.

Bryce lay down, trying his best to block the little one from the view of the guards. He kept his eyes partially opened and watched for the tale-tell sign of the boots in front of him. The beam of a light drifted over him. He heard the guards mumbling to each other from the other side of the room. Slowly the boots thumped closer to Bryce.

His mind went into overdrive. What would happen if they realized he wasn't supposed to be there? He squeezed his eyes shut. He took a deep breath and held it in his chest until he felt calm. All they could do was keep him here. He swallowed hard. He could get through that. He had to find Tiernan anyway. Soon he could see the lantern's flickering flame mirrored in the polished shoes of the guard closest to him. These were the people who couldn't make it as Watchers on patrol. They lacked things like patience, empathy, and the understanding of other ways to handle things besides brute force.

The edges of the boots were right below Bryce. He could feel their eyes on him.

The bed lurched beneath him as the taller guard kicked at the leg Bryce had pulled together with vines.

"Whatcha think we ought to do about that?" the huskier guard said, letting his light move down from the leg of the bed to Bryce's face. He shifted a little, hoping to look natural. It wasn't natural to be stiff as a board when you slept.

"Ain't that the Segal kid?" the tall one said. Bryce winced.

"Looks like he's awake," the large guard said. His fingers snaked around the collar of Bryce's shirt. Bryce lurched to a stance.

"I don't remember him coming in."

"Probably just got hauled in today. I doubt they've finished the paperwork yet."

Bryce's eyes snapped up to the guard's face. Of course. If they had Tiernan, there would be paperwork. If he found that, he could find Tiernan. The guard snarled at him. Bryce felt his muscles relax. He had a plan. Now he just had to get himself hauled into one of the offices without starting a brawl.

"Are you guys going to continue to talk about me as if you didn't just wake me?" he said, brushing some dust off his shoulder and fixing the collar of his shirt, even if it was beyond wrinkled before this whole encounter began. Aer's father would be appalled to see what shape his clothes were in now.

"You better watch it, boy," the huskier of the two said. Bryce couldn't help but grin a little at the wheeze in the man's voice. On the streets, Bryce could have outrun him with no problem and probably come out of a fight okay. But this was the Refuge. Bryce tracked the man's hands. He was fine as long as no one went for the batons.

"Magic ain't allowed in here, boy," the taller one said.

"Magic? You got proof of magic?" Bryce let his arms cross in front of his chest.

"This," he poked the leaves with his foot, "is as unnatural as you."

"Well, someone like you can't appreciate natural beauty. Not with that mug."

"I'm gonna smack you right in the jaw."

"I'd still be prettier than you," Bryce smirked.

"That's enough." The guard reached for his shoulder.

Bryce shrugged him off. "I can walk on my own. I know the way."

"Then get on with it," the tall guard said. The little boy had turned and was looking at Bryce. He trembled. Bryce lifted a finger to his lips and gave the kid a wink. He wished he could have made him sleep with Merin's powers or sent a calming breeze over him. Hell, he would have welcomed a reading from Kor, even though none of them were turning out good. Anything to calm the drumming in his chest.

The guards flanked him as they walked down the twisted hallways. Their lanterns flashed across the walls. Bryce tried to think through a plan before he got to the record room. They always took them there before they took them anywhere else. The last time he was in there he was standing next to the cabinets, crammed in there with three other kids. The drawers weren't locked. The girl standing next to him had been playing nervously with the locks as their punishments were laid out.

"Hey, where are we going?" Bryce asked as the guard made a sharp right down a hallway he hadn't ever been down. He tried to turn around back to somewhere familiar. He could taste bile in the back of his throat.

"Not such a man now, are ya?" The guard behind him laughed and poked Bryce in the ribs. Bryce jerked to a stop.

"Where are we going?" he repeated. He reached for a vine in his pockets, but he had left all the vines back with the little boy. He sucked air in through his teeth for such a stupid mistake.

"I think this place will give you some time to think about that little attitude of yours," the guard said as he jabbed the baton in between his ribs. Bryce grimaced, but he said nothing. His muscles tensed.

"You can be the first one to try out this room," the second man said.

"Aww, you should save the best for last," Bryce said, trying to regain his composure. The bile still coated his throat, making the words hard to get out.

The guard twisted the baton. "Get in there," he said, and the last bit of light was lost behind the big steel-framed door.

MERIN:

Merin paced around her bedroom. She couldn't sit still for three minutes before she had to stand again and move.

Merin sighed and picked up the pillow. She straightened the edges of the ribbon fringe with her fingers. Then punched it. Her stomach lurched.

Bryce was in the Refuge because she couldn't hold on to Tiernan. And if she had to admit it to herself, she had been afraid of him. A little boy. Regardless of the fear in his eyes, the heat rising from his palms had scared her, and she had let him go. The guilt made her take another turn around the room. Every shift of light made her jump, hoping it was Bryce's plants on her windowsill like before.

Instead, he was in his own version of hell. She had seen the ways his eyes were distant whenever they talked about the Refuge. She had felt him pull away whenever they were near the building. And yet he was back in the Refuge, probably starting some fight to pretend he wasn't scared, wasn't as terrified as Tiernan had been. And here she was, stuck staring out the window, and pacing in a recursive pattern, wearing a line in the plush carpet on the wood floor.

"I should be there," she said to the pillow before flopping back onto her bed. "I should never have let Bryce go." She wanted to blame Aer. But the lurch in her gut felt like rocks were piling up. Bryce had the right to stand up to the treatment he had received. Aer couldn't be blamed. Merin knew it was her fault. And losing Tiernan was her fault, too.

"I can't sit here anymore."

"Merin Elia?" her mother called from outside the door, "Just who are you talking to, my dove?"

"Myself, Mother."

"Well, if you could, darling, your father has a few knots in his shoulder from work. These little rebellions are really causing a strain," her mother chimed from the other side of the painted white door. Merin scowled.

"Sure, Mother," she said, looking at herself in the mirror, making sure her face wasn't tangled in the rage her stomach was twisted in.

She dragged her feet toward her father's study. Was this really what her parents wanted for her? To stay here and be her father's personal healer for any minor discomfort? To stay hidden and ignorant of what was going on around them? To be thankful for what she had?

She was thankful. She didn't wake up with nightmares like the others. She had a bed and clothes. No one molested her as she walked down the street. No one second-guessed her coming and going.

She stopped, her hand poised over the brass door handle to her father's study.

No one second-guessed her coming and going. Not even her own parents seemed to care where she had been the last few hours.

She could use this to her advantage, and with that she turned from the door handle. She went back to her room and put on the light blue dress Bryce would love, and she walked out the front door.

It was a quiet walk downtown. Most people were home, so there was no one but the clerks and messengers inside the office buildings. She sighed. The Council Members were at the actual building when it was attacked. It was as if someone had warned them Aer was coming.

Merin was going to find out who.

"Who are you?" asked one of the clerks who had put his feet up on the front desk.

"I'm sure you know my father, Mr. Pomry," she said in her most posh way of speaking.

"Why did Pomry send his daughter?" the clerk asked skeptically. He looked her over from head to toe. Merin knew she looked like her father, and her clothes screamed wealth. There was nothing that was going to tip him off.

"He's been having a bit of trouble with the messengers." Merin took a stab in the dark.

"Can ya blame them, Miss?"

"Most certainly, not. The times as they are," Merin said. The clerk sounded a lot like Rachael, and it made it easier to talk to him.

"What can I help you with?" The clerk sat as straight in his chair as he could.

"My father needs all the documents you have so far on the events of the last few days and Operation Fire Bird," she said. She tried to say everything in a calm and collected manner, but her hands were sweaty, and she could feel beads beginning to form on the sides of her face. "Lots of legal things to take care of, in this mess," she said hoping it gave the clerk enough of a reason to let her see the documents.

"I can't let you take them out of the building." His smile grew as he looked her over again. A smile she wished she could beat off his face. Maybe she was spending too much time with Bryce.

"Would I be permitted to read them here? He does need this information, and I have a very good memory. Top of my class."

"Sure, I'll put them right over there where I can keep my eye on you," he said with a wink. Merin forced a smile.

The stack of papers was the size of her head. She wasn't sure where to start. She thought about what Kor would do.

He would look for anything that had to do with the Watchers knowing they were coming and anything about the operation. Everything else could wait.

She spread the files out in front of her a few at a time. As she glanced through them, she set them into different piles. Useful, not useful, potentially useful. Her useful pile wasn't growing as fast as the other two.

The files were filled with boring things. Shift changes, job placements, parade uniform orders. The list went on and on. She stopped. Parade uniforms. Weren't the men all dressed up when they had first found Tiernan? They never did hear anything about anyone special coming. She flicked through the file. Parade uniforms ordered for all members at the prisoner processing centers, and for all men in the Refuge. That was strange.

She shuffled aside order and size charts to find a logged date and a reason. The Head General of the Hadranian Army was coming to inspect progress on Operation Fire Bird.

She took a look around the room. The clerks were busying themselves with puttering, and the head clerk seemed to have grown bored of her already. No one was watching. She pulled the paper carefully from its bindings and slipped it into the purse at her side.

She shifted through the next few folders. She had stopped on some page filled with legalese when the clerk came to check on her. She tried her best to use every piece of jargon she had ever heard her father use. The clerk moved on. She kept looking.

There were several mentions of Operation Fire Bird in the files, but nothing explained what it was.

There were only two files left in her potentially useful pile, when she stumbled on letters sent from the General of Hadran. They were cryptic.

"The animal has been released. He should fall into your trap soon."

Another read: "The animal wasn't with the idiot wall rat. But the weather girl will do fine."

Another dated from last night read: "They'll be there as promised. Let's hope they bring the Fire Bird. I am growing impatient. That animal needs to come home."

Was he ... was he talking about Tiernan? Was it all a plan? The General was behind it all. Letting Tiernan escape, supporting Sid, telling the Watchers.

The last one was dated from earlier that day: "After tomorrow, no one will care if you destroy all the garbage. They will beg you to do it."

Tomorrow. Something was happening tomorrow. Operation Fire Bird. She had to get to Korvo. They were going to have to get Bryce out of the Refuge.

CHAPTER 10

AER:

THICK STONE SURROUNDED HER. She felt stripped bare without her winds. Not that it would have mattered. She had no energy to control them, listen to them, talk to them. Everything hurt. At least one rib had to be cracked, and she was trying not to breathe deeply enough to figure out if anything else was out of place. Her eye was swollen and starting to close. There wasn't much to do but sit.

She stared out at the darkness that must have been a ceiling, but she couldn't make out any details. At least they hadn't taken the jacket from her. She could still feel the remnants of her powers even after so much work. They should have been depleted, but with the jackets, they should have been unstoppable.

"How did the Watchers know we were coming?" she whispered into the darkness, not expecting a response to come.

"Because I told them before I told you," an icy voice said from the other side of the door. She jumped. There was a jangle of metal as the key scraped its way into the small keyhole. The door scraped against the floor as it opened. Aer scrambled up to a standing position.

"There's no need to stand, Aer," the voice said with a laugh. She knew that voice. She squinted.

The Ice Man.

"You?" Aer moved, but her eyes almost blacked with pain. "You said you were with us."

"I beg to differ."

"You're a liar."

"You're an enemy of the state, a danger to society, and a good-for-nothing Magic. Does it really matter if I lied? Which I still do not believe I did. I don't like to leave loose ends like that."

"But you knew Kor."

"I did and do. He was a special guest of mine before he escaped his cell. Which you will not be doing. So don't get any ideas."

"Who are you?"

"Korvo may have mentioned me. The General of Hadran?"

If there was color left in Aer's face besides the budding bruises, it drained into the ground. Kor had talked about him. The General. The man—how could she have been so dumb—the man with the ice-blue eyes.

"I was hoping to see our good friend Korvo, but it turns out he's gone soft. I doubt he will even try to rescue you."

Aer didn't want to admit that she had hoped Kor would come sneaking into the cell and steal her away in the night. That he could use the cards to find her even when her winds couldn't, but the General had just taken that last shred of hope from her. He hadn't bothered to close the door behind him. He knew she couldn't get past him.

"Kor wouldn't be that stupid," she said finally.

"No. That's why I had to send the boy."

"The boy? Was Sid a spy?"

"That pathetic creature? I wouldn't waste my time with someone like him. The little Fire Magic. I let him go so he could put all of this in motion."

"Tiernan?" Aer gasped.

"Was that its name?" the man looked at his fingertips rubbing a bit of dirt from them and flicking it toward Aer.

"But these jackets?" she said. She was leaning now against the back wall. Her legs were starting to give out, and she wasn't going to last much longer before she slumped onto the floor.

"Oh, the jackets. They were genius. I'll leave that for a surprise for the real show. It won't be long now."

"Why are you even here?" She spat at him. Her anger gave her the energy to stay standing.

"So many questions from the prisoner, but this one I'll indulge. Your Council asked me to come."

Aer's jaw dropped, causing her split lip to start bleeding again.

"Does that really surprise you? Didn't you see the writing on the wall?" He paused.

Aer struggled with something to say. She had seen it. She had warned Kor. She wasn't wrong. She took a deep breath, ignoring the pain, and called any wind that could hear her with her last amount of strength. At least she would take out this man. She could do that for the cause. For Kor and Tiernan.

The wind came whipping to her, bringing bits and pieces of stone with them. They slammed into the room, hitting the General with all kinds of debris. A sizable rock struck him in the temple. He reared. Aer smiled. His hand went to his head and came away streaked with blood.

"You'll regret that," he said.

"Doubtful." She tried to smile, but her swollen face wouldn't allow it.

She called for more wind. More debris. But even with the help from the jacket she had, she was spent. Her legs gave out the same moment he shut the door, plunging her back into darkness.

BRYCE:

With the guard's hands still on his shoulders, Bryce looked around the new room. It was empty except for a simple chair in the corner. He took a deep breath and unclenched his hands. He had been worried they were taking him to the re-education room. He ran a hand along his wrists. The lack of a table with leather straps helped him feel brave.

"My own private room?" he asked with a smirk. The men didn't respond and only pushed him further into the room.

"Have fun," said one of the guards. Bryce turned his back to them. They shut and locked the door behind them.

The room was the same size as the re-education room. The walls were covered with smooth fabric, and the level of cleanliness and lack of smell made it obvious that whatever this room was for, it was new.

"Hello?" Bryce called to the empty room. No one answered. He thought about sitting in the chair. After all, the day had drained him of his physical and magical energy, but he was skeptical. The chair might not have had any straps to hold him down, but that didn't matter. Nothing in the Refuge could be trusted.

The re-education room had looked different each time he had gone. Every time, there was only a single flat table. Every time, though, it was in a new place, a new position. Sometimes he was strapped vertically or horizontally. Sometimes they poured water over his nose and mouth until he couldn't help but breathe the water in. Other times they switched the bare soles of his feet until they were swollen and misshapen. Always, there were men sitting on the side taking notes.

Once they had strapped him down on his stomach and lashed him through his clothes. He still bore those scars. He had seen Merin's eyes wander over them, wanting desperately both to know their story and make them disappear, but he wouldn't let her. This darkness didn't need to be shared, but this darkness couldn't be forgotten. Or forgiven.

"It's about time we met," a voice said, coming in through a door Bryce hadn't seen.

"I'm a very busy person," Bryce said. He kept his back turned toward this new voice. "I haven't got all day."

"No, you certainly don't. I would say your kind has barely a day left in this entire country."

The chair squeaked as the owner of this new voice settled into it. Bryce turned to look now. A man with bluer eyes than he had ever seen was staring back at him.

"Forgive me for being late, but I was just in a meeting with your friend Aer."

"Where is she?" Bryce asked. He had been trying to avoid thinking about anything that was happening outside of the Refuge.

"I think the more pertinent question, Bryce Segal, is where are you?"

Bryce took a deep breath and strolled to a corner of the room.

"That's a pretty dumb question, General," Bryce said. The man grinned. Bryce was right. The man with the blue eyes was the same man that had held Korvo captive. Now that Bryce had his back firmly against the walls, he felt a little less afraid of him.

"You know who I am? Good. This will make things easier."
The General got up.

"You're a bastard," Bryce said.

"I've heard you've been in the Refuge before."

"Once or twice. I've been around." Bryce tried to sound unconcerned, but with the General walking toward him he knew better than to wipe the sweat away from the edges of his hair. It would only show his fear.

"You'll find this room is different than the ones you've seen before."

"Now that you mention it, it seems rather roomy," Bryce said. The General was only a few feet away. In two quick steps, he could have his hand on Bryce. Bryce tensed. That was not a fight he would win.

"This room was one of the first things I requested when I came to Kaybrum," the General explained. He ran his boxy fingers over the fabric that lined the walls. Bryce glanced at it. Thin bands of cloth wove around metallic strips. It reminded him of the jacket Aer had given him. Bryce risked moving one of his hands behind his back so he could feel the fabric. It felt the same as the jacket, too.

"A great new invention in Hadran," the General explained. "It conducts magical current more efficiently than the human body."

"Conducts? I hate to admit it, General, but I wasn't really allowed to go to school. So if this is something you want me to pay attention to, you're going to have to sum it up for me." Bryce flashed a smirk toward the General. Surprisingly, the man smiled.

"When magic runs through all of your filthy bodies, it uses energy that's connected to the elements around us. Earth, water, air, you know the drill. When it interacts with those elements it creates a channel. This fabric bypasses that channel and makes a shortcut between you and the elements of the world. Makes it faster, makes it use less energy."

"You made a fabric that would make it easier to use my powers and wouldn't tire me out. Then you lined the room with it?" Bryce knew he was missing some very large portions of his education, but he was pretty sure even Merin wouldn't have been able to explain why the General would do that in a way he understood.

"This channel, however, does come with a few flaws."

"Flaws?" Bryce asked.

"Once the fabric helps bypass the system, it also bypasses the system controls. That means it makes it harder for you to control. It makes it harder for you to stop. And eventually, your own magic will consume you."

"Consume me?"

"That is the general idea. Unfortunately, we haven't really gotten a chance to test them. I thought Aer's little ragtag army would have put up a bigger fight. I guess I should have told them to hold off on sending in the heavy artillery. So, you will have to suffice. You are doing a great service for our respective countries."

"I won't let you do that," Bryce said. "I won't use my magic. It's not like I have plants in here anyway."

"I came prepared, Bryce. I just hope you're prepared enough to give this a real try. I need proof it will work before tomorrow. Now then," he reached into his pocket and removed a key, "let's do our best." He returned to the same door he had come in from, the one hidden in the wall, slipping out for a moment to grab the plants he'd mentioned along with some dirt, before he secured the door again and returned to his chair.

Bryce smiled. Just because the plants were in front of him didn't mean he was going to use magic. The General could sit and watch him all day, but he didn't have to do anything.

Bryce sat in the corner of the room, farthest from the plants. He crossed his arms, let his head roll back, and closed his eyes. He might as well let the General watch him get some sleep. Of all the strange possibilities, that he might actually get a decent night's sleep in the Refuge was not what Bryce had expected.

With his eyes closed, he let himself remember what had happened during the day. He tried sorting through it like Korvo would. But the look on Tiernan's face when he had run toward him was haunting. The boy's face was a mixture of terror and anger that should have been beyond such a small person. Bryce's memory switched quickly to the fire that had lit up the sky. Tiernan had such power. It had ripped through his plants and had caused everyone to freeze. If Tiernan hadn't come—Bryce didn't want to think about what might have happened. To him. To Aer. To Merin.

Merin's face floated into his consciousness. The feeling of her lips on his made his blood sing. How could he possibly think of such a positive thought while he was in the Refuge? When he still had to find Tiernan and fix the mess he had created? Bryce shrugged. It wouldn't kill him to think about something good for just a moment. He let himself think about Merin. The way she walked. The way she smiled. The way her hand felt smooth and soft and warm on his cheek.

He drifted into a pleasant dream where there was no Refuge and no one to interrupt him and Merin. His dream shifted then. He was standing in the garden. It must have been late spring because all the flowers were blooming, and he trailed his fingers over every petal trying to find the right one for Merin. The flowers grew at his touch. Not just the leaves, or the stems, but the entire flower grew. Each one expanded until they were like trees. Bryce abandoned his search for a flower, and, instead, investigated the massive garden. Already the flowers were overgrowing their beds and moving through the pathways. He moved on to the trees. This time he held on to them as they grew. He shot up in the tree watching the city disappear below him. Even the Refuge became something that wasn't imposing. The roots cracked the garden walls and spilled out into the city. Bryce felt powerful. He didn't feel afraid. He was on top of the world.

"Where is everyone?" He climbed down the tree trunk quickly, but no matter where he searched in the city, he could not find his friends. He couldn't find anyone. Just greenery.

Bryce's eyes shot open. The corner of the room that had held the small potted plants was now a jungle. The plants were lush and mature.

Bryce glared over at the General. He was inspecting one of the leaves with his thick square fingers.

"I didn't do this," Bryce said, trying to convince himself more than the General.

"I know. That's the beauty of this. You have no control. The part of you that tries to control the magic isn't even in the conversation. It's bypassed."

"But I was asleep," Bryce said, staring at the garden in front of him.

"Must have been a good dream." The General laughed, reaching over to smell one of the fresh blooms.

"Then I'll stay awake," Bryce said standing. "I've gone days without sleeping in this place. Who knew I might be thanking them someday for teaching me that."

"It won't make a difference, but at least you'll make better conversation if you're awake," the General said. He chopped off the flower he had smelled. Bryce cringed. It felt like something had stung him. He checked his arms, but there was no sign of any bug.

The General stripped the leaves from one of the vines. Again, Bryce felt a sting. This time it radiated across his body.

"The connection this makes also means that you can't shut yourself off from the plants," the General said, peeling apart a budding flower petal by petal. Bryce shuddered. He tried to shut them out. But the stings kept coming.

He closed his eyes and tried to calm himself. They were only little stings. He could stand them. He had been whipped. He had been tortured. He could stand these little annoyances until the General got bored. Then he could plan his way out.

Bryce waited. He paced. The plants slowly grew, and the stings came in random bunches as the General toyed with him. But Bryce wasn't going to let him win.

For hours, Bryce wandered around the room looking for anything to do to keep him busy and away from the plants. He tried exercising but using that much energy just seemed to make the plants grow more. He tried the meditations Korvo had tried to teach him. He regulated his breathing, but couldn't quite shut out the needle-like feeling of the thorns the General was removing one by one from the roses.

"While this is enjoyable," the General said, finally leaving his chair, "I'm needed elsewhere."

This is my chance, thought Bryce. When he moves for the door, I'll use the plants to hold it open and escape. And then—but his thoughts were cut short by a direct blow to his lower jaw. Bryce was not unaccustomed to taking a punch, but this one included a gold ring that caught him right on the cheekbone. He flew backward.

Without thinking, he called for the plants. He threw his energy into the plants, and they rose to his bidding. The plants encircled the little chair where the General had stood.

The thorns grew long and pointy. He was one with the plants again, like he had been on the battlefield. He could feel their energy mixing with his own. He wasn't sure where he ended and they began. It didn't matter. They just needed to grow. To protect him.

A flick of light caught his eye. The General was holding a match. He did not seem concerned at all that the vines covered in pointed, hungry thorns were headed toward him. In fact, he smiled. Was this the plan? Bryce tried to jerk himself out from the plants, but they wouldn't let him go. His energy was mixed with theirs.

With a flick of his wrist, the General dropped the match, and despite the plants being lush and green, the fire began to consume them. Bryce screamed. His whole body was on fire. He dropped to the ground in pain. He checked his arms, but the flames hadn't reached him. Just the plants. They drew on his power to try to escape the flames, but the more they grew, the larger the lapping flames rose. Bryce tried to pull back from the plants like he had when Tiernan had lit a fire at the Council, but he was too far gone. He withered on the floor as the next set of plants caught fire.

"I've seen enough," the General said, taking a step toward the door. Bryce thought he might douse the flames, but he just left the room. Bryce was alone. The pain was beyond his ability to comprehend. The plants continued sapping his energy, his life force. They were all he could see. The green and the flames were everything. No people. No General. He was going to burn to death without ever touching a flame.

MERIN:

Merin went straight for Aer's apartment. That was where Korvo would be. She didn't bother knocking on the door. She just let herself in.

Kor sat with his back to the door. The cards were spread out on the table in front of him.

"It's happening soon?" he asked without looking up.

"Tomorrow. Well, I guess at this point today. Korvo, do you already know what's going to happen? Did the cards tell you?"

"The cards have been telling me nothing but bad things for weeks. And now they seem more urgent. I just can't quite figure out what it is." He rubbed his hand. "I'm only getting pieces."

"Well, I got some pieces, too." She laid out all the different things she had found in the files.

"So, something is going to happen tonight." Kor leaned back in his chair. He ran a hand over his black hair, knocking it out of place. "And the Hadranian General is involved." Kor swallowed hard.

"What do we do?"

"I ... I don't know," Kor said, putting his head in his hands. "There is no time for playing nice with politics, and with so many people with the medics there are no people left for war."

"What if it's just us?" asked Merin. "Maybe we just need a few people to stop whatever is coming, and then there will be time for other things. Maybe it just needs to be us and Bryce."

"We'll need to get Bryce out of the Refuge." Kor looked up at her finally. "Are you ready for that?"

It was her turn to swallow hard. She nodded, but Kor's hesitation told her he didn't quite believe her.

She nodded again more forcefully. She could brave the Refuge.

Kor nodded, picked up the cards, and put them in the pouch on his side. She couldn't imagine he would need them for anything other than comfort, but she could use a little more comfort now, too.

They walked quickly in silence. The sun had already crested the wall, and its rays were causing the Refuge to shadow everything else around it. Merin stared at it and wondered if she was seeing it for the first time like Bryce saw it. Sinister, haunting, looming. She had always hated the building, of course, but to know its horrors and to be a part of them were very different. Her hands were sweating; she rubbed them on the blue dress that had crumpled from her haste during the night.

People went about their daily morning routine without any care that others around them were being treated so terribly. It made her blood boil.

How had she not realized this before? Is this what Bryce had been trying to tell her all along? She shivered. All this time she had been incapable of understanding him. She hurried to catch up with Korvo.

"We have to get to him," she said. People looked at her as she passed. Suddenly the eyes of the city felt like they watched her wherever she stepped. She urged Korvo faster. The weight behind those eyes seemed like chains, but it didn't matter what people thought of her. Bryce was more important than what people thought of her.

Merin rushed forward until she almost ran into Korvo, who had stopped. The Refuge.

"I can go in by myself," Korvo said, putting a hand on her shoulder. She smiled weakly back at him.

"I have to go," she said, leading the way toward the door. This time she wouldn't use her ability to pass as a non-Magic to get what she wanted. This time she would use her magic.

The first guard came up to them two seconds after she had stepped over the threshold.

"What are you doing here?" he sneered looking the two of them over. He barely gave her more than a glance. The guard's eyes lingered on Korvo.

"Sending the Council to the Refuge was low," said another guard, coming to stand next to the first. Merin took a deep breath and held it. She was happy not to be their center of attention. "I suppose we should show him the real hospitality of the Refuge," the guard said.

Kor stood without flinching as the men started toward him. Merin reached out a hand to the nearest one. He turned and grabbed for her, but already her magic was flowing. *sleep. sleep.* She calmed the blood in the man's veins and sent a healing river through his body. He dropped his hand. His shoulders slouched.

"What did you do to him?" the other man shouted. Clenched in his hand now was a short club. She knew those could do damage. She'd seen enough of the dark purple bruises clustered together on the Magics she had tended to in the Wall. Kor stepped forward, intercepting him and letting the blow from the club strike him in the shoulder.

"Merin, do it now," Kor said with a grunt.

She tried to send waves of peace and serenity toward the man, but he struggled under her power.

"Concentrate," Kor said, trying to hold the man still. The guard had gotten the club free and was coming toward her. She moved, releasing her magic. Korvo struggled to keep the man twice his size under his control.

Merin took a breath, thinking of her inner light, her magic, and when the blue stream was no longer rippling with her jagged breath and rapid pulse, she reached for the man again. She let the magic rush into him. He dropped the club mid-strike and collapsed onto Korvo.

"Good." Kor shrugged the man to the floor, "Let's get out of here."

"Do you know where he'll be?" Merin asked, looking at the tight spiral staircase that seemed to go on and on.

"I know where to start," Kor said. He dashed to the staircase. At every window, he looked around him, but Merin didn't know what to look for, so she just followed. Every time they hit a landing, she hoped she would see a perfectly fine Bryce just waiting to find Tiernan, but after every disappointment, she became more and more worried.

"Here it is," Korvo said suddenly, turning off the staircase and weaving his way through beds covered in children. Merin shuddered.

"Did you see him?" Merin asked hopefully.

"I talked to him out of this window last night," Kor said, looking around. Merin looked around too, but she couldn't sense anything other than darkness and disease. There were no hints of Bryce here.

Kor moved toward a broken bed. Its leg was shattered and the whole piece buckled under the awkward weight of a small child. The broken leg was covered in vines. Bryce.

"Have you seen Bryce?" Korvo asked the child, waking him from his sleep.

"He was just here," the little boy said, rubbing his eyes.

"Where would he be now?" Korvo asked.

The boy's eyes began to water. Merin moved closer. She held the boy's hand.

"It's very important that we find Bryce," she said, trying to not let the things around her distract from the smooth flow of magic between her and the little one.

"He was with me last night, 'til some guards took him," the little boy said. His fingers went into his mouth, and his eyes drooped back into a sleepy state.

"Too much, Merin," Kor said. Merin stopped the flow of magic, but she kept holding the boy's hand.

"Which way did they go?" Merin asked. The boy shook his head.

"I don't know. If he's not here, he probably got taken to the bad place."

The bad place, Merin thought. What could be worse than this? But then she knew. She knew there were places that Bryce didn't talk about. Not to her. Not even to Kor.

"Where are the bad places?" she asked.

"You don't want to go there," the little boy said.

"I know. But I need to get to Bryce," Merin said.

The little boy pointed and quickly returned his fingers to his mouth. Merin gave him another soothing burst of her magic and stood.

Korvo was already heading back to the stairs. She followed after him.

The first room was empty except for a chair with leather straps. They were obviously there to pin the hands and feet of whoever was unlucky enough to be in the chair. Merin didn't want to stay too long in the room. Bryce wasn't there, and they were running out of time.

The next few rooms were also empty.

"They must have him someplace else," Kor said after the fourth empty room. All of the rooms had the same awful smell, and Merin wished she could give herself a little calm, but her magic never worked for her.

"But where? It will take all day to search this whole place especially if we have to avoid the guards."

"Maybe we need to find them," Kor said. His brow furrowed.

"Find them? You want to find the guards?" Merin asked.

"Find them, and then you get them to spill where Bryce is being kept."

"And how do we make sure we find them?" Merin asked. The furrow in Kor's brow deepened. He was working through a plan.

"We start a riot," Kor said.

"A riot? Kor, isn't that the opposite of the plan? Fighting doesn't help."

"Fighting doesn't, but pretend fighting might. If we tell all the kids in the Refuge to start fighting at the same time, it will bring all of the guards out. We tell the kids as soon as one comes within five feet they are to just sit down silently. No one will get hurt and we take the guard closest to the edge and have him guide us to Bryce."

"You think no one will get hurt?" Merin asked, the memory of the club coming toward her was still fresh in her mind.

"I'm not positive, but it will lessen the likelihood if they all sit down. It's the best option."

"How will they know to start the pretend fight?" Merin asked.

"We'll give them a signal. We could hit the furnace like a gong," Kor said.

Merin was satisfied with the plan. They split off to tell as many kids as they could.

"Pass it on," Merin said to the last kid on the floor. The girl scampered away, and Merin moved to meet up with Korvo. He was coming up the stairs. His eyes gleamed. He looked like he finally had the bounce in his step that he had been missing for the last week.

"Time to go," he said. He held up the broken leg of the bed Bryce had tried to fix. With a small smile, he hit the furnace pipe with the bed leg as hard as he could. The sound echoed through the whole building.

Yelling erupted from everywhere. The kids were going crazy. Piles of kids wrestled around on the ground. Some chased each other from bed to bed, and others threw whatever they could find down at others below them. It was chaos. Everywhere Merin looked there was some sort of fight happening.

Kor pulled her into the shadows. They had to sit and wait. The guards streamed in blowing whistles and banging clubs onto anything that made noise, but it didn't stop the kids. Merin hoped they would stop when the men got too close. As the guards approached, she could see the kids were looking at them through their peripheral vision. When one came within a few feet, the kids dropped to the floor, legs crossed, hands in their laps, silent. The guards didn't know what to do. They whistled for backup.

"That's our cue," Kor said, sneaking out of their hiding place. "Grab the last one that goes by."

Merin nodded. She snagged her fingers around the belt of the last guard. He was young, probably a new recruit. He stared at her for a moment before reaching for his whistle. She sent rapid magic towards him. He hunched over.

"Where is Bryce Segal?" she whispered into his ear as she led him toward Korvo. She could make him tell the truth, but she figured it was better to ask first. She might need all of her power later.

"I don't know," he said. His eyes flicked back toward the fray still unfolding on all the other levels.

"Should I force him?" Merin asked. Kor nodded. She closed her eyes and placed her hand on the man's neck. She imagined her magic covering the man's brain. Brain work took effort and concentration. "Only the truth," she whispered.

"Where is Bryce Segal?" Kor asked forcefully.

"I don't know," the Watcher said.

"Where would they take someone they wouldn't want anyone to find?" Merin asked.

"Maybe the new wing. They just finished a few days ago," the man said.

"Where is it?" Kor asked.

"The next hallway on the right," the man said. His eyes were glossy now, and Merin wouldn't be able to hold on to him for much longer.

"Kor, we'd better go," Merin said.

Kor looked at her, as if he was apologizing, and then he struck the man on the head. She flinched as the guard crumpled at her feet. Instinctively, she reached for him.

"Leave him," Kor said. Merin nodded. She spared one last glance at the chaos and the crumpled guard and sped up to match Kor's pace.

The last door in the hallway was obviously new. It was ornate. It was clear that few were to go into this door, and even fewer were to come out.

"How do we get in?" Merin asked.

"We pick the lock," Kor said, reaching down to pull at the handle. The door came open easily. They looked at each other and then back at the door.

"It could be a trap," Kor said. Merin nodded. They entered the room. It was a small waiting area. There were bits of paper and a small window that peered into a bigger room. A door sat open to the left of the window.

"Be careful," Kor mouthed as he shuffled into the room. Merin followed close behind.

Kor reached for the other door handle. It too came open easily when he touched it. Merin peered over his shoulder into the room.

"BRYCE," she yelled, forgetting at once about the possibility of a trap.

Bryce was lying on the ground. His cheek was bleeding and bruised. His arms and fingers were splayed at random angles, and Merin couldn't immediately tell if he was breathing.

"Is he ...?" Kor asked from a few steps away. His cheeks had dropped. The fire in his eyes had disappeared. Merin shoved her ear to Bryce's chest.

"I think he's breathing," Merin said. She was already pulling up his shirt. She could support his lungs and his heart if she had to.

"Merin, I don't hear anything out there," Kor said, leaning on the edge of the door. "Can you move him?"

"I think so."

She tried to get Bryce's arms to relax enough that she could move them easily. He'd been reaching for something. She looked around. There was only ash around him. She smudged some on her fingers. They left a dark black mark.

She put more of the ash on her fingers and drew a Raven's head on her chest. Then she picked up Bryce.

Kor looked at her drawing and nodded. He shouldered Bryce's other side and the two of them dragged Bryce out of the room and into the hallway. Now they just had to get out.

"Kor," Merin said as they headed back toward the main hallways, "hit the furnace again."

"Do you think they'll do it again?" Kor asked. She could tell he was trying to calculate odds as they limped along.

"It's that or nothing," Merin said. Kor nodded. When he found the broken bed's leg on the ground, Kor hit the furnace.

There was a few seconds' delay. Merin's heart dropped. Maybe they were too scared of the guards.

But then chaos erupted once more.

Now they just had to stay on the edge of it until they were free.

AER:

There was nothing but silence. Nothing but darkness. Nothing but hatred and guilt that felt like a black fire consuming her.

Then a sliver of light cracked into her world. Her heart leaped, but it wasn't Bryce or Merin. It certainly wasn't Korvo.

"It's time to go," a guard said, wrenching her to her feet. One clamped something around her neck. Another tied a gag tight against her mouth. Her hands were bound next. They pulled the rope so tight it burned.

She struggled, and they just pulled it tighter. She stumbled after them into the lit hallway.

"I hope you're ready to watch the world burn," the man said. She mumbled through the gag. The guards just laughed.

BRYCE:

He knew he was being moved before his eyes opened. Bryce settled into the idea that he had somehow survived, only to rot away in the Refuge. He felt like he deserved it. A sob came to his throat. He had failed everyone. He let the tears fall.

"Kor, I think he's awake." Merin's voice drifted into his ears. Bryce tried to block it out. There was no reason to try and recall the beauty of her face and the softness of her skin. He was going to die in the Refuge.

"Bryce," Kor said. "Bryce, are you awake?" Kor shook his shoulder. Bryce finally opened one eye. He was greeted with a soot-streaked Raven's head on Merin's chest. He closed his eyes again. He was back in dreamland.

"Bryce?" Merin asked, leaning her forehead down to touch his. The warmth exploded into his consciousness.

"Merin?" he croaked. His throat was ragged from the smoke and screaming.

"I'm here. Kor, too," she said, rubbing his cheek with her thumb.

"You have to get out of the Refuge," Bryce said. His eyes flew open.

"We are out," Kor said quietly. It was almost a whisper.

Bryce looked around him. They were limping toward Aer's apartment.

"Is Aer?" Bryce asked, but Merin shook her head before he could finish his question. "Tiernan?" he asked. Merin turned away.

"We'll get to them," Kor said, "but first we have to get you back on your feet. Merin won't be able to heal you too much, but she can help with some of the pain."

"Don't bother," Bryce said trying to stand up. He wavered, but Kor didn't grab him, and Merin didn't put her hands on him.

"Bryce, I can help," Merin said. Bryce moved his hand to her face. He was relieved to see that they bore no marks from the flames.

"I don't think anything is physically wrong with me, except too much smoke," he said, steadying himself and checking himself all over. "Besides, you should be ready to help Tiernan or Aer."

"What happened?" Kor asked, setting a hand on his shoulder. Bryce shrugged. He wasn't sure he could explain the pain of being drained of his magic and set ablaze at the same time.

"The Hadranian General is here," he said finally.

"We know. He is planning something with the Council today," Kor said.

"They have this stuff. Some sort of fabric," Bryce said. He crossed his arms around him. "It affects our magic. It drains us. It gives us no control. They were testing it."

"I'm sure it's connected," Kor said, but his eyes were deep in thought. "Bryce, can you walk a ways?" he asked.

Bryce thought about it for a minute. He took a tentative step. Merin reached to grab him, but his legs held steady beneath him.

"I'll be fine. What do you want me to do?" Bryce said. He could make it up to Korvo.

"I want you to go to the Council," Kor said.

"The Council?" Merin asked. Bryce mirrored her shocked expression. If there was one thing he hadn't ever gotten right, it was how to talk to the Council.

"Why me?" Bryce asked.

"You've lived through their terrors. They may actually listen. Just stay calm," Korvo said. Bryce nodded.

"Merin, I want you to go to the Wall District and Uptown and gather as many people as you can."

"What do you want me to say?" Merin asked. Bryce could tell she was nervous. He held out his hand. She smiled at him and grabbed his hand.

"Whatever it takes to get them to the Refuge."

"The Refuge?" Bryce stammered.

"The school is gone. The Council has been attacked. The Refuge is the place," Kor said. His face was settled. He had decided.

"Meet back in a few hours?" Merin asked. Kor nodded and turned away.

"Where are you going?" Bryce asked.

"I'm looking for the rest of our friends," Kor said. He didn't say anything else.

"Merin," Bryce said after they watched Kor walk out of view.

"Yes?" She turned to him. They were still holding hands.

"It looks good on you," he said running his finger over the Raven's head. "But shouldn't you get rid of it if you're going uptown?"

"I think I'm going to keep it. It's time everyone knew who I was," she said with a smile.

Bryce squeezed her hand. He was still too tired to throw his arms around her like he wanted. He wanted to hold her close to his chest and see if her heartbeat could help him feel like he wasn't still trapped in the room with the dying plants. But they didn't have time for that.

"I better get going," Bryce said finally. "It's going to take me a while to walk to the Council." He leaned down and kissed her gently on the forehead.

"Stay safe," Merin said.

"You, too."

KORVO:

Kor rubbed his hand as he half-jogged to Bethlem's. He needed to get to Aer and Tiernan, and the only way to do that would be to get the General to bring them to him.

"Bethlem," Kor called, opening the door to the bar. Bethlem smiled at him.

"You look a little worse for wear, my friend."

"I need the best messengers you can find." Kor sat at the bar. He was tempted to order a drink, but he needed to keep his wits about him.

"What's so important?" Bethlem asked.

"I need to spread this message throughout the city. Hopefully to as many Watchers as possible."

"You want to send a message to the Watchers? I have to say I normally follow your plans pretty well, but—"

"If the Watchers don't know we're creating a disturbance at the Refuge, they may set up for their plan elsewhere. I need the General to bring Aer and Tiernan to me. Otherwise, I might never find them."

"Slow down, Korvo. Take me through this slowly. What plan do the Watchers have?"

"They're planning something today that's going to turn everyone against Magics for good. It involves Tiernan and probably Aer," Kor said, taking the glass of water Bethlem handed him. He downed it in two big gulps.

"What general?" Bethlem asked after a moment of consideration.

"The Hadranian General. The one who kept me captive and destroyed the Magic resistance in Hadran."

"This is heavy," Bethlem said, pouring himself a glass of something much stronger than water. It was not like Bethlem to drink on the job. "And you want him to bring them to you?"

"Yes."

"Are you sure?" Bethlem asked. His eyes stared into Korvo's like he was looking for an answer. Kor nodded. "Then it's done." Bethlem went into the back and Kor could hear him whispering orders to some of the boys who could always be found scurrying around the bar.

"What's your next move?" Bethlem asked, returning to Kor.

Kor took a deep breath. "Wait for everyone to show," Kor said. "Hope we don't all die. The usual."

Bethlem nodded and went about his normal duties at the bar. He wiped clean glasses and put them away. He counted money more than he needed to. Kor knew this was causing the poor man stress, but he had no other ideas. No other alternatives.

Kor lifted all of the cards from his pocket. He rippled the edges over his thumb. They hadn't been much help. But before something like this, he needed to look at them thoroughly. He spread them out face down on the bar and shuffled them around. It wasn't very often all of them were out at once. Finally he selected five cards. It felt like the right number. One for each of them.

Five of Swords: self-destruction

Strength: courage and self-control

Two of Wands: determination

The Emperor: protection

The Hanged Man: sacrifice

He stared at the cards for a long time before he traced the images etched into the front of the cards with his fingers. The future that had been haunting the cards was finally starting to break through. He just hoped it would be in time. He tapped each card once more, letting the fates of his friends sink into his skin.

He gathered up the cards and placed them back in their leather pouch.

That's when the sky lit up with flame.

MERIN:

"Why should we listen to you?" a heckler called from the Wall District.

"You've avoided us until now," another called. Merin wished Bryce were here beside her. But she was alone, and she could handle the crowd. Her drawn-on Raven's mark was starting to drip down her chest with her sweat.

"I am not afraid anymore. And I will not let them sacrifice my friends. Your friends. Your neighbors. To make us seem evil."

"And how in the Twelve God's light will we stop them?" someone in the back asked.

"Korvo has a plan."

"So did Sid, and he's long dead. I don't want to see anyone else get hurt."

"No one is asking you to fight. Just come to the Refuge." Merin looked at the faces around her. They were thin and gaunt. The stress and anxiety from increased Watcher patrols, missing children, and death hung about the crowd like a stench. These people were well aware of the horrors that had caused these things to happen. She didn't need to stand there and tell them.

They didn't need to understand how Bryce had looked so broken and that she didn't know if he would make it. That she had felt helpless and alone when Tiernan was taken by watchers. They understood these things in a way she never could.

"What do you want most of all?" she asked the crowd.

"To be treated like people," an older woman said from the sidelines.

"Then show them your, our, humanity at the Refuge today," she said. She still needed to get uptown.

She set off at a run. There was no time for decorum and people stared at her as she ran. She was dirty now. She didn't even notice. Kor had given her a job to do.

She headed to her old school. It had only been days since she had last been there, but it felt like years. She reached the foyer and stopped, hunched over and out of breath.

The kids were eating. The dining hall shined as if it had been polished that morning. Nothing had changed for them.

Merin imagined the rats crawling over the tables in the Refuge. She closed her eyes and gathered herself into the most presentable way she could before walking into the great hall.

"What makes you a person?" she yelled over the lunchtime din of students. Only a few students turned to look at her, and they instantly turned to whisper to each other. Merin felt the need to cover herself with her arms, but she resisted the urge. Instead, she raised her hands above her head. Her chest heaving up and down with her breath. The Raven's mark was fading, but she could see it reflected in the shine of the wood polish. It made her look dangerous, wild.

"Merin? What are you doing?" a voice squealed near her. Merin ignored it. She yelled again.

"What makes you a person? What proves your humanity?"

"What are you getting at, Merin?" a boy asked. His blue coat was cut to fit him. His hair sat straight against his head.

"With that mark on her chest, and her filthy clothes, I'm betting she's been rolling around with that Magic that chases after her like a dog," a boy said, giving Merin a disapproving glance. The girl looked her up and down and turned her back to her.

"Merin, think of your reputation," the girl who had squealed earlier whispered. The hall was quiet enough now that it was clear everyone was listening.

"You are a person because you can think and feel. What makes a Magic any different?" Her eyes narrowed. She demanded an answer.

"They have no control. No decency. Just like your little boyfriend. He's always trying to pick fights. I heard he's a criminal."

"Do you know any Magics?" Merin yelled. She waited for their response. "Do you know their names? Their stories?"

"Why would I want to?" the first boy said. These were people she had grown up with. People she had played with her whole life.

"And if I told you *I* was a Magic?"

"I'd say, sure, I'd believe that just as much someone one would believe I'm from Hadran," the girl nearest her said. She forced a laugh. "Merin," she whispered, grabbing a hold of her hand, "you need to stop."

Merin didn't need to think twice. She let her magic flow into the girl who had gripped her arm. It rushed through the girl. She was still pulling on Merin's arm. She hadn't noticed. That was exactly what Merin wanted. Her magic surrounded the girl's mind.

"I'll show you," Merin said. But then Bryce's face flashed in her mind. Taking control of someone would only make them fear her. She let her magic fade into the girl's system.

"How?" the girl asked, trembling.

"Who here is hurt? Has a headache? A twisted ankle?"

"I do," said the boy who had called Bryce a dog. Merin swallowed the anger that was begging to be let out.

"What's wrong?" she asked. He pointed to his shoulder. Merin closed her eyes and put his hands on his shoulder. She could imagine her magic spreading over his shoulder like water over a riverbed. She found the problem quickly. She solved the problem even quicker.

"So?" she said.

The boy rotated his arm around.

"I hate to admit it but—"

Merin cut him off. "You have known me your whole life. I have always had these powers. I never lost control. I was protected from the Raven's head by my parents. So I was never forced out of school to be on my own. We have played together. I never attacked you. And society has kept you from knowing anyone else who has magic. They are people just like me. They are being hurt. We can stop that. We have the power to help them."

"Merin?" the girl beside her asked. "How can we help them?"

"We listen. Right now. At the Refuge. We listen. I'm going now."

She turned and left the room. She wasn't sure if anyone was following her, but this was her best bet. She was running out of time to go anywhere else. But these kids were the next generation of councilors, lawyers, and teachers. Even if a few of them came, it would be a start.

She refused to look behind her. She wasn't sure what she would see. Would they have listened? Did they hate her now because she had told them her secret? Would anyone come?

Slowly, she heard the scrape of chairs pushed back from tables, the swish of well-oiled doors opening, and—*yes*—the patter of feet behind her. She smiled and picked up the pace toward the Refuge.

BRYCE:

People were scurrying around the Council Building. Bryce's footsteps echoed as he walked. Everything made him jump: the sound of the messengers turning corners too fast, the ruffle of paper, his own breathing.

He followed the signs in the building. It took him a few minutes to figure out the letters, and even longer to try to sound out what they said. But once he had found the directions to the "Council Room," he turned down another hallway.

Raucous voices were all competing to drown the others out.

"Order, order," came the loudest voice. A gavel slammed down on a table. Bryce followed the sound. He entered the room. The Council members surrounded him in a circle. They had all donned their official robes. They weren't all sitting in their chairs, and Bryce wondered for a second what they had been arguing about. But it didn't take him long to realize that they were talking about whatever the General had been talking about.

"What are you doing here?" the Council member with the gavel in his hand asked. Bryce turned to look at him. He looked like he could be Merin's grandfather. Bryce bowed his head.

"You're Korvo's friend? Bryce, right?" Jacqui asked. Bryce recognized his voice. Kor had taken him to hear Jacqui speak once before on the treatment of Magics.

"Hello, sir," Bryce said bowing his head again.

"Now isn't the best time," Jacqui said, the smile fading from his face.

"I know," Bryce said, taking a step further into the room. "That's why I'm here."

"You impertinent fool. We have no need for you. Be gone with you, Magic," one of the councilmen yelled. Bryce didn't even bother to try to figure out which one.

"You do need me." Bryce let his hands drop to his sides. "You need to listen to me."

"And what could you possibly tell the Council?" another Council member asked.

"The Refuge. I assume by now Council Member Jacqui has told you what he saw in the Refuge. But I have seen it, too. Six times. Every part of that horrible place. Every time the floors were covered in rats and roaches. There aren't enough beds to fit the children you pluck from the streets. The education we get is only pain. I was whipped and nearly drowned. I have nightmares where I wake up screaming. I am angry. I know I get into fights, but nothing in the Refuge has ever helped me be a better person. But my fellow Magics? They took me in. I am here today because they taught me to read." Bryce stopped for a second. Jacqui nodded at him. He motioned for Bryce to continue.

"I know that you are working with the General," Bryce said. Murmurs erupted across the room. The same arguments that had been brewing broke out again.

"Why do you think you know this?" the Council Member with the gavel asked. His face was flushed red. Bryce tried to remember his name but couldn't think of it. His head was still too swimmy.

"I know because he tortured me in the Refuge. He experimented on me."

"I can guarantee that the Council—" the leader started. Bryce lifted up his hand.

"I forgive you. I forgive you for being afraid. I've been afraid in my life. When the men I didn't know came and held me down while they tattooed the Raven on my ankle, I was afraid. When I left my family for the city, I was afraid. The nights I spent in the Refuge, I was afraid. I understand fear. It can cause you to do things you wouldn't normally do. I fought. You called the General."

"As I said before, I can assure you that the Council has no idea what you are talking about," the Council member choked out.

"Let the boy speak," Jacqui said.

"I want to hear this," another said. "Maybe it will clear up some of the questions we've been having." The man glared across the room. The man with the gavel gripped it tightly and leaned back in his chair.

"I will not forgive you," Bryce continued, "if you let my friends be hurt because you are scared of who we are. If you are scared of children learning to read, or a six-year-old who has seen his share of torture and darkness. If you are willing to use this city's fear of us to get rid of us, then I will not forgive you. Because that is not the result of someone who is scared. Those are the actions of someone who wants power over others and will make themselves more powerful by stripping others of what little humanity they have left."

"Tell us more about how the General is involved," said a Council member.

"He can't," the leader shouted, "because there is no such conspiracy."

"If you want to know more, come to the Refuge. And see it with your own eyes."

Bryce turned then, his body shaking, and walked out of the room. Tears ran down his cheeks. Once he turned the corner, he leaned up against the wall and sobbed.

When it felt like his body had given all the tears it could, he continued on his way toward the Refuge.

He had expected there to be people there. Merin never failed in any task she had been given, but the fervor in the crowd was intense. It felt like the first day in the marketplace. Bryce scanned the crowd trying to find Merin or Kor. He needed to be near his friends. He was a shell of a person and wanted a familiar face for an ounce of comfort.

He didn't expect a much different face.

Aer was standing at the front of the Refuge. Her winds whipped around her. Her hair was loose and flying. The wind nipped at her jacket. The same jacket she had been wearing when they had attacked the Council. The same jacket that was made of the fabric from that room.

"Aer!" He called to her and ran toward her. "You have to take the jacket off."

She turned and looked at him. Her eyes were wide. Her brow was pinched together, and for the first time, Bryce noticed the slight chain around her wrists.

"Bryce, stay back," she commanded, but Bryce pushed through the remaining people in the crowd. He had almost made it free when a hand grabbed him by the collar. Another familiar face: Korvo.

"Let me," he said. Fire crackled from the edges of the Refuge. Both Bryce and Kor turned to look at each other. Tiernan. Tiernan was here.

"You get to Tiernan," Bryce said. "I'll get Aer."

Kor nodded. Bryce shifted his attention back to his friend. The winds had only picked up. Merin was running from the other side toward Aer. Maybe together they could get the jacket and chains off.

The crowd was beginning to pull away.

"They brought us here to kill us," a member of the crowd screamed.

"Can't they see she's tied up?" Merin yelled to Bryce. He knew fear was blinding them to what was in front of them.

The Watchers were beginning to move in now. Bryce watched them hesitate, like they weren't sure how to follow their orders. They must be in on it. They were waiting for something to go wrong.

"We have to stop Aer and Tiernan," Bryce said. "They're using them to turn the rest against us."

Bryce reached the platform Aer stood on first. She was beaten badly. He could tell standing was torture and having the magic drained from her was only making it worse. There were large bags underneath her eyes. It was only a few more steps until he could get to her. Lightning cracked across the sky. Bryce stumbled backward, but Merin kept going.

KORVO:

The plan had worked. The General had brought Tiernan and Aer to the Refuge for the crowds. Crowds that, hopefully, were full of Council Members and non-Magics. They would see the injustice happening right in front of them.

But he had to get to Tiernan. Tiernan might have had more control than anyone he had ever met, but he also had more magic bubbling inside his body. He was the flame. And without any control ... Kor didn't finish that thought. He pushed closer to the little boy.

The heat got more intense as he got close to the flames. Tiernan's eyes glowed. Korvo looked away, only to find himself looking at the General. His piercing blue eyes twinkled when Kor came to an abrupt stop.

"Seems my little Magic family is all together now," the General laughed. Kor reeled. He thought it wouldn't bother him to see the General again. It had been years. He was grown now. Instead, Kor felt like the small child that had been paraded around the campground like an animal. He couldn't move. Tiernan sputtered another shot of flames, causing another explosion. Even the heat coming close to him was not enough to melt the stare the General had for him.

"Why did you come here?"

"It's my duty to see that Magics are eliminated."

"This isn't Hadran."

"I know, but soon it will be just as great. After the people out there believe that there are Magics like your dear Aer and Tiernan that cannot be controlled, they will outlaw magic. I'll see you in chains once more."

"Why? Why do you hate us this much?"

"I don't hate Magics," the General said, taking a step closer.

"You don't hate Magics? How can you say that? You have a six-year-old boy withering in pain. You tortured Bryce."

"Why would I have feelings about Magics? They are not something to spend time thinking about. It's like dirt on your floor. You don't hate it. You just get rid of it. No questions asked. No complicated feelings necessary."

"We are people!" Korvo yelled now. He wasn't sure if it was to be heard over the crackle of the flames or because he couldn't contain his anger.

"No, you are not." The General moved back toward safety, away from the rising flames. "You are an abomination."

"Tiernan, you have to come with me," Kor said in Hadran.

Tiernan shifted. His eyes glanced toward Kor's and for a moment, Kor thought it would all be over. But Tiernan's eyes fell away, and the fire began to change in color. Blue flames were the hottest; Kor knew that. He was forced to take a step back.

He needed a plan, and he needed it fast. He thought over the cards he had seen. There were only a few options, and one was sacrifice. He took a deep breath and pushed his hand into the fire to grab for Tiernan. If he could touch him, he might be able to bring him out of whatever trance he was in. Bryce had said they found a way to force a Magic to bypass their own control systems. Tiernan needed to regain it.

His hand plunged into the flame. At first he felt nothing; then the fire burned him. It was so hot Kor wasn't sure it wasn't ice. He could feel his skin puckering as he kept it there. He reached Tiernan's hand. He pulled on it. He pulled Tiernan toward him. The fire turned orange, almost pleasant after the blinding heat that had lapped at his skin.

"Korvo?" Tiernan asked. His voice seemed distant, like he was stuck in a dream. Bryce had sounded the same way.

"We need to get out of here," Kor said. His clothes were singeing from the flames still crackling around Tiernan. What were a few pieces of clothes if he could save Tiernan?

"I can't go," Tiernan said. "I'll hurt all those people. They'll be afraid of me. Like that book Merin read me." Tiernan's eyes began to lose focus, and Kor knew he had limited time.

"Tiernan, together we can help you."

"Collar," Tiernan said. Kor raised his eyes to the woven collar around Tiernan's neck. Is that what was making him do this?

"We'll help you get it off," Kor said.

"I don't think that will be happening any time soon," the General said from the safety of the entrance desk.

"Tiernan, you have to trust me," Kor said. He wasn't sure how to get the collar off, but he needed to. And he needed to do it fast before he lost Tiernan to the flames again.

Tiernan allowed him to pull him out the front door. He was still encapsulated in flame, but it was no longer hurting Kor. Kor hoped that meant Tiernan was regaining control and not that his skin was burned enough that the nerves were no longer picking up pain signals. But there was no time to worry about that.

"That boy is on fire," a crowd member said. Tiernan tensed. He pushed Kor away as the fires began to rise around him.

"They're out of control!" a Watcher cried. Kor looked around at the crowd they had brought here. There were a few Council members in the back. The winds grabbed the edges of clothes and the Councilmens' robes with hungry fingers.

"See," the General said coming from the inside of the Refuge. "We couldn't contain them. They have no control.

This is why your city isn't safe. Until we get rid of them, there is no way I will sleep at night."

The General played the sympathy card well, and in a normal Watcher's uniform no one knew his secret agenda. His blue eyes blended in with the upper class. Only Korvo, and maybe Bryce, were feeling physically ill by his presence. To everyone else it would only look like Tiernan had lost control.

The whites of Tiernan's eyes were bulging out of his head. Bryce still hadn't quite gotten to Aer, but Merin was trying desperately to break the thin chains around her wrists so she could get the jacket off.

This was the time to think. Kor ran through scenarios that could play out. He ran through what he knew.

"Tiernan, you can't stop?" Korvo asked, although he thought he knew the answer.

The little boy shook his head.

"Can you play?"

Tiernan looked at him. Kor saw how tired he was. Tiernan's chest was heaving.

"If you can shape the flames, you won't scare anyone," Kor said. The boy nodded.

He squeezed his eyes shut and the flames started jumping. They pulsed in and out. They spiraled inward, and then burst into spectacular explosions. But slowly they were taking shape. They were wings. Big wings that looked like they were coming from Tiernan's back. They flapped a few times, unfurling to be bigger than Korvo. The crowd gasped. Tiernan dropped to a knee. Kor ran to him. With the flames behind him, it was safe to touch him once more.

Holding Tiernan's hand, Kor felt how clammy the boy's hands were. He held them in his hand.

"You're doing good. Do you think you could make flowers?" Kor whispered. Tiernan barely nodded.

"If he has no control, how can he do this?" Kor yelled to the crowd who had silenced as the wings unfurled. He turned and winked at Tiernan who managed a weak smile. The fire slowly turned into a rose. It looked exactly like the ones that Bryce took care of in the garden.

Someone in the crowd clapped.

"Hold on, Tiernan," Kor said, letting go of the boy's hands. Kor chanced a glance over at Bryce and Merin. They had ripped the jacket with a knife they had gotten from someone in the crowd, and they were working on the top of the jacket. Aer's face was gaunt. Her breath was more ragged than Tiernan's. They didn't have much time.

"Magics have control of themselves," Kor said to the captivated audience. He pointed to Tiernan's rose petals, slowly dropping to the ground and disappearing. "What we don't have is control of our lives. Children are denied an education. Children are forced into the Refuge. People like the Hadranian General here are trying to take even more. You are afraid of us, but we are even more afraid of you. Afraid that you will never see us as people. Afraid that we will end up in the Refuge or a labor camp for simply being who we are. We can control ourselves," Kor was almost yelling now. "But can you control your fear?"

The crowd murmured. Tiernan dropped to his hands and knees. Aer was only being held up by Bryce. They were near their limits. If he took much longer, they wouldn't make it.

The General was trying to blend into the crowd.

"All we ask is for help. Ask the General to let this little kid go. Tell him his hatred has no place in Kaybrum. Save them."

The crowd began shouting. A few of the Council members came forward.

"What is hurting them?" Jacqui asked, coming as close as he dared. Kor breathed deeply, relieved that Jacqui hadn't abandoned them.

"See the collar around his neck, the jacket she is wearing? This fabric limits their control to stop. If they don't stop soon, they will die."

A pitiful moan escaped Tiernan, and Korvo leaned down to put his hand on his back. Trying to control the fire was weakening him faster than Aer. Bryce and Merin supported her enough so she could come over. Kor placed his hand on hers without thinking.

"We can't get the knife through the metal," Bryce said, kneeling down next to Korvo.

"What do we do?" Jacqui asked. He had come to kneel next to them. Another crowd member approached cautiously. The looks on their faces said it all. They were horrified. They finally saw the Magic's plight. Kor looked up to yell at the General that it was over. But there was no trace of the man with the ice-cold eyes that haunted his dreams.

It was too late; Tiernan was dying, and they were going to watch without being able to do anything. He placed his hand on the top of the boy's head.

"Everyone move," Aer said through gasps of breath.

"Aer—" Korvo started to tell her to relax, but when he looked into her eyes he knew. He pulled Bryce backward.

Aer teetered onto her feet. She was unsteady, and it took her a moment to get her balance before she raised her arms above her head. Kor watched her every move. Even though Bryce and Merin had gotten through the sleeves and part of the jacket, it only revealed she had the same collar. It rubbed against her jagged tattoo.

He closed his eyes, understanding settling in him. He wasn't the sacrifice card. The cards were never wrong.

"What is she doing?" Bryce asked.

"She's not going to attempt anything big, is she?" Merin shook Bryce's arm. "She doesn't have the strength. I gave her everything I had left, and it's not enough. We need to stop her."

Korvo put out his hand and held Bryce so he wouldn't run when he saw what came next.

Aer began chanting in the language the winds had taught her over her short seventeen years. They swirled and gusted. They could feel what was happening, too. Kor could feel the hair on his neck rise. Aer was calling the weather. She was calling lightning down.

"Aer—" Kor said. It was almost a whisper, but the wind brought her the words. She looked at him.

"It's my fault. Sometimes sacrifices have to be made."

"Can I stop you?" he asked.

"Could you ever?"

The lightning was cackling now above them. Tiernan had lost any shape of the flower and the flames had gone back to consuming him.

Kor shook his head.

"Goodbye, Aer."

"Kor, no. You can't. You have to stop her," Bryce yelled, but there was no stopping her. She nodded at the three of them once, and, with a secret message to the clouds, released the lightning in one single bolt that went straight to the collar around Tiernan's neck. The bolt shattered the thin strip around his neck.

Aer sank to the ground. Kor let go of Bryce. He ran to Aer, calling for Merin. Merin walked to Aer's side, tears streaming down her face.

"Is she?" Jacqui asked. Korvo nodded.

"She's gone." He rushed to Tiernan and picked him up. The boy was limp in his arms.

"Korvo?" Tiernan said. His voice was faint but there.

"Tiernan. Are you going to be alright?" Kor asked.

"Love?" the little boy asked, putting his hand on Korvo's chest.

"Love." Korvo said, laying his mangled hand over the boy's. He started to cry. "Safe."

BRYCE:

The Refuge was closed for an official investigation. Bryce walked by it every day at least once. He refused to feel scared of an empty building.

He was still not feeling like himself. Even though a month had gone by, he still felt weak. He could swear Tiernan was feeling the same way, but Kor and Merin had him running around learning the common tongue and how to read. Merin had gotten some of her classmates to help volunteer at a new make-shift school. It left Bryce on his own to deal with the shadows of the past.

Jacqui had been put in charge of the Refuge investigation, and he was listening to the Magic community. Kor and Bethlem were away a lot now. Bryce had been asked to give testimony, but he wasn't ready to go back into the building. Instead, he had started teaching the little kids skills around the garden or anywhere else their talents might be needed. Things that could help them get a job. It made him move around the city a lot, but even though he walked by the Refuge, there was one place he couldn't quite go.

He wasn't ready for Aer's grave. Kor and Merin went at least once a week. Bryce figured Kor may have gone more than that. Bryce just couldn't face the fact that he couldn't save her.

Today was the day he was going to attempt it. He circled the block that led to the graveyard multiple times before he finally decided to go in.

"I'm sorry I couldn't save you," he said to the stone.

"She never needed to be saved," Kor said, coming to stand with his arm around Bryce. Merin slipped in and held his hand. Bryce leaned his head against hers. "She saved us."

"We did it together," Merin said.

Bryce sighed. "What did I do?"

"Is that what you're feeling guilty about? You made them listen," Kor said. "If the Council hadn't come, none of this would have been possible."

"I guess."

"That's something I was never able to do. Aer was never able to do. Merin either."

The three of them sat in silence, watching the clouds pass over.

"When are the next meetings about the Refuge?" Bryce asked.

"You mean the newest Kaybrum School for Magics?" Kor said. He clapped Bryce on the back.

"It's over?" Bryce asked.

"The Refuge, yes," Kor said, resting his hand for a moment on the stone tablet, "but there is still a long way to go."

ACKNOWLEDGMENTS

WRITING THIS BOOK HAS BEEN A JOURNEY that without the support from my family and friends, I would not have been able to accomplish. I want to thank my mother for her tireless highlighting of errors in early drafts, my father for always being there, and both of my grandmothers for their joy, support, and push to develop my creativity and imagination.

I want to thank my husband and my dog, Quinn, for their patience with spending walks discussing the finer points of fictional drama. A special shout out to my sister who always calls with sage advice, humor, and a page (or more) of notes when needed. To the teachers along the way that made this possible: Mrs. Reidenbach who taught me the joy of writing, Mr. Reichert who taught me how to see the hidden magic in words, and Professor Nadelson who challenged me to share my work with others.

A million thanks to my students over the last decade. They are generally my first critics and always force me to be a better writer. This book would not have been written without them, and I can't wait in the years to come to read all of the books they write.

I also want to acknowledge the 4th grade me who believed that we would become an author. And while I have

still not become a Nobel Prize winning Olympic ice skater/
paleontologist, I hope I have still made her proud. And I hope
you'll follow along with me online at @emily.k.bray or online
at emilykbraywrites.com

ABOUT THE AUTHOR

EMILY K. BRAY is a high school Creative Writing and Drama teacher in Washington State. She has taught hundreds of students to share her love of writing, stories, and words since 2013. Now she hopes to share this joy with others with her debut novel.

Emily lives with her husband and her dog, Quinn. Besides her love of writing and teaching, she also enjoys musicals, crafting, and spending the day under a large blanket.

Connect with Emily online at:
emilykbraywrites.com
Instagram: @emily.k.bray
Tik Tok: @emily.k.bray

www.ingramcontent.com/pod-product-compliance
Lightning Source LLC
Chambersburg PA
CBHW031214260626
47169CB00007B/2059